Mage Evolution

Books by Virginia G. McMorrow

The Mage Trilogy
Mage Confusion
Mage Resolution
Mage Evolution

The Firewing Trilogy
Firewing's Journey
Firewing's Shadow
Firewing's Hunt

Novel
Upstaged by Betrayal

Coming Soon!
On the Right Track

For more information
visit: www.SpeakingVolumes.us

Mage Evolution

Virginia G. McMorrow

SPEAKING VOLUMES, LLC
NAPLES, FLORIDA
2024

Mage Evolution

Copyright © 2005 by Virginia G. McMorrow

All rights reserved. No part of this book may be reproduced or transmitted in any form or by any means without written permission.

ISBN 979-8-89022-254-1

For Kevin

Acknowledgments

Special thanks to my literary agent, Cherry Weiner, as well as Kurt Mueller, Erica Mueller, and the staff of Speaking Volumes.

Chapter One

"Two formal state dinners in three months is asking entirely too much of me." Having voiced that complaint aloud, I sank with grateful abandon onto the pile of plush embroidered cushions next to Anders Perrin, my husband of five years. We were in the queen's private parlor, where our small group of friends sought escape from the noisy crowd of courtiers and diplomats. "No offense intended, of course, my lord," I murmured to Derek Frontish, the senior elder from the land of Spreebridge, our northern and now-friendly neighbor.

"None taken of course, Mage Protector." The gentleman's smile was a stiff grimace that did nothing to soften the formality of his demeanor or the expression in his eyes as he used my ridiculous title, one the queen spitefully bestowed on me. "Your aversion to formal occasions is well known." The diplomat made an effort to broaden his smile. "And, I confess, if not for the pleasant company in which I find myself at the moment," —he nodded at the rest of our cozy group— "I would be as averse as you."

"Elder Frontish, you surprise and disappoint me. I expect that reaction from Alex, which is one of the reasons I command her presence at these events, but I don't expect it from you, as a seasoned representative of your people." Elena Dunneal, reigning monarch of Tuldamoran, and my very close friend, didn't try to hide her amusement as she leaned over and patted my cheek with affection. She winked at my husband, who didn't bother to hide a grin.

Grumbling, I cast an absent glance around the elegant but simple furnishings, trying to find a legitimate excuse to leave Ardenna in the middle of the night, steal my four-year-old daughter from her doting grandparents deep in the Glynnswood forest, and flee back to Port Alain.

"Alexandra, really—" Anders scolded, using my full name to annoy me further, then adding a sharp tug at a strand of my shoulder-length dark brown curls. "Is that any way for the queen's Mage Protector to act in front of an honored visitor from Spreebridge? Not to mention the fact he's the guest of honor—"

"I'm being civilized."

"She is being civilized, according to her standards," Elena reassured him with a grave smile. "But Alex," —her dark blue eyes feigned innocence as she toyed with her half-empty wineglass— "it's not often that the most-distinguished elder and mage from Spreebridge comes to visit Tuldamoran on a formal mission and—"

Before I could reply, Jules Barlow, Duke of Port Alain, leaned away from the safety of the silk-covered wall at his back, perilously close to a drunken slouch, and tapped me on the shoulder. "In case you've forgotten, oh fierce Mage Protector, not only is the distinguished elder mage from Spreebridge sitting opposite you, but so is the ambassador from Spreebridge."

"Him?" I waved an airy dismissal in Jackson Tunney's direction, where bright green eyes studied me with equal humor. "His eyes are too indecent for the man to be taken seriously as an ambassador, in my humble opinion."

"Don't take her comments as a personal insult."

Elena planted a lingering kiss on Jackson's lips, fully aware Elder Frontish was watching, which made me wonder if she was testing the limits of his tolerance. Spreebridge folk, with the exception of Jackson, had the reputation of conservative, dull behavior and mindset. If we were to nurture a new trade relationship with our northern neighbor, Elena might just be thinking it was best for this gentleman to observe the differences in our behavior. And knowing Elena, who never did anything without good reason, she may have simply been letting him observe different facets of our interaction.

"Alex is jealous of you," Elena told her lover, who didn't need the slightest bit of reassurance, "because for the last five years, her splendid mage talent is no longer unique but a mirror of yours."

"And she'd rather yours had been like mine," Anders cut in with a wide grin on his face, dodging my fist.

"Precisely," I grumbled. "I'm annoyed at both of you."

In five short years, I'd changed from flatly denying my unconventional mage talent, which allowed me to transform one element to another, to rejoicing in the gift. And it was a gift, granted by the lords of the elements, making it possible for me to save Elena's throne from a traitorous coup and, soon after, capture dangerous rogue mages from Spreebridge. During that adventure, Anders and I crossed paths with Jackson Tunney, who'd been sent by the Spreebridge elders to help prevent the renegades from further criminal behavior. When Elena and Jackson came together in Port Alain at the end of the affair, the two had eyes for no one else. The rest, as they say, was history of sorts.

When we encountered Jackson on that journey, he'd offered a surprising revelation. His mage talent was similar to mine. But Anders's magic was still unique, a legendary figure come to life, come thankfully into my life. As the mythical Crownmage, Anders could control and transform each element within itself, a feat of which no ordinary mage was capable. Most mages, like my long-dead seamage mother, had control over one element only. And Glynnswood mages, like my father and half-brother, from the semi-independent Duchy within Elena's kingdom, could only change one element to another, as could mages from Spreebridge, like Elder Frontish.

Trying to get to the bottom of this tangle, I spent the last few years attempting to understand how the mage bloodlines worked, curious as to the type of mage child Anders and I had created. Emmy had yet to show any type of magic, but I believed it was only a matter of time. It would've seemed an unnecessary waste of both Anders's and my mage talent to have a child with no magic. But if it turned out the imp had not the slightest inclination toward magic, it wouldn't change the simple fact that Anders and I adored her.

"Doesn't matter," I shrugged. "I'm better and faster than Jackson, anyway." Ignoring Anders's snide comment, I rolled up the silk sleeves of my gown, which I couldn't wait to rip off in exchange for something comfortable. Closing my eyes tight, I coaxed the internal fire and ice awake, blending them easily into cool warmth that tingled through every inch of my body. "That pitcher of water," —I pointed at the low wooden table between Jules's wife, Lauryn, and Jackson— "will become flame quicker than—"

"Alex." Anders jabbed me with a sharp elbow, destroying my concentration, setting the cool warmth to piercing fire and ice. "You've had a little too much Marain Valley wine with dinner and are apt to start a blaze to ruin Elena's very expensive furniture."

"Stiff-necked wretch," I pouted, turning my back on my husband and challenging the queen instead. "Admit it, Elena."

"Admit what?"

"That you invited Elder Frontish to Tuldamoran simply to get me to come to Ardenna, because you know I hate coming to this infernal, noisy, smelly city." I pulled at Elena's long black hair until she stopped whispering in Jackson's ear to send Anders a sidelong glance that shared their mutual suffering at my hands.

"Fine. I admit it. For no other reason, Alex. Elder Frontish and I had nothing whatsoever of a serious nature to discuss. In fact, considering our new relationship is the most historic event since we opened trade with Meravan, our neighbor across the Skandar Sea, that little point is of no significance. Am I correct, Elder Frontish?"

"Absolutely," the gentleman replied, sitting back on his cushions, seeming more relaxed in our contentious company as time went on.

"See? I knew it." Elbowing Anders, I gave him a smug grin. "You always scold me for being disrespectful to the queen but that's a good example of why I am. If only Brendan were here, I might have more respect for the Crown. And Brendan shows more respect for me."

"Yes," Elder Frontish interjected, inclining his head toward Elena, "I am sorry to miss your heir and brother. Even north of our border in Derbarry, we have heard many good things about the young man."

"Don't ever tell him that." Elena laughed, her dark features reminiscent of Brendan. "He's sorry to miss you, too, but he's finally old enough for me to delegate tasks I prefer not to do." Her grin was openly affectionate. "Brendan should be back within the week, though I fear it will be too late. However, if you still plan to accompany the first shipment of precious gems from your mines in the Keshtang Mountains," —she threw in official business to spite me, I knew it— "I'll send my brother to welcome you."

"That's because she's lazy, Elder Frontish, and can't bear to leave this horrid city to visit her royal subjects." A complete and utter lie, as Elena was rarely at home in the fortress. More often than not, she came knocking at our door in the middle of the night. After a two-day journey south to Port Alain, where Jules ruled as duke, I taught the local children, and Anders plotted with Jules's mother as they gardened together.

"Your majesty." Anders bowed with deep respect from his comfortable perch on the elegant silk-woven rug. "Be assured I keep my daughter away from her mother when she behaves in this fashion.

Emmy will always treat you with respect and—" Anders neatly caught his balance as I shoved him.

"Leave my daughter out of this discussion."

"Poor Anders." Elena reached over to kiss my husband's smooth-shaven cheek. "She mistreats you so."

"She does, you know." Blue-eyed Lauryn, quiet until now, decided to make some abusive noise of her own. "You wouldn't believe what goes on back home."

"I can't believe you would turn on me." I threw a spiteful glance her way. "Just wait until I have your twins all to myself in the schoolroom."

Lauryn tossed an auburn strand over her silk-clad shoulder, dismissing my threat. "I still can't figure out why they adore you so. At eleven, they're old enough to know better.'"

I stared at Lauryn, shocked. "You never side with them against me. Never. Ever. Did my husband bribe you? Did Elena threaten your life? Did—"

"She should do it more often." Jules hugged his wife close with smug pride. "When sweet Lauryn has a nasty word for you, Alex," — he raked a hand through his hair, disheveling his appearance— "it says something pretty clear to me. In fact—"

"Why not shut up and be useful, my lord duke. Pour us some of that Marain Valley wine," I suggested, "since Elena's maid was kind enough to bring in a fresh bottle. Defending my reputation is thirsty work."

"So is offending you." Jules reached behind Lauryn's chair and poured us each a full glass of the rich fruity wine from the new bottle.

Jackson lifted his glass in a mocking salute but stopped abruptly. A curious expression bloomed in those indecent green eyes. He sniffed the contents, puzzled.

"Sour?" Anders held his wineglass close to his own nose and sniffed. "Possibly a bad batch of grapes from Tucker's Meadow. I'm not sure."

"I'm the expert," I said with confidence, sniffing my glass, and then making a judgment call. "I'll let you know." That decided, I brought the crystal glass to my lips and tilted it back as Anders did the same.

But I was the one, the only one, who took a deep, irreversible swallow.

"No!" Jackson leaped across the space between us to knock the glasses from both our hands. "Lords of the sea, Alex, no! Ah, no— Ah, damn."

I sat motionless, the remains of my wine spilled onto my silk gown, trying hard not to panic at the open fear in Jackson's eyes, because I knew what that expression meant.

"What is it?" Elena's voice tensed as she grabbed hold of Jackson's arm and shook it with little tenderness, knowing full well that neither of us was playing a trick. "Tell me! Jackson, what is it? Poison?"

Jackson's handsome face drained of all color. "Worse," he whispered, miserable eyes locked on mine in sympathy. "Feyweed." His voice shook, as he glanced at Elder Frontish, the gentleman's face expressing shock, and then back to me. "For Alex, it's worse than poison."

My eyes never left Jackson's face as I clutched Anders's hand with a death grip, waiting for the inevitable loss. So abrupt and cruel and painful, that I cried out in horror and despair, feeling the deep, cold, unending well of emptiness inside me. Knowing it was useless, still I tried to nudge my mage talent awake, searched for the piercing fire and ice that I so long denied. It was gone, utterly and completely gone, and I was lost. With a child's whimper, I groped my way into Anders's stunned embrace, needing his comfort until I could breathe easy again.

No one moved or spoke in the horrible silence until Elena placed a trembling hand on my shoulder in comfort. "There must be a draught to reverse this disaster. Jackson, surely— Elder Frontish, there must be—" Lost in a fog of misery, I heard the quiet desperation in Elena's voice and the hesitation in Jackson's as he muttered something vague, joined soon after by apology in the elder's voice. But Elena wouldn't accept their answers.

"There's no draught to reverse feyweed's damage." Gathering resolve, I raised my head from the shelter of Anders's chest to face Elena. "I'm afraid I'm useless to you now, your majesty." I brushed dampness from my cheeks with the back of a hand and thought longingly of my daughter. "I don't think the Ardenna Crown Council of Mages, despite their well-intentioned behavior these last five years, would tolerate a Mage Protector who no longer has a drop of magic at her command." I rose from the cushions, pushing free of Anders's protective grip, trying to ignore the cold void inside me. I was desperate to escape the pity I knew would be on all their faces.

"Alex, stop." Elena's dark blue eyes were damp as she tried to prevent my imminent fall into despair. "You're not thinking."

"There's nothing to think about. I—I need to go home."

"It's the middle of the night." Jules gripped my arm, his swiftly sobered eyes dazed with anxiety and shock and, as expected, pity.

"We've crept in and out of Ardenna before in the middle of the night." Not wanting to lash out in anger at my innocent friends, I kept fury and bitterness from my voice. But despair won out, nearly crippling me. "Anders, please—"

Compassion eloquent in his gaze, Anders stood up and led me from the room, away from Ardenna, and away from my pain.

* * * *

"I'm sorry," I whispered. "I couldn't bear to stay there a moment longer." Huddled tight against Anders's chest, feeling safe and sheltered, I was uncertain whether or not he was awake. But I should have known better.

"That's why I led you out of there, against Elena's pleas to stay until morning." When Anders ran a familiar hand along my spine, I shivered. Closing my eyes, I edged closer, snuggling against his bearish warmth. "Only a little longer tomorrow morning, Alex, and we'll be at your father's home in Hartswood." The lumpy bed creaked beneath his weight as Anders eased the tension from my neck and shoulders. Lords of the sea, but he was patient when I needed him to be. With not a single word of reproach, he'd stuffed our clothes into our travel bags while I changed into tunic and trousers, and led me out the city gates to a small inn on the outskirts of Ardenna. "Besides, it'll do you good to see Emmy. It'll do us both good."

Emmy, Emila Rose, named after the seamage mother I never knew and the woman who raised me, Rosanna Barlow. The kingdom's recorded history had never reported a child born of a Crownmage and Mage Protector. Our daughter was a mystery.

"How can I teach Emmy about magic when her own talent surfaces?" I whispered. "They stole that pleasure from me, too."

"We'll find an antidote, Alex. I promise."

"Don't promise something that's impossible."

Frowning, Anders placed a firm hand beneath my chin and forced me to look at him. "It's not like you to lose faith." When he saw the protest in my eye, he covered my lips with his finger and shook his head. "Don't start now."

* * * *

"Mama!" My serious, serene, well-mannered four-year-old daughter shouted in wild abandon when she saw us dismount in front of my father's cottage the next morning.

We'd made the trip south along the Kieren River and then west over the Glynnswood border to Hartswood. The village stood at the center of the deep forest, and we made good time, now that winter's end was in sight. Anders complained not once about the swift, reckless pace I set, anxious to put distance between me and the nightmarish reminder of what happened.

Desperate for comfort, I snatched Emmy into my embrace as she wrapped one tiny arm around my neck and the other around her father's, hugging us as though we'd been gone for a century. "You can't possibly be my daughter." I stared at the child in mock horror as the seagray eyes she inherited from Anders studied me back from beneath long dark curls she inherited from me. "Running about like a wild mountain lion. What will the people of Hartswood think of Elder Keltie's wild granddaughter?" I shook my head gravely and smoothed curls back from her pretty face. "You must be a changeling. Now, tell me, where's my little girl?"

Emmy laughed and hugged me tight. Lords of the sea, but I'd missed her, even for the few short days we'd been away.

"And what is this?" Keeping my expression stern, I plucked a fanciful carved wooden horse from her tiny hand. "Did you make it? Is it a dragon? A wild pig? I can't tell."

"Oh, Mama. It's a pony." Emmy giggled and cast a sidelong glance at my twenty-year-old half-brother. He was a decade younger than me, and had, as ever, crept beside us without the least bit of noise. "Uncle Gwynn made it for me."

"Did he now?" I barely managed to keep my balance under Gwynn's overwhelming hug. "And did he teach you to run about like a wild mountain lion and disgrace your grandfather?" Free from Gwynn's grip when he went to greet Anders, I turned to welcome Maylen Stockrie, my brother's constant companion for the past five years.

"I think Emmy learned wild manners from you." Gwynn's dark brown eyes danced with merriment as he tugged at Emmy's curls, tickling until she finally gave in and laughed. "But I am teaching her to creep up on unsuspecting victims, such as her mother, who still makes far too much noise in the forest."

"Nuisance. When will you ever grow up?"

"Is my son bothering you again? Shall I punish him for troubling the queen's Mage Protector?" My father's gentle, bemused voice shattered the brittle restraints I'd placed on my emotions. Anders instinctively grabbed Emmy from my weakened grasp with a murmured loving promise and shoved the bewildered child into Maylen's unquestioning arms. The moment Emmy vanished with Maylen, I turned for comfort in my father's arms, a far cry from my hostility seven years earlier when Sernyn Keltie unexpectedly entered my life.

"Bring Alex inside." Gwynn's mother and my stepmother, Anessa, appeared at the door to their low, sprawling cottage. "Now, Sernyn," she commanded, taking maternal control of the situation.

With a protective arm still around my shoulders, Father obeyed, guiding me to a well-worn favorite armchair, away from polite inquisitive villagers who may have noticed our noisy arrival. Anessa forced a steaming mug of cinnamon tea into my hands, holding her questions, and everyone else's, until I'd settled down. My trembling hands were saved from scalding when Gwynn's protective fingers closed over mine, steadying my grasp.

The three of them, along with Maylen, were the family I'd long been denied, struggled against, and finally accepted with an open heart. For long years, I believed my father dead, until an innocent venture into the forest to understand my unconventional mage heritage brought me face-to-face with Sernyn Keltie. For two years, I'd hated the man, blaming him for my mother's death. Elder Keltie, a mage as afraid of his own power as I'd been, had made my mother promise never to use her seamage talent when he was near. But Sernyn never admitted the truth to my mother, that he, too, was a mage, never suspecting they would create a child with unusual magical powers. When my mother was deep in labor with me, she couldn't defend herself, never understanding what was happening to her fragile body.

For a lifetime, I blamed myself, and then blamed Sernyn. It was a near miracle I'd found the courage and strength to bear my own child. And five years earlier, I declared a truce. I'd forgiven my father, taking his family into my heart and mind as fiercely as I'd fought to keep them away.

"I'm sorry," I murmured, shamefaced. "I promised myself I wouldn't be weak and make a scene when I got here."

"If you cannot be vulnerable in front of your family, then we are of no use," Gwynn scolded, his hands resting over my own, though they probably itched to tug at his still-misbehaving lock of hair.

"Still, I shouldn't fall apart in front of you." I shot a crooked smile in my brother's direction, trying to lighten his concern. "You'll never let me forget. Worse, you'll tattle on me to Rosanna, who'll claim I might be human."

"True. But she will never believe it."

"Gwynn, leave her be." My father broke into our banter, running a slender, sun-browned hand through his graying hair. He leaned forward, studying my face with care, as though he were a healer like his wife. "Tell us what has happened."

When all I did was sigh, unable to relate the horrifying tale, Anders stretched over to touch my cheek before making himself comfortable on the woven wool rug at my feet. "Someone mixed feyweed into our wine. Alex was the only one harmed," he added, squeezing my fingers in reassurance. "It happened so fast, too fast."

Gwynn's easy voice was fierce. "Who did this?"

"We don't know. I'm sure Elena will do whatever she can to find out." Anders gratefully accepted a cup of tea from Anessa. "You know she won't rest, not when her closest friend has been so grievously hurt."

My father kept his face on mine, though his question was directed at my husband. "Was Alex the only target?"

"I don't know. We were all sharing the same bottle."

"Is it possible one or more of the renegade mages you and Jackson captured five years ago escaped from their Spreebridge prison? Though the two women were out of their minds with madness, the lone man was lucid. Vengeance is something you are all too familiar with." My father's smile was sad as he placed a consoling hand on my arm.

I shrugged, careful to sip the tea without spilling it. "It's possible. But I thought the feyweed potion was a secret known only to the elders of Spreebridge. If the renegades knew how to make feyweed, and had the opportunity, it's very possible they would do to us what we did to them. Knowing what it feels like, now, to lose my magic," I admitted with bitterness and regret, "I wouldn't blame them. It's not something any mage should ever experience."

"It is also possible that Jackson is involved." Gwynn's huge brown eyes locked on mine, daring me to argue, challenging me to counter his words.

Surprising my brother, I managed a wry grin at his handsome clean-shaven face, dangling a possibility in front of him. "Apparently, you've never forgiven Jackson for striking you all those years ago when he captured us."

"No, I have not." Though Gwynn's smile matched mine, his protective fury leaked out. "But that is not why I mentioned him, Alex. I have a sound reason that goes beyond my personal humiliation."

"And that is?"

"Mage Tunney's magic is identical to the rare magic you have."

"Had."

"Stop that." Gwynn frowned in annoyance when I tried to be practical.

The sooner everyone got used to the fact I was without mage talent, the better.

"And do not forget it was Jackson's idea to send the renegade mages back to Spreebridge for punishment and that he introduced us to feyweed to use against the rogue mages. He knows how to mix the potion." When I started to protest, my brother held up a hand with uncharacteristic impatience. Rather than argue, I took another sip of tea before Anessa scolded me. "And yes, so does Anders, though you still do not know the contents." When Gwynn shook his head, bemused at my refusal to know what herbs went into making feyweed, for fear that I'd use it indiscriminately, I grumbled something rude. Ignoring me, he continued his argument. "And there is another point to consider, Alex. The queen has not married Jackson yet, though she is so taken with him. They became lovers soon after they met, so why has she still not wed him?"

Shrugging, I blinked at my brother, who was never this persistent and, in fact, had never broached this particular opinion with me. "I have no idea, though I've wondered, too." Sipping his tea, Anders exchanged a thoughtful look with Gwynn, and then my father. "Stop that," I scolded them. "Jackson's never done anything to make us distrust him. Lords of the sea, Anders, he knocked the glass from your hand."

"Before he knocked it from yours."

"You were closer."

"Maybe."

"That makes no sense. If anything, your mage talent, which is still unique, is even more a threat than mine." I lost patience and slammed my near-empty teacup on the carved wooden table and stood up. "Don't forget that Elder Frontish, a mage from Spreebridge, may I remind you, was also in Ardenna when I drank the feyweed. It's possible he was behind it."

"Alex." My father caught the wool of my tunic sleeve and held me back, though I shook his hand from my arm. "Stop frowning, and hold still a moment. While we may be wrong with our suspicions, and I hope we are for Elena's sake, we should keep an open mind." He held my gaze, his voice even and unstressed, despite my anger. The fact that he so easily offered advice and criticism was testimony to the strides we'd made over the last five years. "Maybe, just maybe, we have been too trusting."

"You mean," I growled, correctly interpreting his careful words, "maybe I've been too trusting." When my father didn't answer, I headed for the door to find my daughter. One hand resting on the wooden frame, I stopped and spun back to face him, aware of Anessa's concern as she stood in silence behind her son. "I've never lived in constant fear, and I won't start now. Besides," —I gave my father a pained smile— "the damage has already been done."

"To you." With eyes locked on mine, Sernyn pressed his point. "What if you were not the only target? Even Jackson may be a target, if we presume his innocence. Anders, then, may also be in danger." My father shrugged; his expression eloquent. "That is why I caution you."

"Lords of the sea, but I hate you when you're right." Grumbling, I went out in search of Emmy.

* * * *

"What will you do?"

Fastening Emmy's wool cloak around her neck early the next morning, I pulled my daughter close, kissed her smooth forehead, and sent her outside to join her father. Gwynn had cornered me in the guest bedchamber at the back of my father's cottage. "Go home, I suppose."

"That is not what I meant, and you know it." Gwynn didn't bother to disguise his irritation, which made me wonder why he was so prickly. His manner and temperament had always been more in line with the serenity exhibited by his parents. I was the contentious, cranky member of the family. To his credit, my father had never intimated I'd inherited that behavior from my mother.

I sat back on my heels, braced against the bed, and matched my brother's sober expression. "Years ago, when you were afraid I'd run away and that you'd never see me again, I told you it was quite all right to be angry with me. You haven't been angry since, well, not really angry, but you're furious now. And I'm not sure I like it, particularly since I don't understand it."

"I am not angry with you." Stubbornness crept into his voice. "But I want to know who was responsible. I am worried about you because—" Gwynn waved a rough hand in a futile gesture, at a loss, and looked away, finally resorting to a futile tug at the rogue lock of brown hair.

"Because?" I prompted, crossing my arms, puzzled.

Gwynn shrugged. "How can I explain it? Sometimes you are tough, Alex, stronger than all of us together. And sometimes I am afraid that with one wrong word, you will—" He hesitated, choosing his words with care as he faced me again. "You are fragile now, vulnerable, and I am frightened for you."

Lords of the sea, how had I ever survived my first twenty-five years without a younger brother? "I'm all right." I stood up, muffling a groan of protest, and ruffled his thick hair.

"Liar."

"That's my line."

"Not this time. I told father I want to go to Port Alain for a little while."

"No. Besides," I added as the immediate protest formed in his eyes, "what will Maylen do without you here?"

My brother looked at me as though I was a mad woman, or a fool, possibly both. "She will be with me, of course."

"I don't want you to come."

"Why not?"

"What's wrong with you?" I shouted, finally losing patience. "You're never this argumentative. You always give in to me."

My brother crossed his arms in open defiance. "Why not?" Though his tone was more reasonable, it was no less stubborn.

"I don't want you to see me like this," I whispered, blinking back tears. "I feel useless, powerless, flameblasted empty, Gwynn. And worse, I don't know what mage talent Emmy has yet, though she's inherited a wild mix of potential. I wanted to teach her, show her how to use it. My mother didn't survive to teach me—" I couldn't go on and turned away.

"I told you," Gwynn spoke in the same gentle, measured voice he inherited from my father, "there is nothing wrong in weeping in front of those who love you. Alex." He edged closer. "From the moment I led you around our village five years ago to keep you out of trouble, knowing you for the half-sister I had never seen, I pledged to keep watch over you. I have been through adventures with you and will do so again. But for now, I just want to be in reach if you need me. Please do not fight me on this." He tugged at my sleeve. "Please. It is important to me."

Wretched nuisance.

I sighed with heavy drama, wiped tears away with the back of my hand, and turned to face him. "Well, I suppose Rosanna could use an extra hand to clean out the Barlow stables."

Chapter Two

"Well, well, well." Sarcasm dripped from its owner's voice. "I can't believe I managed to corner the ill-tempered seabeast in her dark lair."

Ignoring the comment and the speaker, I continued rummaging through the illustrated books I'd spread out on the schoolroom table. Delighted to be back in Port Alain, a short journey south from Glynnswood's forest, I took refuge in my private sanctuary.

"If I didn't know better, I'd think you were avoiding me." When I tossed two books onto the left pile and slanted Rosanna Barlow a nasty look, she shrugged. "What did you expect me to think, young lady?" Jules's mother, hair heavily gray-streaked, left her sentry position by the open doorway. "Well?"

"Can you shut that door, please?" Just in time, I slapped a hand down on the papers primed to fly away as the wind kicked up outside. "Looks like a storm brewing."

Rosanna obeyed, and then came to perch on a low wooden stool opposite me and rested her chin on one plump hand. "Hmm, speaking of storms, I always thought that weather often matched a person's mood."

"Listen, old seawitch—"

"Now, Alex." Rosanna raised one eyebrow, unfazed by my unflattering words. "You know better than to sweet talk me. It never works." When I started to laugh, despite my reluctance to answer, she smiled. "Much better. Now, were you avoiding me?"

"Absolutely."

"One honest answer," she mumbled under her breath. "Let's see what else I can find out that Anders and Gwynn haven't told me yet. Maylen's a bit more close-mouthed and loyal to you, but I'll eventually wear her down. All right, Alex." Rosanna sat back on the stool to give me breathing space and crossed her arms. "How are you? Really? And no nonsense."

"I'm fine."

"Liar."

"You sound like Gwynn. I am fine. Why doesn't anyone believe me?" I asked in frustration, tossing three books onto the right pile to appear my activity really had a purpose. But Rosanna's sudden visit caught me off guard, and the piles were no doubt mixed.

"They all know you better. Alex, Alex, Alex." Rosanna sighed, shaking her head in disapproval. "You're not talking to Lauryn, who has far more patience for your round-about way of getting to the truth, or my daughter, Khrista, who might actually believe you if you said it with sufficient authority. You're talking to me, the formidable Lady Barlow. I raised you, remember?"

"How could I ever forget those years of cruel discipline?" At her sudden frown, my own sigh was loud and equally dramatic. "What do you want from me?"

"The truth. That's all I ever ask."

I could play that game, too. "You want me to be honest with you just like you've always been honest with me?"

Scarlet with emotion, Rosanna defended herself. "Don't you dare throw any past white lies in my face. It's old history."

"White lies?" I laughed, finding it difficult to keep sarcasm from my tone. "My father dead when I was barely a week old, for one thing. Let's see, what else?"

"All right. I was wrong, and Sernyn was wrong. But my intentions were good, and he had his reasons. You know that, or you should if you'd been paying attention for the last five years." Rosanna's sigh this time signaled her resignation to my contentious mood.

I took pity on her. "Your intentions are always good." As she appraised the subtle change in my tone, free of mockery, I went on. "What do you want me to say about what happened? I lived without magic for most of my life because I denied its existence. It frightened the breath from me. So I'll learn to do it again."

"Not so easily."

"No," I admitted, running a hand along the edge of a well-worn book. "But I have no choice. I can't keep thinking about it or I'll go mad. I feel lost. Lost, empty, and useless. Does that make you feel better? And worse, Rosanna, I'm worried someone else will be hurt because of me. I know—" I stopped the indignant protest that sprang to her lips. "It's not rational, but it's how I feel. I thought I knew what feyweed could do when I saw despair in the renegades' eyes." I glanced up at the older woman, not bothering to hide my own despair. "But to be frank, if I'd any idea how devastating it felt, I might not have allowed Jackson to punish them in such a way."

Rosanna played with the old duke's signet ring. "I wish there was some way to make it better for you."

I shrugged, dismissing her worry. "It'll pass. These things always do."

"Yes, of course," she said, not bothering to argue. "But in the meanwhile, what will you do?" Rosanna rested her chin back on her hand, keeping a precarious balance on the low wooden stool.

"You sound like Gwynn again."

"Yes, well. We've been chatting," she said, and then added with a smirk, "while he's been cleaning out the stables."

As though she'd ever make him do such a thing. Having me do it, on the other hand, was an entirely different story.

"I'm sure you've enjoyed numerous chats," I said dryly. "Anyway, since you've asked about my plans, I'm also sure you've thought about an answer."

"You always misjudge me."

Straightening the confused piles of books, I cleared the table of loose documents, waiting patiently, knowing I was right when Rosanna cleared her throat with great delicacy.

"You could, ah, well, travel north to Spreebridge."

I'd thought of that on the journey back to Port Alain while Anders kept Emmy preoccupied with a story about wicked stepmothers.

"Whatever for?"

"To find out if there's a way to reverse the effects of feyweed."

I'd thought of that, too.

Rosanna kept her expression neutral. "And, ah, maybe find out who's behind the attack if Spreebridge was involved, and, well, if there are any other targets."

I'd thought of that, as well.

Rosanna tapped a finger in a sporadic rhythm on the scarred tabletop, waiting for my answer.

"I'm not interested."

Standing, with a very unladylike oath about my lifelong stubbornness, Jules's mother gave me a long, piercing look. "You're not interested at the moment." She sighed and turned away from me, heading toward the door. "I know better. It's not like you to do nothing."

"Go away."

"We'll see, Alex. We'll see."

Watching Rosanna depart, I waited until she was out of sight before taking a blank scrap of paper from the far end of the table. In silence, I held it in the sweaty palm of my hand and called on the fire and ice that had come so easily these past years. I waited in vain. I tried to concentrate, imagining the paper as the flame of a candle, or the drip of water from a pipe, or, even, as a puff of air. But the paper remained paper, and my gut held no fire and ice, held nothing but cold ash that was as bitter as the wind howling outside the schoolroom door. Crumpling the paper into a ball, I flung it across the room and out of my sight.

* * * *

"Elena!" Emmy squirmed like a slithery sea serpent in my arms until I set her down on the hard ground.

"Easy. Easy— Don't run."

Elena? She was holding court in Ardenna, wasn't she? Obviously not. My queen was sitting on a stone bench, dark head bent in close, intimate conversation with my brother, a cozy little scene that set my instinct humming. At Emmy's joyful shout, Elena glanced up barely in time to snatch the imp in her arms, settling Emmy on her lap with a warm hug.

"Don't you have a kingdom to run?"

"Don't you have children to teach?"

"I did this morning. What's your excuse?"

"Queens don't need an excuse, according to your husband. Besides, I left Brendan in Ardenna, allowing my heir the opportunity to see what he can sneak by me when I'm not there." Dark blue eyes shone with amusement as Elena nudged Gwynn. "That's what younger brothers do, cause trouble behind your back when you're not there to stop them."

"They do not." Warring with high regard and affection for Elena, Gwynn's indignation lasted only a brief moment. "Well, sometimes they do," he added with reluctance, though a bright smile lit his face.

"All the time. And it's disgraceful how that unsuspecting child adores you," I complained to Elena, waving at my daughter, quietly content to sit on Elena's lap, swinging her short legs with little regard for the authority of the person holding her.

"She doesn't adore me. We're just good friends." Elena hugged my daughter close again. "And we don't see each other often enough, do we?" When Emmy shook her head as though she'd participated in a delicate three-way trade negotiation between Tuldamoran, Meravan, and Spreebridge on behalf of the Crown Council of Mages, Elena chuckled.

"The child is a traitor," I mumbled, taking a seat on the opposite bench. "Just like her father. I knew I should've booted him out of the cottage years ago."

When Elena bent her head of jet-black hair to my daughter's brown curls, wicked dark blue eyes met solemn seagray ones. "Does your mother always mutter to herself?"

Emmy nodded, after a cautious sidelong glance at me, and then smiled shyly as Elena laughed aloud.

"It's all my brother's fault, too. I should have kept him away until Emmy turned twenty-five. If not for Maylen curbing his trouble-making tendencies—" When Gwynn started to protest, I waved him quiet. "And lords of the sea know what lies and deceptions he's told you just now."

"Not one lie." Gwynn stood, towering over me, making me aware of how tall he'd grown in the past few years. "Not even a tiny deception." With a polite, affectionate nod to Elena, a wink at Emmy, and a ridiculous childish face at me, Gwynn vanished down the garden path, heading back to the manor.

"Fool."

"Yes, all of them." Elena shifted my daughter to her other leg. "But we love them, anyway. And without Anders," —she stroked Emmy's soft, rosy cheek with unaccustomed tenderness— "you wouldn't have this exquisite and sweet-hearted child."

"Who obviously doesn't take after either Anders or me," I said lightly, not sure of Elena's subtle mood shift or why she was visiting, although I had some ideas.

"You're wrong, old friend. She has the best of both of you, though Anders has more favorable traits." Despite her playfulness, Elena's tone was wistful.

"You can have your own little seabeast, you know." When Elena smiled, I paused to think about my next words. For all the secrets we'd shared, I couldn't read her expression. Gwynn's disturbing question some days earlier came to mind. "You're wildly in love with Jackson, as even Elder Frontish must know by now after your scandalous, decadent behavior in front of the poor man," I hedged, trying on a feeble smile, "yet—" I waved a hand in the air, pretending to search for the right word, which didn't fool Elena.

"Why haven't I married him?" She swiftly guarded her expression, a thick wall threatening to crash down between us.

"I don't mean to pry."

"Sure, you do, Alex. But why shouldn't you?" Elena's laugh, though earnest, was uneasy. "I'm always pushing you for explanations when you're being evasive."

"As you are now."

"I suppose."

"Well, then, why not?" Assuming she'd just given me approval to badger her, I watched Elena's face with care, not because I suspected Jackson of involvement in the feyweed incident but because I was suddenly, inexplicably, fretting about Elena.

Thin shoulders shrugged beneath her wool cloak as she closed her eyes to the sunlight. "I don't know. No, Alex." She shook her head slowly, her voice soft and uncertain. "That's not entirely true."

And I knew, without asking, what Elena would say. Yet I needed to hear her speak the words aloud, so that maybe, somehow, I could help her slide past the pain destined to haunt her peace of mind.

"Because of Erich?"

I trod with delicacy. The heartache had never fully healed when her lover, the former Duke of Barrow's Pass, allied himself five years ago with Firemage Ravess to topple Elena from the throne. That same lover, whom I'd pushed into a compromising situation to reveal his treachery, fell into a trap that ended with Elena executing him in cold blood.

"Hmm."

"Jackson is a different animal. Erich was a traitor."

Elena met my gaze. "Though I'd had warning, I never fully acknowledged that ugly truth until the end, until it was almost too late."

"Yes, but we all saw it earlier without our hearts blinding us to the truth. And none of us see ugliness in Jackson," I said with what I hoped was sufficient persuasion, pushing Gwynn's disturbing speculation from my head. "He's as wild about you as you are about him. Lords of the sea, he can't keep his hands off you, even when a distinguished elder mage from Spreebridge is visiting."

Elena's voice was pitched low, not responding to my tease. She toyed with Emmy's curls, the child solemn and content. "I'm afraid, Alex, afraid to take that next serious step that binds us together."

"So was I."

"And look what you now have." She kissed the top of my daughter's head and closed her eyes. "I think Jackson's afraid, too. Marrying me makes him Prince of Tuldamoran. I'm not sure he wants the responsibility and status."

"Does he ever press you on the subject?"

"No." She shook her head, studying me. "In fact," —she laughed with a trace of bitterness— "we speak freely of everything under the sun but where our relationship is heading."

"Maybe you should."

Her laugh this time was genuine and relaxed. "From what Anders tells me, you're a fine one to lecture."

"That son of— Hmm." I coughed with exaggerated delicacy at Emmy's sudden wide-eyed look. "Anders is more loyal to you than to me. Someday, when Emmy's not looking," —I winked at my daughter— "I'm going to throw him out and send him to you." Thoughtful, I tucked my legs beneath me and settled my chin in my hand. "Do you know, since Emmy's birth, you haven't barged into our cottage in the middle of the night? It's distressing to have these civilized daytime conversations. It loses something essential to be sitting in Rosanna's gardens on a chilly afternoon when I ask you why you're in Port Alain."

Elena settled the ends of her cloak around my daughter's wool-clad legs as a light breeze stirred her hair. "I was wondering when you'd get around to that."

"Well?"

"I was worried about you."

"You have more than enough willing spies and conspirators in Rosanna's manor. Surely they've been sending you detailed reports," I complained, sounding no older than my daughter, who never once in her short life had ever whined.

"True." Scratching her head in an absent-minded gesture, Elena narrowed her eyes. "And I didn't like what I was hearing."

"I'm all right."

"You keep saying that. But you can't tolerate being near anyone who openly uses magic or discusses it," she challenged, daring me to contradict her truthful words.

"What else have they told you?"

"That you're prone to weep at a moment's notice, somewhat more contentious than usual, if that's possible." She tossed a grin my way. "And withdrawn more times than not."

Well, yes, that was pretty accurate.

"Frankly, Alex," she continued, ignoring my growing pout, "it's a miracle they haven't sent you off on an adventure."

"Are you planning to send me off on an insignificant diplomatic mission?" When her only answer was a low growl, I said, "All right. I admit I haven't been my usual delightful self, but I'm not that bad."

"I don't believe you." Elena lowered her voice as Emmy drifted off to sleep, so content in Elena's arms I was tempted to send her to Ardenna for Elena's sake.

"Listen," I whispered with a heavy sigh, "I don't know what they expect me to do. For the lords' sake, Elena, do you know how many times I try to feel the magic and use it or, worse, forget it's gone?" I leaned forward, almost losing my balance on the chilled bench. "More times than I care to remember. And each time, it hurts all over again."

"I'm so sorry." Elena kept her gaze fixed on mine. "I wish I could give you an easy answer. Elder Frontish said he'll investigate the matter in Spreebridge, so I hope he finds something useful. In the meantime, Jackson had word from his mentor, Westin Harlowe."

"Wasn't he the one who sponsored Jackson as an elder and allowed him to join the governing council up in Derbarry?"

"Yes. Elder Harlowe confirmed the three renegade mages are still safely imprisoned." Her expression was grave as she wrapped a fallen end of cloak around Emmy's leg. "Apart from you, Alex, we don't know if there are any other targets." When I turned my face away, Elena poked my knee. "What?"

"I was wondering," I chose my words with care, "when you'll make a royal proclamation to your subjects that your fierce Mage Protector can't protect you. A mage without magic is useless. You may as well save the taxpayers' money."

"I haven't said anything, and I don't plan to. Lords of the sea, Alex." Blue eyes flashed in annoyance. "You're not useless, though some days I think you might be witless. You're my friend, which you often forget."

"True, but I'm also your Mage Protector. Wait, Elena, let me think for a moment." I got to my feet and paced away from her bench and then back in her direction until she grabbed my arm to hold me still.

"About what?"

"About how to convince you I'm serious. I can no longer be your Mage Protector. Face it, the Crown Council of Mages would be horrified and scandalized to know that you still consider me in that role. That—"

"You're giving me a headache. Whom I choose to appoint to the role of Mage Protector is my privilege. The Crown Council needn't bother itself with that information." She glared when I started to speak, effectively shutting me up. "Their role is to monitor and guide the local Mage Councils throughout Tuldamoran and ensure everyone is using their mage talent for the good of their people. Although," she continued, narrowing her eyes when I tried to sneak in a word, "they're also supposed to counsel the throne on mage-related matters. I choose to use my Mage Protector for that purpose. In fact—"

"In fact," I suggested, cursing my brother for his suspicion, "you could and should declare Jackson as your new Mage Protector since his magic is identical to mine. Or what mine was."

"Stop that, Alex."

"Well, if he doesn't want to be Prince," I said amiably, not fooling Elena, "it's a respectable position he could fill. Besides, I'd feel better, knowing he was acting in my place."

"I hate to admit it, but you're right about these daytime visits." Annoyed, Elena cradled Emmy in her arms as she stood up. "Apparently, you're more civilized and reasonable in the middle of the night."

I flashed Elena a disarming smile. "That's why Anders married me."

Chapter Three

"Is that the Dunneal royal seal?" Head cocked to the side, Anders peeked with open curiosity at the note I'd just started to read, some weeks later, in the Seaman's Berth. "You carried it into town without opening it? Or even mentioning it? I'm impressed."

"I have patience." I refused to admit, even to my husband, the bad feeling I harbored about the contents and procrastinated until I had some ale in my belly.

"I love you more than anything, Alex, but honest? You have as little patience as your dear departed mother, which was" —Anders grinned as I craned my neck to look at him— "practically nonexistent."

"According to my father, Emila Daine Keltie had no faults." Ignoring my husband's smirk, I waved the note and complained, "Your queen was too lazy to deliver it herself." I signaled Chester, the bartender and owner of the establishment, whose young daughter was a firemage. "Another ale, please?"

"Another?" Anders sank back against the seat. "You think it's bad news." Though I continued to read, I laughed in appreciation, prompting a nudge in my ribs. "Well?"

"Be patient. I just started reading."

"You're too slow."

"All the better to savor bad news."

"Ah. Then it is bad."

"Flameblast it," I grumbled, immediately apologetic as the innkeeper set two mugs of ale on the scarred table, raising his bushy eyebrows. "I'm not cursing you, Chester. It's my husband, who won't let me read in peace."

"Better you than me." Chester grinned at Anders, tossing over his retreating shoulder. "Lords know, I don't want Alex bewitching me into a goat."

"Gee, thanks." Cool seagray eyes tried their best to look contrite as Anders blinked at me. I wasn't convinced of his innocence or apology, but he did sit obedient and quiet, sipping the foam from his mug, until I started to frown.

I didn't look up when he tugged at my tunic sleeve, couldn't quite meet his eyes. "There's no way to reverse the effects of feyweed," I explained, trying hard to keep disappointment out of my voice.

"Yet." When I refused to look up, he repeated with more emphasis, "Yet, Alex."

"You said that already. Be original."

Anders raked a hand through his gray-streaked black hair and exhaled noisily. "Just because there's no antidote now doesn't mean there won't be."

Not wanting to arouse Chester's suspicion, since I'd agreed to keep my loss a secret for the moment, even though I'd trust the innkeeper with my life, I blinked to fight back the tears. "If I believe there's no hope," I whispered, "I won't be disappointed."

"That's the coward's way to think."

"Then maybe I'm a coward."

When I met Anders's stare with a valiant effort at defiance, he met it with an unreadable expression. "Maybe you are."

Without taking the bait, I looked away. "If the surviving renegades are still locked away, and if they're involved at all, so is someone on the outside. They must have had help particularly since only one of them is lucid enough to even plan vengeance."

"Someone in authority." Anders seemed thoughtful when I looked up. "How trustworthy is Jackson's mentor, Westin Harlowe?"

I smacked his hand. "You sound like my brother."

"I'm not implying anything about Jackson's innocence or guilt," Anders said evenly, "only his mentor, who happens to be a Spreebridge elder and mage. Just like" —he sipped the ale, wiping foam from his lips with a finger— "Derek Frontish."

"I forgot that."

"On purpose. You're not that forgetful."

"What should we do?"

"Hmm." Anders's fingers wandered over to mine. "Let's see if we can come up with anything we both might enjoy. Emmy's with Maylen all afternoon, and if you drink up and finish your ale like a good little wife—"

The front door of the Seaman's Berth opened, letting a stream of sunlight shine through, along with my brother, Gwynn, who peered around the crowded room. I waved him inside, laughing at Anders's disappointed frown.

"You should be used to interruptions," I murmured in Anders's ear.

"In the middle of the night." He slanted me a dark look. "But since Emmy was born, Jules and Elena have been quite decent. Though I must say, I miss those late visits from time to time." Confronting my poor brother, Anders demanded, "Is there a reason you followed us down here? Or are you just being spiteful and interfering in my free time with my wife since Maylen isn't available for your enjoyment and— Ooph," Anders caught his breath as I elbowed his gut. "That wasn't necessary."

When I snarled at my husband, guessing from my brother's face that trouble was afoot, Gwynn shot me a lopsided grin that swiftly faded. "Forgive me. I know you wanted to have the afternoon to yourselves." Gwynn tugged at the rebellious lock of brown hair. "But Father is here, with my mother. Alex . . ." He hesitated, brown eyes wide, "I think there is something wrong, but he will not tell me." Shaking his head in frustration, Gwynn complained, "I am old enough now, and still people do not tell me everything."

"Then he'd better tell me." I downed the ale and tossed coins on the table, pushing back my chair.

Anders grabbed my arm. "Sernyn could be here for just a visit."

"Anders." I sighed heavily, trying not to scream, "I've already had bad news from Elena, and it's only the middle of the afternoon. I don't expect the day to end without more bad news."

"You're developing a pessimistic outlook."

I flung my cloak around my shoulders. "If my father's here in Port Alain for a simple, unplanned, neighborly visit, it will be a very pleasant surprise. Then you can say 'I told you so.' But don't count on it."

* * * *

Trouble had come to Port Alain.

I knew the moment I saw the guarded expression in my father's eyes that serious trouble was indeed afoot, and tried to ignore it as we greeted Sernyn, Anessa, and Rosanna in the sun parlor on the Hill. Having given my daughter into Lauryn's willing care, Maylen leaned against the window ledge, her very casualness and appearance sending my instinct screeching as she made room for Gwynn to squeeze in beside her.

"I am sorry, Alex, to visit without sending word. Lady Barlow has been, as always, gracious." With that introduction, my father gave me a brief hug, the one quick squeeze confirming what I already suspected. Anessa did the same, before sinking onto the pillow-strewn couch beside my father, a mirror image of Gwynn and the ever-present Maylen.

Desperate for a hint of normalcy, I dropped to a pile of overstuffed pillows next to Anders before the blazing fireplace and said dryly, "I didn't think we were so formal that you had to send an announcement." Craning my neck in Rosanna's direction, where she busied herself over tea and blueberry scones, making me suspect that she was worried, too, I asked, "Have you changed the house rules?"

When my father smiled as Rosanna started to scold me, I could see how troubled that smile appeared. "If you pester Lady Barlow, I will have to listen for an hour or more as she recalls, with great detail, every insult and indiscretion you have made since our last visit."

"I'd rather that didn't happen. So, tell me then," I drawled, "why you're here without sending word." Resting my chin in one hand, I mimicked Maylen's too-casual demeanor, fooling no one.

"Oh, what am I thinking?" Flustered, Rosanna interrupted my father's reluctant answer as she remembered her own manners. "I'll leave—"

"No, please." My father gave her a warm smile, which did nothing to disguise the underlying tension. "It is a family matter, and you are family." He stole a quick glance at Anessa, who squeezed his arm with reassurance. Taking a deep breath, he said, "Some days ago, we received another shipment of Marain Valley wine from the queen."

"Another?" Fearing the knot growing in my gut, I feigned annoyance and narrowed my eyes to slits. "How often does she share my wine?"

"Your wine? Ah, I've forgotten the vintners boast of the Royal Mage Protector's preference for their fine product." Anders tugged at a strand of my curls. "There's more than enough in Tuldamoran to keep you sated. Don't be greedy. Just be thankful Elena's generous enough to spread the wealth without touching your supply. Go on, Sernyn."

My father's expression was peculiar, and I didn't like not being able to read him. "I sampled the wine." He looked down at the worn leather of his traveling boots, a little trait we had in common, enjoying the comfort of old boots.

"And?" I pressed. Though he fumbled for words, they weren't necessary. I read the truth in his eyes. "Damn them."

"What is wrong?" Gwynn knelt at my side in confusion and concern, missing the point. "Tell me."

My eyes still locked on my father's, I shook my head in despair. "There was feyweed in the wine. Anessa?" I searched my stepmother's eyes with an unvoiced question.

She shook her head. "I did not have any, Alex."

"Thank the lords of the sea. But you— I'm sorry," I told my father.

His even voice and gentle eyes held ancient pain. "I never used the talent, Alex, not for years, not even to help Khrista give birth to Linsey."

Linsey was the child of Jules's sister, Krista, a late-blooming sea-mage, and one of the renegade Spreebridge mages now imprisoned in Derbarry. We believed the child had talent just like mine. Though Khrista had been raped by that mage, her husband Kerrie loved the child as his own. Linsey was much like Emmy in that neither of them had yet to show actual mage talent beyond the glimpses of something we'd had at childbirth. When I was in labor, I was able to control Emmy's raw magic with Anders's help, but it'd taken several of us to get Khrista out of danger.

No one had helped my mother give birth to me, couldn't, because they didn't understand what was happening, which resulted in her painful death. But I didn't throw the hurtful words at my father because I didn't need to say them aloud. Because, finally, after what seemed like a lifetime to both of us, I'd forgiven him.

"That's not true. You and Anessa helped teach Khrista what to expect. Without your help, things would have been more difficult for her, and a whole lot scarier."

"It does not matter." Gwynn's anger cut through my troubled words. "If we do not stop these attacks—"

My father placed a restraining hand on my brother's arm as Gwynn jumped off the window ledge and started to pace, reminding me of Elena in one of her restless moods. "We do not know who else is targeted."

"That's what really troubles me. Before you scold me," I warned Sernyn, "the fact that you, as my father, received a crate of tainted wine, makes me think the attack is somehow connected to me. Gwynn's right. This situation can't go on without resolution." Remembering my own taste of the wine, I had a sudden crazy thought. "But the odor—"

My father sighed with fatigue and shook his head. "They masked it better than when you drank it. By the time I sensed something wrong, it was too late. And Alex," —he gave me a sharp look in warning that I wouldn't like his next words— "this attack on me does not, does not," he repeated for emphasis, "necessarily mean that it was connected to you. It might very well be," he hedged when I started to protest, "but we cannot be sure yet."

Rosanna plucked fingers at my tunic sleeve. "Elena would never send—" She didn't finish her thought, didn't need to.

"Of course not, but Jackson would." Gwynn's usually warm brown eyes defied me to contradict him.

Instead, I stared at my brother for a long tense moment, thinking hard, before breaking free of his intense gaze, unsettled. "Did any note come with the shipment?"

"Yes" My father fumbled in a hidden pocket of his tunic and drew out a neat folded paper, complete with Elena Dunneal's royal seal, the gold crown surrounded by sapphires.

I took the letter from his outstretched hand and read the affectionate, harmless message that ended with Elena's signature, not a single word in her handwriting. Silent, I stood up to stare out the window overlooking Rosanna's gardens, the trees and bushes poised on the verge of blossoming any day as the winter's chill receded. After a moment, Anders stood beside me and took the letter from my tight grasp. When he finished reading, I pulled from my own pocket the note from Elena I'd read earlier in the Seaman's Berth, and handed it to him.

Anders compared them in silence, seagray eyes calm as he scanned the contents and the handwriting. "This note at the bottom from Jackson—"

Disheartened, I shut my eyes tight. "I can't do this to Elena again. I can't—"

Tell her that her lover, again, might be a traitor.

Gwynn joined us, pulling me around to face him. "If it is Jackson's handwriting, perhaps someone made it appear to be his handwriting."

I laughed at Gwynn's suggestion, but the sound was hollow. "Giving him a fair chance, little brother, after slandering his good name in earnest?"

Gwynn didn't blink, though he tugged at the misbehaved lock of hair that hung in his eyes. "It is possible."

"It is possible, Alex. Think for a moment." My father drummed restless fingers against his thigh. "What do we know? Or what do we think we know?"

"What do we know?" With a resigned sigh, I fell back into my seat of cushions by the crackling fireplace, Anders trailing behind. "One: Someone tried to trick me, and you, too, by blocking our magic. Two:

They tried to do the same to Anders and Jackson and Anessa. Maybe. Or made it look like that was true. Three: Jackson introduced feyweed to us." I gave my father an apologetic glance as I waved Elena's recent note to me in his direction. "Four: Jackson claims there's no way to reverse the effects of feyweed." With a not very subtle nudge from Anders, I added, "Yet. Yet. All right. Yet. Who knows? Five: If the renegade mages in prison up north are involved, they must have outside help. Since knowledge of feyweed is restricted to the elders, according to Jackson, then an accomplice may be an elder or someone privy to an elder's secrets." Pausing for breath, I leaned back against Anders. "Oh." I sat forward again as another thought entered my head. "Six: Someone knows my father enjoys Marain Valley wine almost as much as I do."

Rosanna studied me for a moment, tapping her fingers against the wooden arm of her chair, oblivious to my father's similar activity. "Well," she hesitated, her tea forgotten on the low table, when I encouraged her to speak, "there are a few possibilities, given all these things we know or think we know. The intended victims could be those with Crownmage or Mage Protector talent which would account for you and Anders and Jackson at that dinner. Or you and your family, which covers you and your father and Anessa, if only for vengeance or because Glynnswood magic helped create a mage like you, Alex." Rosanna continued to tap her fingers. "The imprisoned renegades could be responsible with an elder's help, possibly Jackson's mentor, Westin Harlowe. Possibly Jackson is involved, possibly not. Possibly Elder Frontish started matters rolling when he was in the capital." She sent Gwynn a guarded look. "Possibly Jackson alone is responsible."

"There's another possibility," Anders murmured, breaking off a piece of blueberry scone and handing me the rest. "The Ardenna Crown Council of Mages, newly appointed by Elena after you defeated

Firemage Ravess, has been very well behaved. Though they offer counsel to Elena from time to time, she depends on you, Alex," he said, reminding me of my recent words to the queen in Rosanna's garden. "Might be" —he shrugged— "they're jealous of your position and behind this little melodrama."

"What about the others? What are their motives?" I demanded, as Anders rubbed my neck with familiar ease to rid it of tension.

Rosanna blinked and stopped tapping. "If the renegades are involved, vengeance, pure and simple. You told me, Alex, the feeling of loss is so terrible that had you known, you might have prevented Jackson from giving them feyweed." Her expression held compassion. "And if Jackson is the culprit, it may be jealousy of your talent and the position you hold in Elena's court, much like the Crown Council of Mages might feel."

"So what you're saying is that we don't know anything."

"Not very much that's certain. Not yet, anyway. Of course," Rosanna added in an exquisite bland tone, studying the wood grain of her chair, "you could always go north to Spreebridge." Watching the wily old woman, I hugged my knees to my chest as she said, "Besides the reasons I gave you days ago, a trip north would give you a closer look at Jackson's mentor and Elder Frontish without their knowledge. And you might be able to determine whether there's any communication between Spreebridge and Ardenna that should concern you." She smiled with mock innocence. "I'm sure you can devise any number of legitimate reasons to suit your needs."

"You mean, we should spy."

"Well, yes." A guarded look crept back into her eyes.

"What else?"

"Well . . ." She started to tap her fingers again. "You might see whether Jackson's telling the truth about not being able to reverse the feyweed's effects."

"Since you seem to have it all mapped out, where do you think we should start? I don't know a soul in Spreebridge, with the exception of Derek Frontish. And I can't very well ask him or Jackson for any introductions." Surprised, though I shouldn't have been, I caught the stealthy look exchanged between Anessa and my father, and wondered what other little secrets Sernyn had decided not to share with me over the years.

"Alex—" My father's cheeks flushed scarlet in embarrassment, refusing to look at me. "I traveled for a time to Spreebridge after Emila—" His eyes were locked to the spot on the lush carpet between his worn boots. "After you were born. An elder mage in Derbarry kept me from ending my life," his voice grew unsteady, "though I tried several times. She—"

"She?" I bit my lip as his flush deepened.

"Yes." His dark head was still bowed. "I stayed with Kimmer Frehan for a year before returning home to Hartswood. I had responsibilities—"

"In Glynnswood." I couldn't keep the bitterness from my voice. "Not Port Alain."

He dragged guilty eyes upward to meet mine. "Yes."

Though I had forgiven my father for abandoning me as an infant, still the pain crept in with stunning force to shake me. I threw off Anders's restraining hand and jumped up, slamming the oak door behind me.

* * * *

"Would it help if I beat Father senseless? Or if Maylen and I held him down while you beat him senseless?"

I laughed with genuine affection at my furious brother, who had dogged my steps, as expected. "I don't think so."

Gwynn sat beside me on a stone bench in Rosanna's garden. "I would like to, Alex. It would make me feel better."

I patted my brother's knee to calm him down. "It happened almost thirty years ago. I don't think it's fair to beat him senseless now."

Gwynn didn't blink. "Well, I do. Alex, look at you." He pulled out a rough handkerchief and wiped tears from my wet cheeks. "It is all his fault. He continues to break your heart when you least expect it."

Not surprised at my brother's fierce loyalty to me, I waved the handkerchief away and gripped his shoulders, forcing him to listen to reason. "It's in the past, Gwynn. I accepted that five years ago. And it's not fair to Father if you're angry over something that happened to me before you were even born."

"When I was born, he still refused to acknowledge you," Gwynn said stubbornly, chin thrust forward, daring me to contradict him.

"I know," I admitted, struggling between tears and laughter, at the protectiveness Gwynn had shown from the first day we'd met, "but I accepted all that. It's what forgiveness means. Everything is different now."

"Oh, certainly, I can see that." One dark brown eyebrow rose ever so slightly in mockery at the damp handkerchief he waved at my face. "But it still causes you pain." He crossed his arms, locking gazes with me, until I looked down at my worn boots, no different than my father, and sighed. "Then let me beat him senseless. It may not make you feel better, but it will make me feel better."

Envisioning that image in my head, I started to laugh and pulled Gwynn upright with me. "Thanks, but no. Maybe some other time."

With a fierce affectionate hug, I dragged him back to Rosanna's sun parlor in her tower, overlooking these very same gardens. When we reached her quarters, I didn't look at anyone but Anders, sitting at ease by the crackling fire. He shifted to make room for me and settled his arms around my shoulders as I leaned against him. I took a deep breath and only then looked at my father, at soulful eyes that, for me, always held a fleeting glimpse of sorrow and regret from the moment I'd met him so unexpectedly in the forest. "I'm sorry." When he started to protest, I held up a hand. "I don't know why, but it still hurts. Doesn't matter. It was a lifetime ago. You were a fool then."

Sernyn nodded gravely. "I was indeed a fool then." He stole a furtive look at Rosanna. "And for many years after."

"You were. I won't deny it, but things are different now, Elder Keltie. However," —I glared, running both hands through my hair— "if you continue to place me in a precarious situation where Rosanna actually suspects I have a heart, I may have to disown you."

At Father's bright smile of relief, Rosanna leaned over to smack my arm. "I know you're not human, so don't try to pretend. It won't work."

Gracing the senior Lady Barlow with a crooked grin, I turned back to my father, who was staring, wide-eyed, at Gwynn. "Come, sit." I patted the floor beside me when Gwynn didn't budge. "Gwynn, it's all right." He exchanged an odd look with my father that held, I suspected, a serious warning. "Flameblast you." I stretched to grab his deep green wool tunic and nearly toppled him to the floor beside me. "I told you I'll let you know when you can beat him senseless," I whispered, loud enough for my father and Anessa to hear, "but not now." Gwynn didn't respond to my teasing, didn't even look at me. Impatient, and more than a little worried, I turned to Maylen, who hadn't budged from her spot on the window ledge overlooking the garden. "I'm holding you responsible for this fool."

Maylen tossed a blonde braid over her slender shoulder and raised an eyebrow in query. "Shall I beat him senseless?"

"Maybe. I'll let you know." When the young woman sent Gwynn an enigmatic look that seemed to ease him somewhat, he still refused to look at me. "I don't know what you see in him, Maylen. Honest."

"Neither do I."

When Gwynn started to protest, I shoved him in the ribs. "Hush. We have work to do." Anessa watched the entire manipulation with a bemused expression, torn between worry for her husband and, I guessed, a perverse pride at Gwynn's undying loyalty to me. "Men," I grumbled, exchanging a smile with the healer before giving Sernyn my full attention again, glad to see he'd finally relaxed. "I did have another thought while I was outside trampling Rosanna's blossoms. Or weeds, I'm not sure."

"You wouldn't dare." Rosanna peeked over Maylen's shoulder at her beloved gardens. "They're on the verge of blooming. My roses, my sunflowers, my—"

"Weeds. Given the incredible talent you and my father have shown over the years for keeping secrets from me . . ." I was gratified to see them both turn a brilliant shade of scarlet. "You didn't happen to, ah," —I glanced sideways at Gwynn, who looked puzzled— "well, since you were there for a year . . ." I fidgeted with my tunic sleeve, brushing away an invisible speck of dirt. "You didn't leave any Spreebridge children behind, did you?"

"Lords of the sea," my father exploded in a mix of urgent emotions, his flush the deepest I'd ever seen. "No! Alex, of course not. I—"

"All right." Patting his hand in reassurance, I was afraid he'd faint. "Just making sure." When Rosanna coughed with delicacy, I said, "Don't scold. I have every right to know if I have other siblings, and so does my brother."

"I didn't say a word."

"You were thinking volumes."

"I love these family gatherings." Anders snuck a kiss to the back of my neck. "They're always so—" When I jabbed his stomach with my elbow, he winced, "painful."

"Have you been in contact with this, ah, lady elder? Kimmer Frehan, is it?"

My father smiled openly now, amused at my feeble attempt at discretion. "We exchange news from time to time." He patted Anessa's hand. "We are still good friends, Alex, after all these years."

"I'll bet. But you don't think—" I hesitated, reluctant to say the wrong thing, suddenly serious again.

My father was a step ahead of me. "I believe we can trust her, if that is what you fear, but I still think you should be cautious. Kimmer has a good heart, but people change over the years, and sometimes you cannot be sure what they think or in what political situation they may find themselves. I have not seen her for many years," he added, taking a sip of cooling tea, "and cannot guarantee she is trustworthy."

"Well, just don't tell her we're coming."

"We?" Anders nudged me, deftly avoiding my elbow.

"Too old for an adventure?"

"You know I'm not too old. As a matter of fact, before your brother interrupted us at the Seaman's Berth, I was about to carry you home and show you how young I am." Embarrassed, I put a hand over his mouth. "But—" He tried to talk around my fingers.

I jabbed him quiet, and turned to Gwynn. "Are you and Maylen coming to Spreebridge, too?"

My brother blinked in honest confusion, and tugged at his unruly hair, slanting a look at the young female scout. "Of course. But you will not try to stop us?"

"I'd rather keep you where I can see you. And so would Father, I'd guess," I added dryly, craning my neck to look at Anessa. "You don't mind, do you?"

"I wish none of you had to go, but, no, Alex, I do not mind." Her reassuring laugh spoke of maternal affection. "I could not stop him, anyway."

"Maylen? I'd hate to drag you into this trouble."

Blonde hair catching the afternoon sunlight, she crossed her arms and leaned back against the window ledge. "Someone has to keep an eye on you."

"I hope you're referring to my brother and Anders."

Maylen schooled her face to utter neutrality. "Of course, Mage Protector."

"Anders?" I shifted around until I faced him. "What about Emmy?"

My husband looked thoughtful as he pursed his lips together. "We don't know if she's a target, but Emmy might be safer hidden away in Glynnswood. Harder to reach than here," he explained to Rosanna, and then glanced at my father and Anessa for agreement, which they readily gave. "That would fit in if we all leave together. We don't want Elena or Jackson to know where we've gone or why. Or, for that matter, Jules." Anders sent Rosanna an apologetic glance, expecting her to understand the unspoken thought that if Jules knew, so would Elena, sooner or later.

"Do we have a reason for this family holiday?" I asked, catching a ghost of humor in Anders's gaze as he turned back to me. Suspicious, I threatened to jab him again, but he held my arms tight at my side.

"If we send word that we're off to Glynnswood because you've been cranky and depressed and contentious—"

"No one will believe you," I grumbled, trying to shake free of his firm hold.

"Alex," Rosanna patted my head as though I were a lapdog. "That's the only thing no one would ever question."

Chapter Four

"Mama! Oh, mama, come look! Hurry—"

In response to Emmy's unbridled shout of joy, I ran from the pantry, nearly tripping in my haste to reach the clearing behind the cottage. And stopped cold in my tracks. Anders, kneeling beside our daughter, shot me a miserable look when he saw me frozen in place, an expression that matched the unhappiness on my brother's face.

"Mama, watch me, please."

Forcing a smile to my lips, I obeyed Emmy's proud entreaty and leaned against the wall of our cottage, attempting a casual pose that I knew fooled neither Anders nor Gwynn. I tried to ignore the pain and nausea in my gut, as my daughter held a fair-sized rock in her tiny hand, changed it to crumbly dirt, and then, lords of the sea, to water. Shoving aside my own selfish grief and replacing it with maternal pride, I knelt in front of Emmy and hugged her close, kissing her cheek.

"That's wonderful! Do you know not even your father can do that?" I encouraged the child, meeting Anders's worried eyes over her curly head. "Or me, either. You've done something very special, sweetling. Is this the first time it's happened?" The child pulled away from my arms and nodded, her excitement bringing a glow to her eyes. "All right. Then listen to me." Assured of my daughter's complete attention, I sent Gwynn and Anders a guarded look, warning them. "I think we should keep your mage talent our secret for just a little while. It's a very special gift, and we don't want anyone to get jealous, do we?"

"No, Mama." Emmy shook her head gravely as I ruffled her hair.

"I'm so proud of you." Giving the child one more hug, I brushed the curls from her eyes. "Run up to the manor house now with Uncle

Gwynn and tell Grandpa Sernyn and Grandma Anessa what you just did."

The little minx beamed with pride and delight and bolted in the direction of the path leading to the manor, she stopped as another thought occurred to her. "Can I tell Maylen and Grandma Rosanna, too?"

"Yes, of course. But Emmy—" I alerted Gwynn, unnecessarily, with a swift look. "No one else. Not until your father or I tell you. All right? Promise?"

"I promise." With a nod and another fierce hug for me followed by one for her father, she scampered up the path, little legs flying in haste.

"I am sorry, Alex." Gwynn threw over his shoulder as he started after the imp. "It happened so fast, and—"

I waved away his apology with another forced smile. "Just keep her out of trouble. That's all I care about."

As Gwynn vanished up the forest path in Emmy's wake, Anders pulled me to my feet and wrapped his arms around me, letting me sag against his chest. "If I'd known she'd call for you so quickly, Alex—"

"It's all right."

"No, it's not," he murmured, running a gentle hand down my back. "I know it hurts you to see magic. But lords of the sea, Alex, she's got your talent and mine. In my wildest dreams, I never thought it possible, even though it was logical."

"We don't know the extent of her mage talent yet," I mumbled into his chest. "She'll need you to keep close watch over her as it develops."

"And you."

At his reproachful words, I shut my eyes tight against the pain and emptiness. "I didn't expect her to be using mage talent," I said, bitterness leaving an ugly stain on my heart. "She was so excited. I had no idea why she called me, thought only that maybe Gwynn taught her a new game." I shivered as Anders stroked the back of my neck. "How can I keep watch over her? I can't even keep watch over myself."

"That's it." Anders yanked at a strand of my hair. "I'm going to tell Rosanna you're feeling sorry for yourself. And you know how she chides you."

"I have a right to a little self-pity," I pouted, pulling away from his embrace.

Dragging me back, Anders smiled. "Yes, you do. But I'll only allow it to last a few moments." He kissed me lightly. "There. Your time's up. Now come along." Without waiting for a reply, he half-dragged me up the hill.

"Maylen and Gwynn have taken Emmy outside to distract her," Rosanna informed us when we joined her in the parlor, sitting with my father and stepmother. "It might be best if you kept Emmy out of sight until this mystery is solved. She's a child and excited, with good reason. You can't expect her not to test the limits and see what else she can do, despite the fact she's so well behaved. Word will get around, Alex."

When I didn't answer, my father agreed, though I wasn't prepared for his next comment. "Glynnswood is no better or safer than Port Alain. My people adore Emmy and would do her no harm, but since she was born" —he sighed in resignation— "they have all wondered what kind of magic she would have. Even the most well-meaning tongues will wag, Alex. If there is somewhere Anessa and I can take her for a time in privacy—"

"There is such a place." Rosanna looked at me as she toyed absently with her beloved husband's ducal ring. "Alex knows where it is."

Adamant and irritated, I shook my head and stared out the window. Early evening shadows only added to the bleak empty feeling Emmy's display caused in the pit of my stomach. When Rosanna called my name, I faced her with a fair amount of stubbornness. "No."

"He," she said, without identifying who "he" was, "doesn't have to know anything."

"It's not right, and you know it."

"These are extraordinary circumstances."

Anders coughed diplomatically until we both stared at him in annoyance. "Who and what are you arguing about?" Though I suspected he knew who and what and why.

Rosanna crossed her arms and leaned back in the armchair, glaring at me. "My son has a place that he keeps hidden." She met my angry stare without blinking. "Only a few other people know its location. I'm not one of them, but Alex is."

My father rested his chin in the palm of his hand and looked at me curiously. "Under the circumstances, you do not think it is right to use this place without telling Jules?"

"She's developed a late-blooming case of ethics," Rosanna cut in.

I ignored her, recalling, with a shudder, my midnight journey over the terrifying bridge by Jendlan Falls to bring Jules home when his twin boys and sister were kidnapped five years earlier. That episode left me cold, not only for the personal challenge I faced by crossing that bridge alone in the dark, twice, but also for the ugly emotions and ill feelings it created among Elena, Jules, and myself for months.

"Would it help if you tell Jules you want Emmy protected without explaining why? Must he be told about her magic? Simply that she is your daughter would be enough." My father looked thoughtful. "He would understand. The duke has two children of his own."

"Perhaps this may help," Gwynn said quietly, explaining, when I glanced in his direction, "Tell the duke that you will be there alone."

Irritated, I threw up my hands in disgust. "Then I'll still be exposing his secret to other people without telling him. There have been enough lies among my family and friends. I can't. It's not right."

Anders narrowed his eyes. "Then you go with Emmy alone, and I'll take Gwynn and Maylen to Spreebridge."

"I can't. And not because of the—" Stopping the word "bridge" from bursting out of my mouth, I turned my back on Anders and stared out the window at the darkness surrounding the gardens, looking for answers. "I can't protect Emmy." I bit my lip hard to fight the grief. "I have no magic to wield in her defense. I can't help her. I can't help my own daughter." Resting my head against the windowpane, I hugged myself tight. When Anders put his arms around my waist, I leaned back, grateful for his warmth.

"Either you trust my son to keep Emmy's secret safe from Elena, so Jackson doesn't find out, or you trust Emmy to keep her own secret," Rosanna said into the uneasy silence. "It's your choice, Alex."

"And Anders's choice." I kept my face averted, thinking hard for a long, tense moment when my husband stayed silent. Then, "Gwynn?"

"Yes?"

Prepared for an argument, I faced my brother. "I need you to stay with Emmy in Glynnswood."

Defiant, he shook his head. "I am going with you to Spreebridge."

"Emmy may be in danger."

"So may you."

I smiled, torn between conflicting urges to laugh and cry. "I've already been hurt. Please stay with her. Please. For me." While Gwynn considered my request, I turned to Anders, searching for approval in his eyes, uncertain what to do if he disagreed with my choice.

"It's all right with me," he said softly. "Gwynn can take Emmy into the forest every now and then to allow her freedom to practice."

"Gwynn?"

"All right, Alex, all right, though I am not happy. I hate to let you go so far without me." Tugging at the rogue lock of brown hair, he announced, "Maylen will go in my place."

"No. She needs to stay with you and Emmy," I countered, knowing how inseparable the two of them had become these past few years.

A flicker of stubbornness appeared and vanished. "I do not think so." Before I could protest, he added, "That is my condition, Alex. Take it or leave it."

Without answer, I glanced over at his mother, who smiled. "It is not in my nature to be so willful, Alex," Anessa said wryly. "It must be inherited from his father."

* * * *

We left Port Alain two days later on a bright sunny morning, parting company at the outskirts of Hartswood to avoid meeting any of the villagers. I pushed aside my lingering hesitation and watched Emmy go with Gwynn and her grandparents. My heart was heavy at leaving her behind. "I never quite got around to thanking you for coming with us."

"It will be good to have Gwynn miss me for a little while. He has been taking me for granted lately." With a sly grin, Maylen glanced up from rummaging through her travel-worn leather pack, tossed to the ground when we decided to set up camp for the evening. "And more important, there is no need for thanks."

"You Glynnswood people are so damn civilized," I muttered, flicking dirt from my scuffed boot. "Of course, there is."

Blue eyes slanted a mischievous glance in Anders's direction. When he shrugged, disowning any part in this conversation, Maylen said, "Alex, from the moment Gwynn decided that I was not the pest he thought I was, with your help," —her bright grin recalled my brother's inexperience with the opposite sex five years earlier— "the

Kelties have taken me in as one of their own. They have always treated me with warmth, but now, I, well, you understand— I am with Gwynn, which means I am with them." The young woman wrapped her dark wool cloak tighter about her slender body. "So, if I am part of the family, how can I not help you? And truly, Alex, even if I were not, I would still be here."

I rolled my eyes at Anders and collapsed against the tree trunk in mock despair. "She's been with my brother too long."

"Be nice." Anders looked about to suggest that I start a fire, as he always did. Instead, he busied himself gathering dry twigs.

"I can do that," I said quietly.

"Sure, you can. But then you'd complain I never lift a finger to help. Be right back," he called over his shoulder as he disappeared into the woods.

"Don't get lost. I'll have to send Maylen to find you." He grumbled something rude, and I sat cross-legged, lost in thought. Staring at the small mound of dirt my boot heels had kicked together, I focused, calling on the fire and ice which I knew was hidden deep in my soul. It just needed a little persuasion to emerge. With that stubborn mindset, I envisioned the dirt as a blazing campfire, then a whirlwind, and, finally, a pool of water. But the soft moist earth mocked me, and I kicked it hard, scattering dirt across the hard ground.

"Alex?" Maylen knelt beside me, her gaze filled with worry and compassion. "You cannot lose faith."

"It's hard not to," I whispered, bowing my head in shame.

"I know. But, listen to me." Maylen squeezed my arm. "If you lose faith, we are all lost." When I gathered the courage to meet that young, vulnerable gaze, I found strength, too.

"You're right. I'll be damned if I let them get the better of me."

"Thank the lords of the sea." She grinned, sitting back on her haunches. "I was afraid you had become a changeling in the night."

Chapter Five

"I never thought the great and esteemed, though no longer legendary, Crownmage of Tuldamoran," —I paused to chuckle without mercy— "would be queasy on a riverboat sailing along on water that's smooth as fine glass."

Poor Anders turned a deeper shade of nauseous green as he muttered a curse bare moments before bolting back to the tiny cabin below, which didn't offer very much in the way of creature comforts or fresh air.

"You are being cruel, Alex."

"I know." I winked at Maylen, who made a feeble attempt to disapprove and failed, her own smile escaping. "For all the grief that man has given me over the last six years, surely you can't blame me for taking advantage of a glaring weakness he kept hidden? All this time, I've had to listen to how all powerful and potent he is when the mere rocking of a tiny wave sends him scurrying to hang his prideful head over the side of the boat. I had no idea. But it explains all those lame excuses he's invented to avoid going out on the bay with us."

"Dangerous for him to have you know this weakness." Maylen settled back comfortably against the polished wood of the small craft and crossed her short legs. "Your brother complained just the other day that I pay too much attention to how you abuse Anders."

"Good." I trailed a hand over the side through the cold waters of the Jendlan River. We sailed upstream toward the Keshtang Mountains, the source of the gems and minerals Spreebridge hoped to sell through the fledgling trade between our kingdoms. Meravan, our other major trade partner, couldn't offer such goods, a fact that the crafty Spreebridge elders used in their negotiations. The Keshtang Mountains loomed closer in the distance, separating Tuldamoran from Spreebridge, just north of the Duchy of Ardsbrook. "I hope you demonstrate whatever you learn from me whenever the opportunity presents itself."

"Always." Maylen hid her grin behind a raised hand as Anders reappeared back on deck, wiping his slick brow with a wet cloth. "Feeling better?"

"You think I don't see that smirk, Maylen, don't you? Everyone thinks you're so shy and reserved, but there's mischief in you. And you, woman," Anders grumbled at me, taking a seat well apart from us, "you were raised in Port Alain, so you're used to sailing with Jules and the family. Have pity."

"I'm used to sailing on rough seas out on the bay, not this smooth surface. But you were raised in Belbridge Cliffs. What's your excuse?"

"The village was well inland."

"Obviously."

Anders turned away in disgust and faced Maylen with an almost pleading look in his eyes. "How much longer do I have to suffer?"

"As long as you remain married to Alex," the young woman replied with a bright smile. "But if you are referring to this voyage, we are only a day's journey from the north end of Ardsbrook."

Grunting, Anders shaded his eyes and squinted against the sunlight, tugging his cloak around his broad shoulders as a cold breeze swept across the deck. "I can see the Keshtang Mountains. Funny, in all the years I traveled for your mother, Alex, gathering information and spreading news, I never came this far north."

"You had no reason to."

"I suppose."

"Spreebridge always kept to itself until recently, so Elena's father never interfered. The old king didn't want to" —I bit my lip to hide a grin— "rock the boat, so to speak."

"Cute."

"I have never been across the border, but some of our scouts have traveled to Derbarry and beyond." Maylen hugged her legs close to her chest, resting her chin on her knees. "Although the river continues through the mountain range, the boat cannot pass that way. The waters are too rough." She covered a smile as Anders's skin turned a pale shade of green. "Besides, border guards block the route, forcing all travelers to go by land through Coglan Pass. Even though the queen is negotiating trade now between our kingdoms, Spreebridge gets edgy every now and then and watches who comes and goes with more scrutiny. As they do now. But there have always been travelers between the two lands."

"For legitimate purposes?" I asked, intrigued at this version of neighborly relations that only a sneaky Glynnswood scout would know.

"Some, but most not. Although formal trade has never existed," the scout explained, stifling a yawn with polite motion, "Marain Valley wine has been known to grace the tables of some Spreebridge elders."

"Well, at least they have good taste. Maybe we can steal a bottle or two for our time and trouble."

"That's unethical," Anders scolded, eying the deck with alarm as a small fishing boat passed by, causing us to rock. "Assuming that this boat doesn't sink. Since it can't travel as far north as we'd like to go, we'll have to make other arrangements."

"Alex and I thought it best to—"

"When did you two have time to decide anything?" Anders interrupted Maylen with a suspicious glance at me.

"We've had a number of hours alone while you were, ah, plunging your head over the railing." I smirked, jerking my hand from the water as a fish swam by.

Anders turned a darker shade of green. "Don't remind me." Narrowing his eyes to slits, he stared at Maylen. "Well? You said you had a plan."

Forgiving his nausea-induced curtness, the scout shrugged slender shoulders and wrapped her cloak tighter around her body to keep out the chill breeze that seemed to increase every mile we sailed north. "We thought it best to leave the boat before we reach the border and avoid Coglan Pass. There's a small dock a few miles south of the mountains, where some, ah, shady and disreputable characters often disembark."

"How do you know all this?"

"I am a Glynnswood scout."

"No offense" —Anders wiped his brow again— "but you're a forest scout. Besides, you just said you haven't traveled this far north."

"I have not crossed the border, but I have traveled this far north. Many times," Maylen added, her smile mischievous. "How else could Glynnswood scouts uphold our reputation and be of such use to our people and the queen?"

Anders digested her words for a moment. "Then what? Do you propose we walk across the border?"

"Yes." I eyed Anders with skepticism, judging his condition. "You should be all right once you're on land."

"Alex, that is not the only worry. You—" Maylen's voice, as her words faded, held just the right amount of hesitation to make me suspicious.

Drying my fingers on the edge of my cloak, I folded my arms across my chest and glared. "I what?"

"There is a way to avoid border inspection at Coglan Pass and possible trouble if anyone should recognize you or Anders."

"I see."

"Well, I don't," Anders grumbled.

Maylen cleared her throat with great delicacy and studied the smooth, worn planks beneath her feet, tracing the grain of the wood with one sun-browned finger.

"I'm waiting with admirable patience," I said, tapping a swift rhythm with my fingers against my arm, as I locked gazes with our evasive scout, instinct in an utter uproar over what she would admit.

"There is a, well, a—" Her smile was feeble. "A smaller, little-known pass exists through the Keshtang Mountains."

"How little-known?"

"Very."

"I suppose it doesn't even have a name."

Maylen's eyes went very wide. "Oh, but it does." When I continued tapping, she shot me a wry apologetic grin. "Lunatic's Crossing."

"How very reassuring."

"Your father said—"

"My father?" With that addition, I practically jumped down Maylen's throat. "My father said something about this pass?" When Maylen nodded, eyes wide, likely wondering whether I'd throttle her in my father's absence, I threw up my hands in disgust. "He couldn't take the civilized route? I'll even wager he carved out the hidden passage himself. In fact—"

"Calm down, please, Alex. Have pity." Anders's eyes pleaded as his face changed colors. "You're rocking the boat. Besides, you don't even know why it's called that."

"I can well imagine, considering how hesitant our secretive young scout has been to even mention this little change of scenery until now." I stared at Maylen, whose face turned bright crimson with guilt. "Well?"

"There are narrow passages and cliffs and— Alex, it might be best if you could see for yourself."

"Bridges?" I demanded, when the poor woman couldn't force the word past her lips. "I know there has to be a perilous bridge somewhere, or my father wouldn't have sworn you to secrecy. And if there's one that's anything like that bridge in Edgecliff—" My threat to Anders faded as I shuddered, remembering the terror I'd felt, "I'll—"

What would I do? What could I do?

"I'll carry you across." Anders winked at Maylen. "And she makes fun of me being queasy on a riverboat."

"All you do is throw up. My heart can stop on a bridge. What if these crazy northerners have a different interpretation of the word 'bridge'?" I continued ranting, already feeling cold sweat trickle down my back. "I'm doomed."

"A bridge is a bridge. You'll see."

* * * *

"I'll wait here."

It was obviously that a bridge in Port Alain, or even Edgecliff, was not a bridge in the sparsely populated Keshtang Mountains. My heart dropped to my feet in clear horror when I saw the northern version of a bridge. Far, far worse than the bridge in Edgecliff . . . which still haunted my dreams every now and then.

How could I possibly cross this abomination?

We'd left the boat quietly at Plymborne-on-Jendlan, just south of the border in the Duchy of Ardsbrook, and trudged up through the rough foothills of the Keshtang Mountains without a single problem, until this point. Crossing the pass to reach Derbarry by this circuitous route and find Kimmer Frehan was impossible. No sane person could have conceived the suicidal, intricate, zig-zagged rope bridges that spanned the chasm.

Only a lunatic, indeed.

The bridge over Jendlan Falls, north of Port Alain, was a breeze, a short swift gallop, compared to this nightmare. The bridge at Edgecliff, though terrifying, at least offered a plunge into the river and a scant chance of survival. But the bridge in the Keshtang Mountains, appropriately named Lunatic's Crossing, offered a plunge into a black, bottomless ravine, annihilation, and a painful death. My vivid imagination painted the scene in my mind in excruciating detail.

"I'll wait here," I repeated, when neither Anders nor Maylen responded to my earlier comment.

Anders stood at my back, hands resting on my shoulders. "Unlike my poor judgment in Edgecliff," he said quietly, running a hand along the back of my neck, "I'll change the rope here to stone and you'll be able to cross without worry the bridges will sway."

"You can't."

"I'm the great and esteemed Crownmage, Alex, and I'm on solid ground. No more puking. Of course, I can."

"You can't."

Anders peered around my shoulder to stare at me, hearing in my voice indisputable fact. "Why not?"

"The rope isn't natural. It's made of some peculiar fiber."

Cool seagray eyes, filled with skepticism, didn't blink. "How can you tell?"

"I was raised in Port Alain," I said evenly, fighting the urge to flee. "I've tied more sailors' knots than you could ever dream about. Trust me."

"Well," Anders began, sounding unconvinced, "At least, let me try." With confidence, though knowing full well my fear wasn't imagined, Anders faced the nearest span and concentrated on nudging his mage talent awake. I watched my husband's rugged face as his calm features transformed from confidence to confusion and, finally, to defeat, his shoulders slumping in resignation. Sending Maylen a sidelong glance, Anders turned a somber gaze in my direction. "We'll take each span very slowly. Maylen and I won't let you cross alone."

I set my pack down on the ledge. "I'll take my chances by boat. I should be able to bribe a local to cross the border."

"Fine." Another glance at Maylen. "Then we'll meet you at the dock in Derbarry. Be careful, and don't trust anyone. Let's go, Maylen. We're wasting time. I want to reach the end of the passage before dark."

Without another word, Anders blew me a kiss as though he were heading into Port Alain for the day, tested the narrow span for steadiness, and began to cross. Maylen followed him in silent concentration, her pretty face neutral, guilty eyes avoiding mine. Envious and yet appalled that Anders would leave me behind to take a separate route, I watched them inch their way over the first span, testing each one before and after crossing. Anders never looked back, didn't see my wet cheeks or clenched fists, or hear my angry, terrified, whispered curses. I lost sight of them as the chasm veered westward. By that time, my sight was so blurry from tears, I wouldn't have noticed Anders if he stood on my toes. Forlorn, I leaned back against the cool cliff face, lonelier than I'd been in a long, long time.

Lonely and lost and sorry for myself.

No mage talent. No courage. Not a drop of self-respect.

With a rough move, I wiped my eyes and cheeks with the back of my hand. I'd come this far to find my enemy. I didn't need to be one to myself.

Shouldering my heavy pack and strapping it firmly in place, I took a deep breath and a tentative, shaky step toward the first bridge. Clutching the rope tight, knuckles stretched white with strain, I refused to look down or even think about looking down. I put one foot cautiously on the span, and whimpered as the bridge swayed, though it steadied swiftly. The lunatic who built the bridge wasn't a complete fool. Stronger than it looked, the span held firm. Shutting out the void below, the cliffs to either side of me, and the never-ending sway of the rope, I lost count of my steps and the spans, focusing only on my boots, setting one foot in front of the other for what seemed a lifetime.

Until I bumped my head into Anders's chest as he caught me at the last span, holding me close without a word.

* * * *

"Be honest. Was this border crossing my father's idea of a jest or was he exacting vengeance for all those years I was angry at him?"

Maylen, usually ready with an answer, was at a complete and utter loss.

"Leave the girl alone," Anders scolded, as he sat by my side, outstretched hand holding a chunk of raisin bread and soft cheese.

"When we get back—" My words faded as an uneasy thought penetrated my head, a thought I had tried to deny.

"What?" Anders peered at me, though I had the distinct impression he knew what was on my mind. He hadn't said a word all the previous night, just tucked me into my coarse bedroll and held me close until I stopped shivering and banished the fear to murky dreams.

"Do we have to go back that way?"

"Depends on what we find in Derbarry."

"Hmm." Considering his vague answer, I stared past Maylen, lost in thought, and suddenly grinned. "I suppose," I drawled, batting my eyelashes at my husband, "we'll cross that bridge when we come to it."

As Anders shoved me over, Maylen smiled in obvious relief. She'd been worried, keeping it well hidden from me. Now that the mischief had returned, I indulged a perverse urge to rattle the girl. "Well?" I demanded.

Confused, Maylen stared at me, wariness in her eyes. "Well what?"

"Was it a jest or vengeance?"

"Oh, that."

"Yes, that."

Toying with the end of her braid, she avoided looking at me, and then snapped her head up. "Alex, you know it was neither. Sernyn was very worried about you."

"I'll bet."

"He was."

"You could have told me about the crossing before we left Port Alain."

"I wanted to," she admitted, and I didn't doubt her intent. "But Sernyn made me promise not to say a word. He knew you would fret from the moment you left Glynnswood."

"I'm so pleased to know that everyone has the highest confidence in me. I— Oh, forget it." The truth was that everyone's fierce overprotectiveness stung. Irrational maybe, but I'd managed well enough for most of my life without the whole Keltie tribe worrying about me. Having only the Barlows and Elena fret was more than enough to handle.

"Lady Barlow," Anders smoothly cut into my thoughts, "will be interested to hear you're feeling sorry for yourself again." I sent Anders a black look, which he ignored. "Whenever you're ready to move on—" He brushed a lock of gray-streaked hair from his face and kissed the tip of my nose.

"Why don't you go first," I growled, "so I can shove you headfirst down the slope."

"Maylen is our scout." Anders kissed my lips this time. "And I'm rear guard."

"Then guard my rear."

"That's my plan."

* * * *

I don't know what I was expecting, but Derbarry was no different than any medium-sized inland town in Tuldamoran, except it was colder. We stopped to catch our breath not far from the loading docks and to make discreet inquiries for decent lodging.

Anders shaded his eyes against the late afternoon glare, searching the busy dock for a harmless bystander to interrogate. Scanning the crowd, his body stiffened as he lowered his arm and stepped backward, out of sight.

"What is it?" I whispered, alert to danger. When he muttered inaudible words, I persisted, "Anders, what—"

"Hush." He gripped my arm, eyes fixed across the calm water to the parallel dock. My stomach lurched as though I were on board a ship in rough seas when I recognized what held his rapt attention. Across the short space of water, an earnest conversation between a weathered seaman and an anxious young man was taking place.

Maylen gasped at my side. "We must follow him."

"Yes. I should think so. Come on." Anders slanted me a bleak look as he shouldered his heavy pack.

I sighed and followed after, ill at heart, to trail Jackson Tunney.

Chapter Six

Following Jackson at a discreet distance, my heart heavy with dread and foreboding, I pushed aside all thoughts of Elena and speculation about why Jackson was this far north. Was it simple chance that made our paths cross again? Or were the lords of the elements more active in their interference than anyone really imagined? Two miles down a meandering road that had the feel of a very drunken road builder, Jackson came to a halt in front of a neat, though weathered, cottage. Rapping smartly on the wooden door, the queen's lover glanced from side to side, doing nothing to improve my mood. Even from our distance, I could see his slender form taut with some visible emotion.

Before I could make the suggestion, Maylen shot me a quick grin. "I will go. After all," she added, "I am quieter than you, Mage Protector, no offense."

"I hate when you spend time with Anders and Gwynn." As Maylen crouched to dart across the road, I grabbed the young woman's cloak. "Be careful."

With a nod, she was gone to eavesdrop the moment Jackson slipped inside the small building. Anders stayed close beside me, both of us hidden in the late afternoon shadows, while we watched and waited for what seemed an eternity, until Maylen returned.

"It seems Jackson has lost his magic." The scout's expression held none of its usual mockery or dry humor as she whispered the surprising news.

Huddled in my cloak against the damp chill, I blinked. "What? How?" Before she could answer, I asked a more important question. "Do you think he's telling the truth?"

"Why wouldn't he?" Anders looked puzzled.

"Jackson might somehow know we're here. Maybe someone recognized us on the riverboat or when we arrived in Derbarry. Or," I added, thinking out loud and trying to solve the puzzle, "he might be trying to fool whomever he's telling."

"The cottage belongs to Westin Harlowe, Jackson's mentor." Maylen held my gaze as she pulled the edges of her coarse woolen cloak around her shoulders when the wind picked up. "I think he was telling the truth to Elder Harlowe. Another thing to consider, Alex, is that Jackson—" She looked past Anders, pressed her lips together, and turned back to face me. "He seemed truly upset, claiming someone in Ardenna tricked him into drinking feyweed."

"What was Harlowe's reaction?" When Maylen frowned as dry leaves scattered in the wind, I pressed her for an answer. "What is it?"

The young woman shook her head. "I could not read his expression. Elder Harlowe was sympathetic, surely, but not given to much open emotion. But that says nothing, Alex," —she offered a small smile— "because Spreebridge people are more reserved than, well, people in Tuldamoran, especially those who live in Port Alain."

"Including Glynnswood? Or do you put yourself in the more polite, restrained category of your northern neighbors?" I teased back, watching the younger woman's furtive glance at Anders, trying to figure out what was bothering her when she didn't respond to my jest. "What else, Maylen? There's something you're not telling us."

"Elder Harlowe sent Jackson off to sleep, explaining that tomorrow—" Maylen bit her lip, while I waited, fighting the temptation to pull the words from her mouth. "Alex, he plans to take Jackson to visit Kimmer Frehan tomorrow."

"Kimmer— Lords of the sea, what mess have we gotten tangled in?" I sighed, knowing nothing much would make sense until I had peace and quiet to sort it all out. "I'll take first watch. I can't sleep just yet." I shrugged. "And tomorrow we'll just tag along. At least, we won't have to ask for directions."

* * * *

Tailing Jackson and his mentor for several miles in broad and brilliant daylight was a challenge. For the hundred thousandth time, I wondered why mages were blessed with marvelous ability but not invisibility. Was that too much to ask? We tried our best to stay as close as possible to catch any loud conversation, as impossible as that was for spies darting constantly behind trees and avoiding undergrowth along the sides of the road. I was thankful for Maylen, who made up for the numerous mistakes Anders and I made.

We stopped a short distance from Kimmer Frehan's home, a small building that appealed to my sense of what home should be. Not so very different from our cottage in the woods back in Port Alain, though a bit larger. As Anders and I settled back to let the expert scout ply her trade, Maylen scooted ahead with enviable stealth.

I guessed that the woman who opened the door was Elder Frehan, judging from my father's warm, though decades-old, description. Standing in the bright sunlight, she greeted Harlowe as an old friend and Jackson with a reserved, but welcoming manner. Tall and slender, she wore her hair, blonde streaked with silver, unbound. Falling past her shoulders, the long strands caught the sunlight's brilliance. It wasn't hard to imagine her thirty years younger, or understand why my father lingered awhile in her company, despite his responsibilities in Glynnswood.

And despite me.

I kept my thoughts to myself, though Anders gave me an odd look when I sighed.

When Kimmer ushered her guests inside, Maylen edged closer, cautious and discreet. Anders and I watched and waited, impatient to find out what was being discussed. My imagination was wild with speculation when our scout returned some time later. Maylen's expression showed clear confusion, but we held our questions until Jackson and Westin departed. Only then, when we moved silently to a hidden thicket back from the road that still provided an unobstructed view of the cottage, did I shake Maylen gently to grab her distracted attention.

"What is it?"

Maylen scratched her head, looked at me, then at the cottage, and back at me again. "There was a man inside—" She stopped, rubbed her eyes, and hugged her knees to her chest. Though all that activity was far too much fidgeting for Maylen Stockrie, I waited, with patience this time, despite the loud clamor of instinct. "Elders Frehan and Harlowe seem to be on friendly terms," she said, sheepishly aware of my restraint. "She knows Jackson, but I do not think she knows him well. They spoke of trouble in the elder council in Spreebridge once Jackson explained what happened to him and to—" Maylen glanced at me then away, "to others. Jackson did not mention your name, Alex, only that other mages in Tuldamoran had been similarly harmed."

Anders tapped his fingers against his leg. "Did they seem surprised?"

"Yes. Jackson had not told Westin Harlowe about the others." At my questioning look, she added, "Perhaps he was too weary last night."

I yawned, barely covering my mouth. "Sorry. I can understand that, although it doesn't make too much sense to leave out that kind of information. And?"

Maylen gave me a cautious grin, still uneasy, and I couldn't figure out why. "They were both horrified. Even Elder Harlowe's expression, this time, was clear."

"And the trouble they spoke about?"

"I am not certain what the trouble is." Smoothing her braid, and then her cloak, Maylen caught her restless actions and brought them to a halt before I did. "But that is how I knew there was someone else in the cottage. A man, Alex." The scout scrutinized every single crushed blade of grass between her boots, avoiding my eyes.

I didn't know where this discussion was heading, but I knew my father was involved somehow.

Maylen's blatant reluctance spoke volumes. "The other man— He was young, Alex. He mentioned trouble in the elder council, something that did not seem to surprise either Elder Frehan or Elder Harlowe. I would guess it is because they are both involved in council politics and know what is going on."

I knew I should have stayed in Port Alain and played games with my daughter. "They must have given some kind of hint about the situation."

Maylen shrugged, entranced by a particular blade of grass that clung to her boot heel. "There seems to be a power struggle. Elder Frontish is involved, so they claim. Kimmer Frehan admitted that her son, Sloane, supported Derek Frontish, which troubled her."

"Sloane is the other person who was there?"

"Ah, no. There was another young man, who said that Derek Frontish was a threat to the stability of the Spreebridge council."

"There go Elena's plans for a trouble-free trade relationship." I rubbed my bleary eyes, dreaming wistfully of a steaming hot bath and soft bed. "All right. Three questions leap to my confused, tired, and hungry mind. Is there a connection between their council trouble and our feyweed trouble? Who is the other young man in Kimmer Frehan's house? And last, do we trust any of them?" I leaned against Anders's warm body, thinking hard.

Anders wrapped his arm around my shoulders and drew me closer. "To your first question, I'm inclined to think the answer is yes. Derek Frontish, the supposed senior elder from Spreebridge, was in Ardenna when you drank the feyweed potion. So I think we need to be suspicious. As to your third question," —he ignored my raised brow when he skipped to the last question— "if we assume that Elder Frontish means trouble and believe that Jackson is innocent, I think we can trust them to a point. We may have to confront Jackson back in Ardenna, on our own turf. I just don't know. If we talk to Kimmer Frehan, we needn't tell her everything unless we trust her. Your instinct is usually sharp, and Sernyn hasn't mentioned any reason not to trust her. So we'll take a calculated risk, all right?"

"What about my second question?"

"Ask Maylen." Anders removed his arm from my shoulder and stretched, doing a fair imitation of someone who wasn't the least bit interested. But I knew better.

During our little discussion, the young woman in question had been busy destroying the grass at her feet as we turned to look at her.

"I do not know who he is." Her expression was bland, expressionless, and evasive. In other words, clear as glass.

Flameblast my father.

"All right." I hugged my knees close to my chest and rested my chin on top of them. "Who do you think he is? Be honest."

"Alex—"

"It's all right, Maylen. I have a very open mind. Go on."

Anxiety flashed across her young face as she glanced up and sighed in resignation. "He looks a little like you, Alex, and a little like Gwynn. And," she added, poised to flee at the merest hint of trouble from me, "a lot like your father."

I shut my eyes tight and clenched my fist, banging it softly against my leg.

"Maybe he didn't know," Anders suggested, tugging at a strand of my curls. "Give him a chance."

"Why?" I demanded, opening my eyes to snarl at my husband.

Anders stole a furtive look at Maylen and winked, before turning to me. "If Sernyn didn't know, then no harm's done. But if he did, Gwynn will have a chance to beat him senseless."

"Remind me" —I punched Anders in the arm— "to ask my father when we get home where else he's traveled. Lords of the sea know where else I have kin."

Chapter Seven

Clear blue eyes studied my face with polite intensity before cautiously appraising Anders and Maylen, and then returning to me. Kimmer Frehan recognized me before I'd uttered a sound. "You are Sernyn Keltie's daughter."

"There are quite a few days when I wish I wasn't his daughter," I muttered, jumping as Anders discreetly pinched my backside. "Yes. Yes, I am." Her eyes strayed back to Anders, who met her gaze with infuriating calmness. "My husband, Anders Perrin."

"Crownmage." Kimmer nodded with respect as I introduced Maylen and waved us all inside her warm cottage, graciously restraining her curiosity. "Alexandra. No," she corrected herself with a smile before I could snarl. "Alex. Is that right?"

"Yes. Listen, Elder Frehan, I'm sorry we didn't send word. It's rude to just show up on your doorstep." Gratefully accepting a glass of cool wine, I discreetly sniffed the contents to be sure there was no taint of feyweed when she reached for another glass, and then took a sip and raised a brow in feigned surprise, remembering Maylen's words about smuggling across the border. "Marain Valley?"

"The same." She smiled in appreciation, offering a glass to Anders and Maylen before pouring one for herself. "Is there any other that can match its quality?"

"Not to my taste, no." Eying Anders to warn him that it was safe, I took another small sip and leaned back against the pillows stuffed behind me. "I didn't know it was traded north of the border."

Her smile intensified. "There are ways."

"Ah. Well, understandable, under the circumstances. But again, I'm sorry—"

Kimmer raised a hand to stop my apology. "Sernyn's daughter is always welcome here, as is he, though I have not seen my friend in many years." Blue eyes narrowed in concern. "Is your father ill?"

"No, he's as strong as a seabeast," I reassured her, pushing aside all thoughts of feyweed and our mission as curiosity took over. "And sends his warmest regards."

The Spreebridge woman flashed a smile that was filled with open affection, shedding years from her face. Easy to see how my father found comfort in her arms so long ago, as well as honest friendship. "Your stepmother? She is well? And Gwynn?"

I matched her smile. "Anessa suffers only from the presence of my father and her son, both of whom drive her to distraction. As for Gwynn," —I gestured in Maylen's direction— "she keeps close watch over him."

"Indeed." Kimmer sipped her wine as she reappraised Maylen. Turning again to me, she added, "You have a daughter."

"A little minx."

"She's no such thing." Anders elbowed me without bothering to be discreet.

Laughing, Kimmer added her own opinion. "According to Sernyn, she is perfect. I would guess that is her father's opinion, too."

"Sernyn tends to be a typical grandfather, thinking the world revolves around his granddaughter. As for my husband—"

My words stopped cold as a young man rushed in from a back room at the far end of the cottage. A young man who looked, well, a little like me and a little like Gwynn and a lot like Sernyn Keltie. I studied the newcomer, roughly my age, with avid interest. Taller than both Gwynn and me, he shared our dark Keltie hair, as well as Gwynn's deep brown eyes. Maylen exchanged a furtive glance with me.

"Your pardon, Mother." The young man flushed bright red. "I did not know you had visitors."

"My son, Corey," Kimmer said evenly, taking careful note of my silent exchange with Maylen as she inclined her head in our direction. "Corey, our visitors are kin of an old and dear friend I have not seen in many long years." Giving only our first names, she concealed whatever thoughts were running through her head. Well, yes and no. Her tight grip on the wine glass threatened to shatter the crystal, and I was glad to see Elder Frehan wasn't quite as sure of herself as I'd originally thought.

Corey nodded with absent courtesy and excused himself with a rushed, though genuine, apology, scrambling out the cottage door. Kimmer watched his departure, undisguised affection in her eyes, which she then focused on me. It was obvious she knew I was aware of his parentage.

I cleared my throat and gestured in the direction Corey had gone. "Handsome young man." Keeping my tone exquisitely neutral as I'd learned from years of being on the receiving end of Rosanna's blandness, I took a sip of wine. "Is he always so, ah, rushed?"

"Only when he is late." Kimmer matched my tone. "And today, he is very late. In fact, I thought he had already left." She kept those clear blue eyes fixed on mine as I reached for my glass again and took a sip. "He teaches the village children."

I choked on my wine. Anders patted my back until I waved him away, but not before I caught the mischief in his eyes as he handed me a linen handkerchief to dab at the wine splattered across my dark tunic.

"Shall I get some water?" Kimmer met my gaze with an odd expression in her eyes, part mischief, part concern, and, damn my father, part fear. When I shook my head, she said quietly, "Your father does not know about Corey." When I stayed silent, uncertain how to respond, she clenched and unclenched the fist she held on her lap. "Sernyn was suffering enough guilt about leaving you behind, Alex. I could not add to his burden."

Burden? Is that what I was to him?

Before she could read the reaction on my face, I pushed the bitterness aside with effort. "Does Corey know about Sernyn?"

"No, Alex. My son believes his father dead—" At my involuntary movement, in spite of the tight restraint I'd placed on my emotions, her eyes softened. "Sernyn wrote to me some years back and told me how you hated him when you encountered him so unexpectedly in the forest. I could not do that to myself. I— Alex, I did not have the courage." Gathering her resources, Kimmer shrugged with gentle grace in calm acceptance of a decision she'd made so long ago. "If I lost Corey's affection—"

"Don't you think Corey has a right to know? My father, too?" I couldn't keep the heat from my voice.

"It's not your affair."

When Anders gripped my arm with subtle pressure, I flung him away. "Corey's my half-brother. Just like Gwynn. How can you look at Gwynn and me and then tell me Corey isn't my affair?"

Anders took my face in his hands. "Because he's not. It's different. Elder Frehan made that decision long ago. Judging from the Keltie blood that runs through your veins, I'd say she runs a grave risk by telling Corey the truth at this point in his life."

I despised Anders when he was right. Dragging my eyes away from his, I turned back to face our hostess.

"I have another son, Sloane." With a grateful look at Anders for taking her part, she added, "His father, my husband, died only recently. My sons are several years apart, Alex. I could not pretend Sloane's father was Corey's, though they are separated by more than just age."

She managed a cautious smile. "Corey could easily fit the Keltie name, but not Sloane. He is ambitious for power without responsibility, a follower in search of those who can give him that power. He supports some of our more outspoken elders who crave control of the elder council without thought of the damage they will inflict." Abruptly, she stopped talking and poured herself another glass of wine. "I am sorry. Those are my troubles. It was thoughtless of me to go on so. You do not need to hear all that."

"Actually, we do." I sent Anders a covert look as she put the bottle aside. "And I think you'll understand why." Curiosity flashed in her eyes as she straightened. Despite my father's letters over the years, I wasn't quite sure she knew what to make of me. Instinctively trusting the Spreebridge woman, though I didn't agree with her decision about Corey, I made myself comfortable, tucking another cushion behind my back. "It's rather a long story, if you have some time."

"Corey is gone until late afternoon. And Sloane . . ." She sighed in maternal resignation. "Well, he does not live here any longer."

"All right, then let me tell you why we've come to Spreebridge."

* * * *

"I do not think Jackson is lying." Kimmer ran a slender hand through her unbound silver-blonde hair. "However, I do not know him as well as I do Westin. But what purpose would it serve Jackson to claim he has lost his mage talent if he has not?"

I stretched to ease the muscles in my neck and shoulders, barely catching myself from purring as Anders massaged my neck. "Hopefully none. I don't want him to be lying."

"After hearing your tale, I think that Elder Frontish connects your trouble with mine, though I cannot explain why."

"Instinct?" Anders moved his hands skillfully to my shoulders, pushing my head down so he could loosen the tight muscles.

"More than anything else, but what could Derek Frontish hope to gain by hurting you?" Kimmer asked me. "How could it help his positioning for power in Spreebridge? He has already claimed the seat of senior representative. And before he left Derbarry to visit your queen, Derek seemed more than content with the new trade agreement." Puzzled, Kimmer scratched her head and looked to me for answers. "Unless I have missed something vital, I am at a loss."

"Maybe destroying Alex's mage talent is just an extra perverse enjoyment on his part. Maybe Derek Frontish is connected to the imprisoned renegades somehow." Maylen broke her lengthy silence, looking at each of us in turn. "Perhaps there is a link—"

"I cannot think why there would be." Kimmer shook her head and poured us all another glass of Marain wine. Somewhere in the middle of our story, she had brought out cheese and spiced beef rolls, along with another bottle. "I remember when Jackson sent the renegades back to Spreebridge. Derek was furious at what they had done in Tuldamoran and supported their punishment."

"Perhaps it was an act." Anders stopped massaging my shoulders and sat back against overstuffed cushions.

"Have you seen the renegades?" I asked, wondering if we should investigate further. "Are they still safely locked away?"

"As of last week when I visited them, yes." The older woman smiled at my surprise. "Part of my duty as an elder is the security of political prisoners. I can tell you for certain that the two women are mad, and the man furious. But still, he is without magic. Looking back on Derek's reaction to their capture," Kimmer added, sipping at her wine glass, "he was not happy that such odd talent even existed. Add to that, Alex, the fact the mages wielding such odd talent were not under his control seemed to be of particular irritation. So, no, Anders, I do not think Derek's anger was an act. I believe he wished those mages stripped of their magic power and kept out of sight, which makes me wonder about his intentions concerning Jackson." Kimmer looked pensive as we digested that insight, and then frowned. "But one thing is very clear. If Elder Frontish is involved, then so is my son."

"You don't know that Sloane is involved," I protested, not wanting it to be true, for Kimmer's sake.

The woman's eyes were tinged with sadness, so like my father. "Ah, but I do know that, Alex, to my sorrow. From the moment Sloane was old enough to understand the intricacies of power and politics and magic, he latched onto the edge of Elder Frontish's cloak. Derek gave Sloane what we could not, and would not even if we could. To be honest, I despise what Derek represents." Kimmer stood up and walked toward the window, where late afternoon shadows had grown prominent. "Corey should be back soon. You may want his opinion on this matter. There are times, though not recently, when Corey can make Sloane listen to reason."

"I'm sorry to add to your troubles."

Kimmer turned from the window to face me. "You have only added to what I have tried to avoid. And if Sloane is involved, it is my responsibility to give you whatever possible help I can, if only for the damage he has caused. I cannot continue to turn away from what I suspect to be true." The woman stood tall, authority covering her like a cloak. "I, too, am an elder of Spreebridge, and must do something before others are hurt."

"Who has been hurt?"

We all turned at the unexpected voice from the doorway. Well, there was proof of Glynnswood blood. Sneaky, every one of them.

"Mother? Who has been hurt?" Corey demanded, sitting down when I waved him to join us before Kimmer could answer.

"It's a long story, Master Frehan. If you have some time, let me tell you why we've come to Spreebridge."

* * * *

Lords of the sea, but my newest half-brother had Gwynn's passion for outrage. I liked Corey immediately. "We don't know for certain that Sloane is involved," I reminded him when fire flashed in his eyes. It had been difficult to tell the story again without speaking of his father or his half-brother or me, his half-sister. But I held my tongue, almost slipping once or twice and saved by the grace of Anders's delicate and timely interventions.

"He is involved. I know it. I do know it— And so does Mother." The accusation was muttered with pained conviction as he turned dark, brooding eyes in my direction.

"Do you have proof?"

"Yes. In here." Corey touched his heart, avoiding his mother's eyes. "And," —he sipped the Marain Valley wine his mother had poured after his outburst— "Sloane spoke to me recently of feyweed." Though Kimmer's eyes widened in surprise, she stayed silent, until Corey slid her a sideways glance, a very guilty sideways glance, from the corner of his dark Keltie eyes. "I did not tell you because I knew you would be upset." When Kimmer nodded her understanding, Corey continued speaking to me, failing to notice the force with which his mother bit her lower lip. "Alex, Sloane told me Elder Frontish had gathered large quantities of feyweed in secret. Sloane was trying to find out what the elder intended to do with it. I am not certain, but I think Sloane really didn't know what Derek planned. Or if he did know, it is obvious

Sloane does not trust me all that much, after all." Corey's shoulders slumped with his admission, unable to disguise the bitterness and old pain that crept into his voice.

"How long ago was this?" Anders nibbled at a chunk of cinnamon bread that Kimmer set down on the low table.

"Shortly before Elder Frontish visited Ardenna."

Anders sipped the wine to wash down the bread, before he asked quietly, "Do you know—" He shot a glance my way, and then back to Corey. "Did Sloane say anything about a way to reverse feyweed?"

"My brother said Elder Frontish claims there is no way to reverse the damage, but Sloane did not believe him." Corey shrugged in apology. "I do not know who or what to believe. It may be possible that there is a draught to unblock the mage talent. For those innocent victims afflicted with the potion, I would hope so."

Uneasy, I caught Corey's attention. "If you'll forgive me, I need to ask you something. Not to be intrusive, but because it's important." When Corey nodded after a reassuring glance from his mother, I went on, "Your mother told us you and Sloane aren't on the best of terms. Why would Sloane speak openly to you? "

Corey smiled that sorrowful, resigned Keltie smile. "Sometimes my brother remembers that I am not his enemy."

Anders touched my arm to get my attention. "Perhaps we should reserve judgment until we're certain what's what."

"Anders is right. Though I believe Sloane is involved just as you do," she informed Corey, who was about to protest his mother's assessment, "I also believe Anders is right. And maybe, if we are lucky, Sloane is getting tired of Derek's manipulations."

Corey agreed with open reluctance before turning back to me. "Did you know Elder Frontish is returning to Tuldamoran in three weeks? To Ardenna?"

"No, I didn't." I raised the glass to my lips and drained it, enjoying the fruity aftertaste on my tongue. "I know he's planning to travel to Port Alain with the first shipment of gems, but that's not for some time. He didn't say anything to Elena when we had dinner together. And she hasn't mentioned it to me, though we have been traveling the last few days. Do you know why he's heading south again?"

"No, sorry, but Elder Frontish has kept this planned journey secret from all but those close to him. Sloane told me when we spoke of the feyweed. Although Frontish claims to be in favor of this new trade agreement," Corey said thoughtfully, echoing the idea that had drifted through my mind, "I fear he may be, in reality, against it. Some of the elders want Spreebridge to remain apart from affairs to the south, fearing corruption and dilution of our, what they call, traditional culture. There are many in the council who fear exposure to the uncivilized ways, your pardon, Alex," —his grin was reminiscent of Gwynn as he apologized— "of Tuldamoran. They worry too much interaction may hurt our people in the long run. Mother and I disagree."

"But why do you think Derek is one of these naysayers?" Kimmer asked her son, studying his handsome features as he broke off a wedge of hard cheese and popped it in his mouth. "If he is against the trade, everything he's been saying is a lie."

"It very likely is, Mother. I place little trust in anything Elder Frontish says, and I respect him even less. So, Alex, if it is all right with you," —Corey nodded to me as I tilted the glass back to catch the very last drop of Marain Valley wine Kimmer had snuck into the goblet— "I will meet you in Ardenna to tell you what I have discovered about his clandestine journey."

I choked. Shoving the glass into Anders's hand to keep him from slapping my back, I tried to catch my breath, slanting Kimmer a wary glance.

"Ardenna should be all right, I think," the Spreebridge woman murmured, toying with a wedge of half-eaten cheese that had lost its appeal. "After all, what can happen where the queen's reign is favorable and the queen's Mage Protector is on hand?"

Struggling not to laugh, or cry, I managed to keep my voice even. "Ardenna would be perfect. No need to wander around the countryside. Never can be too safe about brigands on the road and in the forests, even though Elena keeps the roads relatively free of trouble. And there's an excellent inn not very far from the east gate—"

* * * *

"If my son knew who you really are, I think he would be pleased."

I blinked at our hostess, still groggy from too much wine and a deep, dreamless sleep in a soft bed after a hot bath that was more delightful than I had any right to expect. "Lords of the sea, Kimmer, I'd no idea he'd suggest coming to Tuldamoran." I rubbed my eyes and gratefully accepted a steaming cup of tea from the older woman.

"Well, neither did I. But he is committed to your cause." She poured herself a fresh cup of tea. "Alex—"

"I won't tell him who I am."

"Thank you."

"However, we'll have to keep my brother away from him." I gave the Glynnswood scout a warning glance as she busied herself with hot cinnamon rolls and a sliced apple. "Maylen, that's your job."

"I know, Alex. I have already thought of that." Another set of blue eyes appraised me, and I caught the barest twinkle of mischief. "Gwynn would guess the truth immediately. He is nearly as smart as you."

Before I could reply to the backhanded insult, Kimmer intervened. "I am sorry to put you in such a difficult situation, Alex," she apologized, pouring a fresh tea for Anders when he drained his cup. "But you must understand my dilemma."

"Oh, believe me, I do. But it's not your fault. Anyone who is even distantly related to my father puts me in a difficult situation." I shrugged, smothering a rude yawn. "I'm used to it."

The Spreebridge elder started to reply, caught Anders's eye, and shook her head, laughing. "I can imagine," she said, trying with little success to keep a straight face, "that you have more than made up for the lost years you did not share with your father."

Anders smirked, eying Kimmer through the rising steam of his teacup, "Next time you write to Sernyn, ask him how gray he's become in the last five or so years."

* * * *

"Can you set the dock on fire?"

A few hours later, after we'd made our way back to the wharf in Derbarry, Anders studied me very carefully from head to foot. "Kimmer sent you off with a warm enough farewell, didn't she? Or are you still cold?"

Maylen looked first at Anders, and then at me, as though we'd both gone mad.

"Can you?"

"Yes, if I use that cook fire beneath the teapot by the group of sailors."

I studied the distance between the cook fire and the men conversing lazily along the dock. "All right. Can you make sure the fire heads toward land?"

Anders narrowed his eyes to slits, trying, I guessed, to imagine what I was planning. "Yes, of course." He puffed out his broad chest. "I'm the great and esteemed Crownmage who serves the queen of Tuldamoran and lords it over the queen's Mage Protector and—"

"Hush. Just do it."

"I thought you wanted to hurry home to our daughter."

"I do." Grateful we would soon be heading south, I leaned back against the rough wall of the supply shop we'd just left a little richer. "But there's one more thing I want to see before we go home."

"Jackson—" Maylen's loud whisper brought Anders's head swiftly around to follow her intent gaze.

Anders turned back to me, mischief lighting up his eyes. "And you accuse Rosanna of being a devious old witch."

"She taught me everything I know."

Anders laughed and planted a kiss on my lips, and then started to wave his arms, but I slapped them down.

"Do you think you can avoid theatrics? I don't want to be noticed." Pouting, he muttered something unintelligible under his breath. "Pardon?"

"Nothing, dear. Yes, wait—" Anders turned suddenly anxious, and I could read his guilty thoughts as though they were written in bold letters across his forehead. "Shouldn't you go for a walk or something? Just until I'm finished—"

"I've been walking away enough." Clamping a tight grip on my shaky insides, I nodded. "Sooner or later, I have to be able to deal with the fact I can't wield magic, Anders, but thank you." I kissed his smooth-shaven cheek, surprising him. "Go ahead. I'll be all right. Maylen," —I grinned at her concerned expression— "if I turn deathly white or start to fall over, catch me. Anders won't be able to." Nodding, she kept her expression serious. "I'm joking. Lords of the sea, you're both— Never mind. What I'm thinking isn't grateful. Anders, hurry and get it over with before he decides to leave."

"Great mage talent can't be rushed," he intoned, and then proceeded to rush. Eyes focused on the cook fire, Anders stayed very still.

I watched the flames beneath the old tin pot flare and scoot toward dockside, edging nearer to Jackson, nearly lapping at his boots, as he waited to board the smaller vessel that would bring him downstream to the riverboat at the border. When I feared no one would notice the danger in time, the flames flared once more and Jackson turned, shouting for water, yelling in frustration and anger, as he tried without success to use the mage talent that had forsaken him.

Satisfied, and saddened, I tapped Anders on the shoulder. "Let's go home."

"By bridge?"

"I did it once, and it didn't kill me," I said, disregarding the nausea that threatened to overtake me at the mere thought of the passage I faced. "After all, it's better if we cross the border in secret. We stand more of a chance of being discovered on these small boats before we even reach the border if your pitiful stomach starts vomiting again."

"Now, Alex—"

"Home, husband." I pointed south. "That way."

Unfortunately, I was almost sorry we did go home.

Chapter Eight

"Emmy's sound asleep," my father whispered, slanting a wary expression at Anessa. "Wait, Alex." He gently but firmly gripped my cloak as I tiptoed toward the small cozy chamber where my daughter slept. "There is something you must know before she wakes."

"All right." I forced my expression to utter casualness, fooling no one, especially my father. Keeping my back to the welcoming blaze of the fireplace, though it was warmer so many miles south of the Keshtang Mountains, I waved a hand at him. "Tell me."

"Sit, please."

When he tried to lead me toward the armchair closest the fireplace, I resisted, crossed my arms, and met his worried gaze. "I don't need to hear bad news sitting down. I promise I won't faint or do anything foolish. Now tell me."

My father's sigh was loud. "Someone slipped feyweed into Emmy's milk."

Ah, no. She was only a child. My child.

"Alex." Anders stepped past my father to slip his arms around my waist.

"How?" I ignored my husband, keeping my gaze fixed on Sernyn. "Did she use her magic in front of anyone? Was she showing off?"

"Of course not." Sernyn shook his head. "We were all careful with her. Even Emmy knew it was a secret, and you know how well-behaved she is." As Anessa inched near to stroke his arm, he sighed again. "There were some traders in the village, a new young man among them. He must have spied Emmy and Gwynn deep in the forest when they thought they were alone. It never occurred to me—"

"Can we find him?" Anders held me close, as though to stop me from fleeing.

My father hesitated. "He is no longer a problem. We tried to capture the man unharmed to question him, but he attacked Gwynn and tried to kill him. I—" Sernyn left Anessa's side and turned away, walking with weary steps toward the window. "I made certain he would never hurt anyone again."

Lords of the sea, what more would happen? "I'm sorry." I pulled free of Anders's protective grasp and hugged my father close. "I'm so sorry."

"No, Alex. I am sorry. We let you down—"

"Stop it." I shook him with easy affection. "How could you know? How could any of us know?" I caught the swift glance that flashed between Anessa and my father. "What is it? Is Gwynn all right?"

Anessa sank down into the armchair, trying to keep tears back as Maylen knelt by her side. "My son is gone, and we do not know where. He blames himself—"

"Flameblasted fool. We have to find him. Maylen?"

An odd expression in the younger woman's eyes made me pause and feel more confident. "I will find him. There are several places he may have gone. One, in particular, I think." She stood up and strode toward the door, resting one hand on the wood. "Do you have any message, Alex, when I find him?"

"Oh, yes. Tell my brother he's a coward," I said, angry, but not at Gwynn. As Maylen faced me, her expression unreadable, I whispered, blinking back hot tears, "And tell him—Tell Gwynn that it's my fault. I should have brought Emmy to Jules's lodge." The tears fell unhindered. "My fault, Maylen, not his."

"It is not your fault either, Alex." With no other words for me or from me, Maylen vanished into the night.

Respecting my silence, though like as not disagreeing with what it implied, Anders trailed me into the chamber where Emmy lay sleeping. I stood in the doorway, not wanting to wake the child, but some instinct stirred her awake.

"Mama!" Tiny arms snaked around my neck as I knelt by her bedside, Anders beside me. She threw one arm around his neck, never letting go of me. It took all the restraint in my power not to weep for her. "I can't do magic anymore," she whispered, starting to cry.

"Hush. It's all right, sweetling." I hugged her tight. "Didn't Grandfather tell you what happened to me when I was as little as you?" When Emmy pulled back from my arms and shook her head gravely, I smiled. "Silly." I pushed the curls from her face and wiped her tears with a handkerchief Anders made a production of pulling from his tunic pocket. "Well, he should have told you. Now I'll have to scold him." I shook my head in mock disapproval. "When I was little, I could only do a small bit of magic, and then, one day, I couldn't do any, not one bit. I thought it had disappeared."

"What happened?" Huge seagray eyes, her father's eyes, studied me as she listened with an adult's intensity.

I shrugged with a lightness I didn't feel, as though my experience had been nothing to worry about. "I don't know why it happened. I couldn't do anymore magic until the day your father showed up at the door to my schoolroom." I made a ridiculous face at Anders behind my hand to make her laugh. "And then, all of a sudden, he taught me how to do magic all over again."

Anders touched her damp cheek and smiled. "If your mother could learn to do magic again, then so can you. After all, you're a lot smarter than she is." Anders ducked my fist and hid behind Emmy for protection, both of them shrieking. Laughing as he tickled her, she hugged him again.

"Go back to sleep." Kissing the top of her head, I leaned on the bedpost to stand upright, watching Anders tuck her in until she was warm and snug. "And if you tell anyone, especially grandmother Rosanna, that you're smarter than me, I'll dangle you by your fat little toes over the Skandar Sea."

Anders waved me away in dismissal and winked at her. Emmy smiled sleepily, yawned, and blew me a kiss as Anders led me from the room.

"She'll be fine in time," he reassured my fretting father as we joined them back in their sitting room. I plopped back against the inviting cushions on the armchair beside the cottage fireplace.

"I do not worry so much about my poor granddaughter. It is you, Alex. Will you be fine?" My father glanced with meaning in my direction as Anessa handed me a steaming cup of cinnamon tea. She'd added a hint of Marain Valley wine, another trick she learned from the senior Lady Barlow.

"Yes."

"I am not convinced."

Fully aware of the irony, I glanced at the man who, not so very long ago, wouldn't dream of confronting me. "It's Anders you should be worried about."

"Me?" Anders looked confused.

"My guess is that you're their next target."

"I'll be careful."

"We were careful with Emmy, and look what happened. I want you to go somewhere and hide. Travel. Take a holiday." When Anders gave me a long-suffering look, I exploded, "Flameblast you, Anders! If Elder Frontish is behind these attacks, I need your precious Crownmage talent intact."

From the corner of my eye, I caught my father's open curiosity. Well, we hadn't had time to tell him anything of our journey yet. As Anders related what we uncovered, with the tactful omission of just who Corey was in relation to my father, I let my thoughts wander until they rambled around and about the long way back to Emmy. And how I'd failed to protect her. I never noticed my father kneeling beside me until he stroked my wet cheek.

"Don't tell me it's not my fault," I whispered. "That's a lie."

He studied me for a long silent moment. "You made a choice, Alex. Maybe it was not the right one, but you chose, believing at the time that it was the best choice. No one could predict what would happen."

Anders knelt opposite my father. "And I went along with the decision."

"Not to listen to my nagging—"

"Stop it. You're implying I'm henpecked. It's my fault, too. Now enough nonsense." Anders stood and pulled me to my feet, with a wink at Anessa. "Besides, it's time I tucked you into bed. We haven't been alone in, what— Months? Years?"

Chapter Nine

"Your daughter was smarter than you from the very first moment she opened those gorgeous seagray eyes and smiled at me."

"I can't believe she'd tell you that."

Rosanna kept her expression bland, a very old Barlow trick, very much like Anders's far-too-innocent expression, and sat across from me as I found my usual refuge sorting through books and papers in the schoolroom. "She didn't have to. It's obvious." I gave Rosanna the same long-suffering glare Anders often gave me, to no avail, as usual. "Well?"

"Well what?" I snapped, annoyed Rosanna had cornered me so fast after our recent return from Glynnswood and an uneasy farewell from my father.

"Feeling out of sorts?"

"Damn it, Rosanna, my daughter's been robbed of her fledgling mage talent, my foolish brother's a coward and hiding from me, my father's feeling guilty about the whole horrendous matter—"

"And you're not?" Eyes wide with innocence and an upraised brow stared me down from the top of my head to the soles of my worn boots. When I didn't bother to answer, her tone softened, "Alex—"

"All right!" Having heard enough, and not wanting to hear any more, I slammed a heavy geography book on the low table, sending papers flying across the wooden floor. "I should have taken Emmy to Jules's lodge instead of sending her to Glynnswood and damn all Jules's rights to privacy. Is that what you want me to say?"

"Of course not."

"Then what?" I listened in utter amazement as Rosanna rolled her eyes toward the ceiling and uttered a very out-of-character unladylike oath, much like her daughter-in-law, Lauryn, when she was exceptionally annoyed at me. "My, my. Listen to you. If your grandchildren could hear those words—"

"I'm glad you did. Maybe you'll get my point." Rosanna glared at me. "Don't you know the difference between my pestering and my honest concern?"

"Is there a difference?" I grinned, bending to retrieve the nearest scattered papers from the ground.

"Ungrateful child."

"So you're concerned now, I take it?"

"You know I am."

I put the papers aside and leaned forward, catching her off guard as an impish thought entered my head. "Did Anders tell you everything?"

Rosanna blinked. "Well, now, that depends," she hedged, shrewdly suspecting a trap. "What's everything?"

I cocked my head to the side. "Corey?"

"Corey?" The senior Lady Barlow scratched her gray head, thinking, or pretending to think. "Kimmer Frehan's oldest son?"

"Hmm, yes."

"What about him?"

The old woman looked sincerely ignorant, but she'd lied to me before. Maybe Anders hadn't told her the whole story. Then again, maybe he had. "What did Anders tell you about Corey?"

"Quite a lot." She grinned, earning a scowl from me. "As always. But apparently," —Rosanna narrowed her eyes— "not everything." When I didn't enlighten her further, she poked my arm with a pudgy finger. "Well?"

I learned quite a bit from the woman who raised me over the years, including the art of sidestepping. "Do you think Gwynn will show up in Port Alain once Maylen kicks his butt and he finds the courage to face me?"

Perplexed, Rosanna blinked again. "Gwynn? Yes, of course. Once Maylen convinces him he was very foolish to run away." She shoved aside the geography book, propped both elbows on the table, and planted her chin on her hands. "All right, Alex, I've been alive far longer than you. What does Gwynn Keltie have to do with Corey Frehan?"

I knew I'd hook her sooner or later. Shrugging carelessly, I explained, "I just can't let Gwynn follow me to Ardenna next week when I meet Corey."

"Why not?"

"Anders really, really didn't tell you?"

Rosanna shook her head. "No."

"Ah, then. If he didn't think it important, then neither do I." A bland expression covered my face as I started to clear away the books and stack them in a lopsided pile.

Rosanna grabbed the sleeve of my tunic. "You're being exceptionally difficult."

"I'm trying very hard."

"You're succeeding."

"All right." Laughing, I straightened the pile of books, pulled them in front of me, and leaned an elbow on top of them. "I'll take pity on an old woman who has nothing better to do than listen to local gossip."

"Now you're being disrespectful."

"You deserve it."

Huge eyes, expressing hurt feelings, stared me down. "Do I really?"

"The wounded look isn't very convincing at the moment." Smacking her arm lightly, I lost, and then caught, my balance on the pile of books. "Now think, Lady Barlow. Why would I have to keep my half-brother, Gwynn, away from Corey?" When Rosanna concentrated, unable to make the connection, I grew impatient. "Lords of the sea, woman, don't think too hard. It's unnerving."

She gasped, muttered another oath, and narrowed her eyes. "Oh, Alex!" Knowing she'd finally snapped the puzzle pieces into place, I started to laugh again, losing my balance as the books fell. She grabbed my arm to hold me steady. "Is it true?"

"Oh yes."

"Does your father know?"

"No."

Rosanna sat back and studied me. "You didn't tell him?"

"Kimmer didn't want me to say anything."

Rosanna's fingers tapped an anxious rhythm against the tabletop. "In your case, that usually doesn't matter."

I held her gaze, daring her to say the wrong thing. "Kimmer's afraid Corey will hate her, or feel betrayed. Can you imagine such a thing?"

"No, Alex." Rosanna's eyes widened again in mock innocence. "I can't imagine anyone reacting that way."

"Neither can I."

"What's he like?"

Considering my answer, I sat back on the stool, sighing heavily. "You'd like him. He's a bit like me and Gwynn and my father, all rolled into one. Rosanna—" When she said nothing, waiting with her usual patience, aware that I'd grown serious again, I admitted, "My father really should know about Corey."

"Agreed." She patted my hand and said softly, "But not from you."

"No. Not from me."

* * * *

"Why didn't anyone tell me you were back?" Jules poked his head through the doorway of the schoolroom moments after his mother left. If he'd arrived a few moments earlier, the conversation might have been a little different and a whole lot dicier.

"You probably didn't ask. Or maybe you didn't care."

Raking slender fingers through disheveled light brown hair, Jules shook his head. "No one knew when you'd be back. You didn't bother to send word like a decent human being," he scolded, which meant he'd been worried. "Not to mention Lauryn's going to hang me by my toes from Mother's balcony if I don't tell her you've arrived safe and sound."

"Don't bother. Your mother is probably on her way there now." Jules came into the spacious room and sat on the low wooden table, tapping two letters against his knee. I studied his handsome face. "You'll break the table."

"I will not."

"All right. Be stubborn. But if you do break it, I'll insist the ducal treasury, not Lauryn's half, pay for another." I pointed at the letters he was waving, squinting to get a better look. "What's that? Aha, they have the royal seal. Must be important."

"Yes, unfortunately." Jules's expression turned abruptly grim and, beyond that, apologetic on my behalf. "Someone's attacked Jackson with feyweed. He's lost his mage talent, too." He handed me the other letter. "This one came for you."

Following my instinct, which usually led me in the right direction if I didn't count my recent decision to not use Jules's hunting lodge for Emmy, I thought it best for the moment not to tell him I knew all about Jackson's trouble, or how I knew. Too much awkward explanation and too few solid answers. I broke the seal and scanned the letter, reading Elena's worries about Jackson and me between the lines. It was good she didn't know what happened to my daughter or father, despite the fact Sernyn never used his magic. It was still a loss and a violation, and Elena would be heartbroken for both of them.

"I know just how Jackson feels."

"Does it get any easier?" For a pleasant change, Jules was sincere. "You lost it once before as a child."

"Yes, but that was before I really had it, or, honestly, enjoyed it. My fault, thank you for not reminding me, Jules. After all, most of that lost time was due to the fact magic scared me half to death, and so I didn't want to have it." At the ugly reminder of our earlier shared history, I shrugged, trying hard to disguise my grief. It wouldn't serve anyone's purpose to have Jules worrying more than he needed to worry. "I suppose time will make it easier for us. I don't know. I still reach for the magic like a missing arm or leg. Sometimes I do it on purpose, just to see if maybe the whole incident was a nightmare and never really happened."

"Can't anything be done?"

Stretching the kinks from my back, I gave Jules a sly grin. "We've some ideas to play with." As his eyes widened with a hundred thousand questions, I wagged a finger at him. "Don't ask."

"All right, but that's not fair. In fact—"

"Alex!" In moments, I was nearly knocked from the low stool by a crashing tidal wave of children and adults as Hunter and Carey, Jules's twin eleven-year-old boys, pulled me to my feet and swept me around in a circle. Khrista and her daughter, Linsey, trailed along with Lauryn, my own Emmy running between them, face flushed with excitement and joy at being back home in Port Alain.

"Why didn't you tell us you were back?" Lauryn scolded, light blue eyes flashing with genuine annoyance. "Not that any of us missed you, of course, but we did miss Anders and Emmy."

"I'm sure you didn't miss all the noise."

Khrista grinned as little Linsey entwined her small fingers in her hand, the child nearly as serious as my own daughter. "Not a bit. In fact, just the other day, Kerrie and I told Chester, over a pint or two of delicious ale down at the Seaman's Berth, how much we loved having you gone."

"We missed you, Alex." Hunter, the twin who favored Lauryn's gentle, perceptive temperament, hastened to reassure me. "Didn't we?" he nudged Carey, the other twin, Jules's twin, as his grandmother always proclaimed, the one who couldn't stay out of trouble for very long.

"Sure. Especially since Mother's a harder taskmaster when she takes over the school lessons." Carey scampered out of my reach, a broad grin on his handsome face, as he hid behind my adoring daughter.

"By the way, Alex," Jules cut in, with a wink at Emmy, who smiled shyly, "Did your little journey to Glynnswood make you any less cranky?"

No wonder Carey was the way he was. I folded my arms across my chest. "What do you think, my lord duke? Care to take a wager?"

* * * *

"Imagine the nerve of your son implying I was anything but pleasant. Even Khrista," I complained, smothering a yawn, "had bad things to say in front of the impressionable children. I expected better of your daughter. After all, we did spend a lot of time in our childhood plotting against Jules and Elena, now that I think of it."

"Completely unfounded accusations, Alex. I'll see they're both properly chastened." Rosanna accompanied her dry response with a sly glance at my traitorous husband. "After all, I did raise my son and daughter to have better manners. You, too, for that matter, which brings me to a point I've been pondering for a very long time. I've come to a definite conclusion over the years."

"I can't wait to hear it."

Rosanna's grin was eloquent and, beyond that, wicked. "Well, the point is this. I believe that it must be, in fact, has to be, your influence that makes my usually well-behaved children misbehave."

"You can't possibly be that blind. It's their influence on me."

"Hmm. Somehow, I don't think so."

We were tarrying in Rosanna's parlor some evenings later after the rest of the noisy clan left us in peace to put the children to bed. I shifted Emmy in my lap where she lay peaceful and asleep, curled like a well-fed, contented kitten. Brushing a wayward curl from her face, I sighed deeply, my thoughts wandering far from the bantering with Rosanna.

"We won't be gone for long," Anders responded to my sigh.

"I know. I just hate leaving Emmy behind again." I smiled at his attempt to make me feel better. Glancing at Rosanna, I added, "Not that I'm worried for her safety, mind you. They've already damaged the poor child. It's a selfish reason. I'll miss her."

"And she'll miss you, too. Both of you. So be sure to return as soon as you can." Rosanna squeezed my arm, offering comfort where I could find none. "Now tell me. If Gwynn comes here to Port Alain, with or without Maylen, what should I tell him?"

Emmy stirred in my arms and turned her head, settling herself against my stomach. "If Gwynn doesn't come here in the next few days, I don't think he will. Maylen knows we're to meet Corey in Ardenna. But, listen, if he does—" I looked at Anders, uncertain what to say as my daughter murmured something I couldn't understand, whimpering in her sleep. Had the poor child been caught in nightmares, as I had been?

"Tell Gwynn to return to Glynnswood until we send word." Anders's voice was a soothing and confident counterpoint to my uncertainty. "Make sense?"

I shrugged, unable to think clearly. "I suppose. I just wish he hadn't run off like that. It's not like him, and—"

Soft, persistent knocking at the chamber door cut into my words.

"I'll see who it is," Anders muttered under his breath as he struggled to his feet. "It can't be Elena. It's not late enough, and we're not in bed, though she no longer visits in the middle of the night, nor does Jules. I never thought to admit it," he tossed over his shoulder, "but I really do miss those uncivilized visits."

I grinned, turning toward the door, just as Anders poked his head out, muttered something sharply, shook his head, and shut the door. "Anders? Who is it?"

My husband opened the oak door again, with infinite slowness, and stood in the doorway, arms folded across his chest, blocking my view of our visitors. "We were just saying nasty things about you."

"Gwynn?" I scrambled to my feet as Rosanna pulled Emmy from my arms, tucking my daughter onto her own lap, whispering sweet words at the abrupt movement that disturbed the child's sleep further.

"Yes, Alex, it's your brother." Anders's voice was flat, which made me immediately suspicious.

Not sure what to expect, I peered around Anders's broad shoulders at the trio that stood in the hallway, awkward as newborn ponies. Maylen, with an exquisite bland look on her pretty face, stood beside Gwynn, as always. But it was the third person, Corey Frehan, who had a hundred thousand emotions flashing across his face as he stood quietly on the other side of my brother.

"Lords of the sea," Rosanna snapped in exasperation, lowering her voice to avoid waking Emmy. "Are you this inept in your own cottage, Alex? And Anders, really, I might expect this rude behavior from your wife, but you? Have either of you no manners? Let them inside, will you?"

Chastened, Anders stepped backward, right onto my toes. Wincing from the pain, I smacked him on the shoulder, losing my balance. Gwynn caught me as I fell, looking very uncertain and very young.

"Fool." I hugged Gwynn hard. "If you ever do something that stupid again—"

"You mean, almost let you fall?"

Stepping back to take a good look at my brother, worried at the obvious sleeplessness in his eyes and the shadows beneath them, I punched his shoulder hard. "You know what I mean. And another thing, remember those times you said when I was angry, you were afraid I'd leave?" My words rushed out in a torrent, most of the things I'd planned to say drummed out of my head by the sheer relief in seeing him in one piece. "How did you think I felt when you were gone?"

"But I'd failed you," he whispered, looking miserable. "Alex—"

"I failed Emmy. It was my decision not to send her elsewhere, which Anders respected and trusted. My fault, not yours," I scolded, shaking him hard.

In answer, Gwynn hugged me to his chest, relieved, right before flashing me that all-too-innocent Anders's look. Stepping aside, he let the other two come into Rosanna's parlor, a feline smile on Maylen's face.

Corey, here with Gwynn. Lords of the sea, now what?

"Rosanna, ah, Lady Barlow." I avoided meeting not only her eyes, but Corey's, as well. "This is Corey Frehan of Spreebridge—"

"Your half-brother, Alex."

Ah, well. I turned slowly at Corey's words, eying his face with great care, then Gwynn, who was grinning like an idiot, and then finally Maylen.

Tossing a blonde braid over one shoulder, as though dismissing both of my half-brothers, she said with a hint of smugness, "I did not tell anyone anything, Alex. Corey came south to Glynnswood on his own."

I spun around to face Corey. "At least you had the decency not to make your statement when I had a glass of wine near my lips."

"Mother warned me you had a, um, tendency to choke." All of a sudden, Corey lost his composure under my fierce glare, flushing hotly from the top of his head to his tunic collar, his voice a trifle shaky. "Are you angry?"

"That I didn't choke again?"

Flustered, he turned to Gwynn, who patted him on the back. "She can be very difficult at times. You will get used to her."

Insulted, I shoved Gwynn away from Corey. "Leave him alone." With another fierce look at my new brother from Spreebridge, I added, "And don't you believe a word that fool says. Gwynn has absolutely no credibility."

Corey nodded hastily, new to our family dynamic. "But, well—" When I gestured him to go on, his expression turned somber. "I must know, Alex. Are you angry Mother told me the truth about you and Gwynn and father?"

Lords of the sea, save me from moronic younger half-brothers. Gwynn had asked the very same thing of me, more than five years ago. I turned to Rosanna, one hand planted on my hip. "Why are all the men in my life complete fools?" Before she could offer an acceptable answer, I tapped Corey on the chest. "Of course not. I wanted your mother to tell you the truth because I thought you had a right to know." I paused for a breath, a little shaky myself. "The question should really be whether you're angry."

"No." His expression revealed an odd mixture of emotions. "No, she told me about Father and you, and, well, what happened when you discovered he was still alive." Corey flushed again, embarrassed. "No, Alex. I do understand."

"But I don't." Puzzled, I scratched my head, searching Corey's face for the answers. "What prompted your mother to tell you? She was adamant when we left Derbarry that you not know the truth."

Corey's expression abruptly changed. "Sloane is dead."

"Ah, no." Sensing his grief, I gripped Corey's shoulders tight, wanting to hug him, not sure it would be welcome. "I'm so sorry."

Corey shook his head in resignation. "I knew it would come to this sad end, sooner or later, Alex. So did Mother. But still, we hoped."

"Come sit down." I pulled him toward the armchair opposite Rosanna, though he paused before sitting to peer shyly at my daughter.

"This is Emila?" Corey turned questioning eyes over his shoulder. When I nodded, he touched her curls with affection. "She is as beautiful as Gwynn said she would be."

"Just what she needs, another uncle to spoil her," I muttered to no one in particular as I plopped down at Rosanna's knees, ignoring her bemused expression.

Corey exchanged a shy smile with Gwynn, and then sat down as Anders poured cinnamon tea all around. Maylen and Gwynn, removing their cloaks, joined us, side-by-side in front of the fireplace, as though they'd never been parted.

"Tell us what happened."

"We have no proof, Alex, but I hold Derek Frontish responsible for Sloane's death. I think, and so does Mother, that Sloane was creeping too close to whatever trouble Elder Frontish has been brewing here in Tuldamoran." Corey paused to take a cautious sip of the hot tea, nodding his thanks at Anders. "The last time I saw my brother alive, Sloane told me large crates of feyweed were being sent in secret with the first trade shipments of gems and ore on the Stoutheart's maiden voyage down river. They'll be coming here, down the Jendlan River, across Shad's Bay—"

"To Port Alain." Thinking, I stretched out my legs and settled back against Rosanna's chair. "On a ship called the Stoutheart."

"That is why mother sent me south. And because of Sloane, truly." His expression turned mischievous. "And to, um, meet my father."

"What was his reaction to you?"

"He has not yet seen me or even knows of my existence."

"Hold on. I'm now completely confused. If you're traveling with Maylen and Gwynn, then how—"

"We met along the road," Maylen explained, leaning into Gwynn's shoulder. "It was quite a coincidence, if one believes in such things."

"Knowing the Kelties, well, knowing Sernyn and Gwynn Keltie, since I hold Anessa innocent, I no longer believe in coincidence," I grumbled, turning to Corey as a wicked thought entered my head. "Well, good, I'm glad he doesn't know about you yet, because I want to be there when the two of you meet. That man swore he had no other children."

"He didn't know," Rosanna hotly defended my father, "and besides, Alex, vengeance is not something you should be after."

"Normally, I'd agree with you, but when my father is involved, all the rules change." As a companionable silence fell, with Anders acting as host and serving the trio cheese and sausage bread, I started thinking about the implications. "Why bring the feyweed to Port Alain? Why not smuggle it across the border by land?"

Maylen met Anders's eyes, the two of them smiling.

"I admit Lunatics' Crossing isn't the friendliest route, but it's more isolated. Unless they're just arrogant and plan to ship the feyweed right under our noses, while the royal heir welcomes them with open arms."

"That's my guess," Anders said, handing me a wedge of cheese.

"Well, esteemed Crownmage, since you agree, will Port Alain be a central distribution point? Will they then travel along Shad's Bay to the mouth of the Kieren River, and sail north to Ardenna?" Frustrated with the tidbit of information that told us nothing, I added, "And why? What's their objective?"

"The one point Derek and my brother disagreed on was mage talent. Sloane craved power and was desperate to be a mage, any kind of mage. Unfortunately, for my poor brother, Sloane never had a glimmer of talent." Corey shot me a sorrowful look. "That is one of the reasons Sloane was never completely comfortable with me. I have the magic he always desired. And although Derek is a mage, Sloane could tolerate the fact because the elder offered him the opportunity to become involved in the plot he was planning to unleash."

"My, my." I laughed, able at the moment to think of my father's unused magic without bitterness for the price my mother paid in childhood. "Imagine my father's horror at having three mage children? I definitely want to be in Glynnswood when you tell him about yourself. What tricks can you do?"

Corey's face turned scarlet. "The opposite of Gwynn. Fire to earth."

"My, my."

"Alex." Rosanna tugged sharply at a strand of my hair. "Leave him alone."

In response, I waved a hand in dismissal. "I forgot to warn you, Corey, about Lady Barlow. But what was it about magic," I asked him, serious again, "did Sloane and Derek disagree about?"

"Elder Frontish, along with some other of his cronies, think it a perversion of pure mage talent to have any type of power that differed from the Spreebridge kind, which is essentially what Glynnswood mages share. We can change one element to another, and that is all. Until, that is, Jackson Tunney came along, and then you, Alex, who share Glynnswood blood." Corey glanced down at his hands, rubbing them as though they were chilled. "I think there is fear that another mage like you will happen again, so they wish to prevent the possibility. The fear is simple ignorance, fear of the unknown, fear that someone more powerful will come along and destroy whatever power they hold."

"So the trade agreement is a cover?" I asked, thinking out loud.

"Might be. Corey's theory explains the attack on Jackson. He's an oddity like you," Anders said thoughtfully. "Don't you think?"

I shook my head, not certain whether or not to be insulted by his choice of words. "It explains the attack on Emmy, too," I said, "but not my father. And what about our own mages here in Tuldamoran? Seamages, firemages, windmages, and earthmages? Their talent is a perversion, too, if you accept what Corey is saying. After all, although they can only wield magic within one element, it still differs from Spreebridge magic." Angry and frightened at the implications, I scratched my head with vigor, trying to clear away the cobwebs in my mind. "What gives them the right to come south and judge utter strangers who have done them no harm?"

"Narrow-minded fanatics, Alex, believe they have the right to mold the world into their own image of what is right and wrong. If that is their purpose, to judge Tuldamoran mages, it might explain the large shipments," Maylen added, eyes half-closed as she nestled against Gwynn.

"Possible. Why else send crates when only a small pinch would be enough to attack the rest of my family," —I shot a glance at both brothers, both mages— "and possibly your granddaughter," I warned Rosanna, whose face paled at the thought of Linsey and the child's latent magic, the product of a renegade Spreebridge mage and her seamage mother, "particularly if they know what happened to Khrista in Edgecliff?"

"Hold on, Alex. What about the Crown Council of Mages in Ardenna?" Anders turned Rosanna's attention and worry away from her granddaughter. "You humbled the old Crown Council by defeating Charlton Ravess in the Mage Challenge and then exposing him to Elena when he returned from exile."

"Yes, but the present Crown Council is new, handpicked by Elena with Jules's help. The others have been removed from office."

"True," Anders agreed, though I felt I was missing his point, "but you defeated them all symbolically. Do you think any of them have any real affection for you? Especially when you consider your mother's well-known disregard for all Mage Councils. The Crown Council in Ardenna, including the local council here in Port Alain, may respect your position as Mage Protector, and hold their peace, but only because Elena demands it. I don't know. Maybe they're involved." He shrugged, looking as tired as I felt. "Maybe they're not. But who's to say that on Derek's upcoming visit to Ardenna there won't be any secret meetings with Elena's Crown Council?"

"Hmm. Then what about Jackson?" I asked, not sure that I was sure about anything anymore.

Rosanna gave me a crooked smile. "Jackson is wedged even closer to Elena than you are, in a different way. Were she to marry him, Elena would have all three of you locked inside her circle. You, Alex, as Mage Protector, Anders as Crownmage, and Jackson, with talent identical to yours."

"Elena doesn't have Jackson's magic or mine anymore." It was difficult to keep bitterness from my voice, as I hugged my knees close and rested my chin on top of them, lost in self-pity that had crept in unawares.

A yank on my hair was accompanied by, "You're feeling sorry for yourself."

When I didn't bother to answer, Corey offered tentatively, "Sloane believed there was a way to reverse the damage feyweed causes. There is still a chance, Alex."

I studied my new-found brother, neither denying nor affirming his words. Another yank on my hair prompted a growl from me. I reached back to grab Rosanna's hand and found myself clutching a tiny one instead. Emmy's wide-eyed face peeked at me. I tapped her on the nose, as she fell laughing into my arms.

"Uncle Gwynn!" Nearly head over heels, the imp scampered out of my lap and into Gwynn's outstretched arms, hugging Maylen next.

Corey watched shyly until she turned those huge seagray eyes on him.

"Emmy?" When she turned to me, one eye still on Corey, I explained, "That's your Uncle Corey. We found him when we went away on our journey."

Emmy turned her full somber attention to me. "Was he lost?"

Lords of the sea. I started to laugh, as Corey reddened. "Yes. I guess he was."

Emmy squirmed out of Gwynn's sheltering arms and into Corey's, who looked bewildered when she wrapped her tiny arms around his neck and hugged him. "I'm so glad Mama and Papa found you."

Rosanna sighed. "She can't possibly be your child."

Chapter Ten

"But how can you be leaving?" Lauryn demanded to my rigid back as I stood motionless, staring out the window overlooking her mother-in-law's gardens, most of which had burst into full colorful bloom. "You've only just arrived."

"It's important," Anders answered for me, seeking to placate my concerned friend. "Alex and Jackson have both lost their magic. We have—"

"Yes, I know," Lauryn, without her usual polite and patient manner, interrupted my husband. "But you've both—"

"Emmy has lost her magic, too." I spun on my boot heels to meet Lauryn's shocked blue eyes. "As has my father."

Caught off guard, her face ashen, Lauryn turned to Jules, who shrugged helplessly, not having known about the latter two victims. When her sister-in-law, Khrista, glanced at her own husband, Kerrie, the steward of the Barlow manor, I wondered whether Khrista was thinking about her own child.

She would, soon enough.

"I don't want to go away again so soon," I admitted, "especially because I have to leave Emmy behind. I've been doing that all too often, but we have some ideas about who might be responsible. Khrista—" Meeting her eyes, the fear was evident. "You need to watch Linsey very carefully. We're not sure whether the assailants are after me and my family, or anyone with special and different mage talent. Since we're not certain what Linsey can do and we don't know who knows about her lineage," —I stepped with care on delicate ground— "keep her near you and safe from strangers."

Kerrie, lords of the sea bless the man, loved and treated Linsey as his own child. So it didn't surprise me that it was Kerrie, rather than his wife, who answered. "I'll alert Chester, down at the Seaman's Berth, to be on the lookout for strangers. Anything I should tell him?"

"Only this," Anders said, offering a tentative smile to ease Khrista's fears. "There's to be a shipment of trade goods from Spreebridge, the first one between our lands, due to arrive in a few weeks. The ship's name is the Stoutheart. If it docks earlier than scheduled, before we've returned, send word to Ardenna immediately. And alert Jules, too." Nodding at the duke, who had started pacing the length of the parlor, much like Elena when she was thinking, Anders touched his sleeve when he passed by. "Jules?"

"Yes, of course." Running weathered fingers through his disheveled brown hair, Jules added, "In fact, I'll have some of my troops unobtrusively keep an eye on the docks and the roads coming into Port Alain. What's coming on the ship besides the gems and the ore?"

"Feyweed." At my quiet but emphatic word, they all stared at me. "We need to find out who's targeted and how. That's why I have to leave. There are a few important stops we have to make before coming back to Port Alain," I apologized to Lauryn, who looked forlorn. "I need to visit Glynnswood, and then Ardenna."

"Glynnswood again? You were just there. Alex, is your father all right?"

"He—" I stopped, remembering that none of them knew we'd really gone to Spreebridge rather than Glynnswood, nor did they know about Corey, and started to laugh. "At the moment, yes. Though when I arrive with my escort, he might not be."

"Alex—" There was definite scolding in my husband's voice, which I chose, as usual, to ignore.

"But why?" Honestly curious, Lauryn pursued the subject. "Who's going with you as escort? Anders, I presume. Maylen and Gwynn? Yes, all right, of course, they're going, and that polite young man, Corey, is it? The one from Spreebridge who was sitting in the garden this morning?"

I hadn't known that Lauryn had seen my brother. Tongue in cheek, I asked, "Did you take a good look at that polite young man?"

"I only got a glimpse of him, Alex." Lauryn narrowed her eyes, most likely seeing the young man in her mind's eye. "He seemed a little familiar, but I couldn't quite figure out why." When I started to leave the room without another word, a smug grin on my face, Lauryn grabbed a fistful of my tunic sleeve and shook my arm in annoyance. "You're not going anywhere, Alex Keltie, not until you tell us what's going on. Who is he?"

"Unbeknownst to my father,"—the smile escaped—"Corey Frehan is my, uh, slightly younger half-brother."

"Half—Oh, Alex." Lauryn gasped, shaking her head as the image of Corey's face probably popped back into her head. "Your father will be—" Lauryn blinked. "What will he be? How do you think he'll react?"

"Gwynn and I figure he'll be terrified of me. After all, I'm the beast in the family. So poor Sernyn will expect me to be angry. But I'm not," I reassured Lauryn, as she instinctively searched my face for truth. "My only problem with Corey is that he's as annoyingly polite as Gwynn. Well, as polite as Gwynn used to be until he started hanging around with my nuisance husband."

Lauryn leaned forward to hug me close. "You know, Alex, for someone who didn't think they had blood family only a few years ago, you have to admit the Keltie house is getting a little crowded."

* * * *

The precise moment my stepmother, Anessa, caught sight of Corey's face, she knew the truth. As we entered their warm and welcoming home, the noise was deafening, with embraces all around at our surprise return. Stepping back from Anessa's hug, I leaned against the cottage wall, arms crossed, watching as she studied Corey's face. Her shoulders abruptly tensed as she slid a furtive glance first at her own son and then her husband, and finally me. Anessa's eyes widened in guilt as she caught me staring at her. When a tiny smile tugged at my lips, her whole slender body visibly relaxed.

Lords of the sea, was I really that much a beast?

When my father turned to find Corey Frehan waiting patiently at the back of the crowd, he offered a hand, an affectionate smile on his face. "You must be Kimmer's son. You have a look about you that reminds me of her face." When Corey slanted me a sidewise glance that seemed to make my father cautious, Sernyn was perplexed. "Have I offended you? Have I said something out of turn? If I have, then—"

"No. No, of course not. Elder Keltie—" The young man flushed bright crimson, looked to me for rescue. "Alex—"

Poor fool. I took pity. "Elder Keltie," anticipating this moment, I pushed away from the wall and bowed in a mockery of court formality, "may I present the son of Kimmer Frehan and" —I bit my lip hard to keep laughter from bursting out—"yourself."

"My—What are you saying? Alex, it— That Corey—" My father couldn't quite get the words out. For a moment, I thought he would faint.

"Oh, and by the way," I responded without directly responding to his unspoken query, "he's a mage, too." With that, I turned on my heel and went outside.

* * * *

Anessa found me a little while later, sitting against an oak, or maple, or elm, maybe, not that I cared, except it was huge and offered perfect shade, enough for a lazy nap on a cool spring afternoon. She sat beside me, not waiting for an invitation, her slender legs, encased in soft leather, crossed beneath her. In the last five years since she and I had become friends, the gray had become more visible in the long, thick brown hair that hung below her shoulders. An attractive and openly affectionate woman, Anessa was a wonderful stepmother, as caring of me, the orphan child, in her own way, as Rosanna was in hers.

"When you left the cottage, I was not certain if you had changed your mind."

"Changed my mind?" I hugged my knees close to my chest, puzzled, still half drowsy. "About what?"

"When you first arrived, I had the distinct impression you found my husband's predicament," she stressed the word, one eyebrow raised, "well, humorous, since he had been so adamant about not having any other children."

"I did, and do."

"Ah. But then you left—"

"Yes, I did, didn't I?" Thinking back on my departure, I laughed. "Two reasons and only one respectable. The first is I wanted the two of them to have time alone, to get acquainted. The other—" I rested my chin on my hands, wondering if she would guess.

"To make your father think you were angry, even though you are not." When I grinned, not the least bit guilty, Anessa shoved me sideways onto the lush grass. "Alexandra Daine Keltie, you are a terrible, terrible child."

"No, she is not," a male voice drifted across the clearing. "But I am a terrible, terrible father." Sernyn offered a hand to help me sit back up, kneeling beside his wife. "Alex, I honestly did not know Kimmer had borne my child."

"Didn't anyone ever teach you the facts of life?"

Dark brown eyes stared soulfully at me for a heartbeat before he released his breath in a huge sigh. "Anessa is right. You are a terrible, terrible child, but I count myself blessed to be plagued by you." His smile was relieved as I leaned over to kiss his smooth-shaven cheek. "And I must warn you. I am afraid Corey, unlike Gwynn, has no idea what to do with you."

"Well, I'll just have to straighten him out about that, won't I?"

* * * *

"You mean to test Jackson again." Not a question, but a statement of fact, from my brother, Gwynn. "Alex? Is this true?"

"I'm convinced Jackson is telling the truth about losing his magic and," I stressed, glaring at Gwynn, who wasn't bothered in the least, "that he's above suspicion, but yes, I do mean to test him again."

"Good."

Maylen elbowed him, knocking my brother from his perch on the bench beside her. "When Alex is satisfied that the queen's lover is innocent, will you finally accept the truth and leave us all in peace and quiet?"

"If I must."

"Gwynn has some of your stubbornness," Anders said dryly before I could argue with my brother's bull-headedness. "Commendable," he added, "under some circumstances."

"Good thing you added that last point."

"I'm no fool, Alex."

"No, you're not. In fact—"

"Alex—" Corey tentatively broke into our banter, flushing as all eyes turned to him, including my father and Anessa. "Will the queen suspect me? I am, after all, a foreigner from Spreebridge."

"Ah, yes." I slid a glance at my stepmother, who had the presence of mind to hide a smile behind a delicate cough. "But, Corey, you're Elder Sernyn Keltie's son. And since Anessa has graciously accepted you into her home, as well, how can you possibly come under suspicion by the queen?"

"Alex, really—" My father's chiding faded swiftly as I raised one eyebrow in silent challenge.

"True or not? The fact that Corey is your son—"

"I would hope that Elena would trust my family," Sernyn's own quiet challenge dared me across the space of the sunny parlor, "no matter where they live."

"He's got you there."

"Hush." I glared at my husband. "Corey was asking a serious question and deserves a serious answer."

"You didn't give him one."

"I did so. In fact," —I turned my attention to Corey and my back to Anders, so his antics wouldn't distract me— "it's a question that concerns me, too. I doubt Elena will have any problem with Corey, but I can't speak for Jackson. He knew you and your mother in Derbarry," I reminded my newest brother. "But Jackson also knew Sloane, and that may turn out to be the problem. Not you."

"Jackson respects my mother. I can only hope he respects me, too."

When Corey stared down at his hands, I wondered how difficult it had been for him growing up, to love a brother who sometimes returned that affection with hate. All my life, I'd been missing a brother or sister, and now I had two younger brothers, a father I'd finally been brave enough to welcome into my heart, and a stepmother who offered unconditional acceptance. And above all that, Anders and Emmy, the Barlows, and Elena. To say that I'd been blessed would be insufficient. The loss of my magic, considered from this perspective, was meaningless. I had to believe that, or my life would turn bitter.

Glancing across the room at my father, I met his somber gaze and smiled, sending a message I wasn't certain he understood. But something of my mood must have made its way into his heart, because his smile was filled with peace.

"I think Jackson will respect you," I reassured Corey, "though he may press you for information. Just be honest. Be yourself." Thinking about Elena and the task before me, I admitted, "It will be hard enough for me to be honest, to admit to Jackson, in front of Elena, that even for a moment, we suspected him of treachery."

"You are the queen's Mage Protector," Anessa said, breaking her silence. "You could do nothing else. If Elena were to take a hundred lovers," she cut off my protest before it had even formed in my mind, "you would have been within your rights to watch every one of them." Huge brown eyes held my gaze, defying me to argue.

I gave in, and laughed. "No wonder your men have no say in this household. All right, so Corey will come to Ardenna with Anders and me, and—"

"Do you like him better than me?"

"What?" I stared at Gwynn in disbelief. "Corey needs to first tail Elder Frontish and find out what he's up to in Ardenna, and then he has to speak with both Elena and Jackson. You, on the other hand, don't need to do either of those two things. However, I do need you elsewhere, if your parents don't mind the peace and quiet of having you gone."

"Mother will miss me." Gwynn shot Anessa a grin.

"I will not, Alex. Please send him far, far away for many days."

"My pleasure, though it will only be Port Alain. And if Maylen will keep him out of trouble" —I waited for the young woman's nod of agreement— "I'd like the two of you to give Jules a hand in keeping watch in town. I don't doubt the skill of his troops, but there's no sneakier people than Glynnswood folk."

"Have we just been insulted?" Gwynn asked our father.

"Alex would never insult us," Sernyn reassured him before turning to me. "Would it help to have our scouts keep watch along the river? If the ship should come downstream early, we could send word even sooner."

"Yes, thanks. Send word to Ardenna and Port Alain. I'm not sure where we'll be, but wherever it is, there's bound to be trouble."

Chapter Eleven

Though I might have trusted my new-found half-brother with my own personal secrets, I had no right to trust him with Elena's secrets. That meant taking the long way around Blane Woods and into the city of Ardenna through the main gate, rather than slip in through the tunnel like a thief. However, it certainly didn't mean I had to wait for a civilized hour to visit my beloved queen.

"You do not mean to wake the queen at this hour?" Corey stood blinking in the lamp-lit corridor outside Elena's private apartments, ill-at-ease under the guard's unsmiling expression. "Alex, it is the middle of the night and—"

"Yes, it's the perfect time to visit. When the queen's Mage Protector and Crownmage," I said for the benefit of the stern guard, "arrive at this time of night, it means we have important business to discuss that cannot wait one tiniest moment, even if it means disturbing the queen's restful sleep."

"Have pity," Anders scolded, as he handed the guard a bottle of Marain Valley wine with which to bribe the queen, along with a second bottle for his personal consumption when he went off duty. "It might be a good idea for Corey to wait outside for a little while until we set things straight with Elena." When the guard disappeared into the suite, without argument, as well-used to us as we were to him by now, and Corey visibly relaxed, my husband sent my poor, bewildered brother on his way to a padded bench in the corner. "Take a nap, my lad. We may be a while."

The guard returned waving us inside with a bemused shake of the head and then took up his position outside the huge double doors. Inside, Elena and Jackson were both up and waiting, matching silk robes neatly tied at the waist, the bottle of wine cradled in Jackson's arm. A cloud of sorrow hung over them both, and I could only sympathize with the loss Jackson was feeling, the same loss that had yet to leave me in peace.

"I'm so sorry," I said to the Spreebridge mage, wishing I could erase the pain from his indecent green eyes and make him laugh. "I know just how horrible it feels."

Jackson's nod was grateful, before he went, without companionable urging, to open the bottle of wine.

"I heard from my spies you and Anders left Port Alain for a time." Not bothering to stifle a yawn, Elena sprawled like a cat among a pile of fluffy pillows, eyes studying the emotion, or lack of it, on my face. "But not where."

"Or why?"

"I assumed it was because you'd been so—" A smile tugged at her lips, though her intended teasing word changed, whether from consideration for her lover or my own grief, or both, I wasn't sure. "They said—"

"They? Who have you commandeered into your spy corps this time?"

"Jules. Rosanna."

Although Elena didn't include Jules's wife in that well-meaning group, I was convinced Lauryn snuck in a word or two, as well. "They said what, precisely?"

Unsure whether or not I was searching for an argument, Elena chose her words with care. "That you'd been very unhappy since my last visit."

"Yes, well, I was, and still am." Not volunteering anything more, not yet, I plopped onto the decadent lush carpet across from my friend's reclining body. Like Rosanna, Elena always had plenty of soft pillows scattered on the rug for her friends who preferred to stretch out on the ground.

"I was away, too," Jackson said, handing out glasses of wine, his voice barely more than a whisper. "I went north to Spreebridge." When neither Anders nor I gave away our knowledge, in fact, didn't even dare glance at each other, but nodded encouragement, he went on. "I wished to find out what I could about the attack on you and me, Alex. I went to Derbarry to see Westin Harlowe, my mentor, and then to Kimmer Frehan, both elders, both people in whom I have had, and still do, a great deal of trust. I do not know Kimmer as well as Westin, but her reputation among my people has always been impeccable. But they could tell me nothing more than that they would investigate the matter, and that—" He sighed. "That they did not know of any antidote to counteract feyweed. Though Kimmer, perhaps seeking to keep up my spirit, told me she had heard rumors of such—" Jackson's voice trailed off, as he sipped absently at the fruity wine.

"Did you see Derek Frontish?" Anders's voice was neutral, asking only out of curiosity, or so he would have wanted Jackson to think for the moment. "While you were in Derbarry, I mean? I thought I heard the elder had been traveling, had, in fact, come south recently." So Corey had found out, bringing us disturbing news only hours before, about the elder's activities. "It might have been a misunderstanding. Alex always gets things wrong."

Wary, though unsure what game we were playing when I elbowed my husband, Elena narrowed her eyes and studied Anders though he gave no sign he noticed anything amiss in her demeanor. Instead, she said, "I didn't know Derek had come back south. If he visited Ardenna," —she watched my face with care as I sipped the wine— "his trip was unannounced and informal."

"I did not hear he had returned either." Jackson glanced at Elena, bewildered. "If so, it would be odd for him to not let us know he was in your city. I would hope it was a misunderstanding," he said to me, before answering Anders's original question. "When I was in Derbarry, I heard Derek had returned to Spreebridge, but I did not see him. However, Kimmer did mention there has been recent trouble back home in our elder council." At Jackson's use of the word "home" Elena flinched, and I wondered whether she'd forgotten these past five years that her lover was a foreigner. Oblivious, Jackson added, "There have always been factions and squabbles, but this particular trouble seemed more serious, in her opinion, and more devastating to our people should matters get out of hand. Her son, Sloane," Jackson went on, brushing hair from his eyes, "is a close associate of Elder Frontish, despite the vast difference in age."

Had our moods been more light-hearted, I would have remarked about the vast difference between my young thirty and Anders's midforties, and how we managed to "associate," but Jackson was not in the right frame of mind for our banter. And if I had to be honest, neither was I just then.

"That troubles her?" I asked instead, taking off my boots to stretch my toes.

"Yes. It has been a heartache for Kimmer these past few years. And truly, Alex, because of my long-standing respect for the woman, her reaction to her son's association with Derek makes me suspicious of the older man." Jackson paused to sip his wine again, falling silent, lost in troubled thoughts, judging from his somber expression.

"Sloane is dead," I said into the heavy quiet, earning a look of surprise from both listeners, though Elena's dark eyes were expectant, "and Derek Frontish rumored to be responsible for his unnatural death."

"How do you know this?" Jackson demanded, setting his glass aside with an abruptness that had Elena reaching for the crystal before he shattered it. "You do not even know these people, Alex. You do—"

Raising a hand to stop his urgent questions, I glanced at Anders, who nodded his agreement. "I do now, Jackson. I know them all. Anders and I, along with Maylen Stockrie, met them when we traveled north to Spreebridge, and Derbarry, in particular, for the same investigative reason you did."

"Why didn't you tell me?" Anger flared hot in Elena's eyes as she glared first at me, and then Anders, demanding answers, suspecting we'd been up to no good once again.

Stifling a yawn to avoid provoking her even further, I asked calmly, "Must the queen's Mage Protector report every movement, every tiny suspicion, to her monarch?"

"When the Mage Protector is sworn to protect the queen, and then leaves the kingdom and her queen unprotected, without a single, solitary word of warning, then yes." Elena sat up straight, ready for battle, wide awake. "Damn it, Alex, yes. Absolutely."

"Oh, well." I sighed with more drama than was necessary, hoping to coax a smile from my friend. Finding my weak attempt unsuccessful, I admitted, "Since you're already annoyed, I might as well get the whole mess over with."

"Get what whole mess over with? Lords of the sea, Alex, what have you done now? What's going on?"

Ignoring her frustrated queries, I decided to confront Jackson first and get that part of the ugly mess over with. "I'm very sorry about the fire on the dock in Derbarry." When his eyes went wide with utter confusion, I explained, "Anders started the fire, though it was at my insistence, to test you."

"You tested Jackson? You did— Why?" Furious now, more than frustrated, Elena looked ready to demand her guards put me in chains as her lover stood up and walked away, edging into a darker corner of the spacious parlor. "Alex, tell me. Tell me right now what's going on or I swear, by the lords of the sea, I'll—"

Her threat went unfinished as Jackson interrupted. "It is all quite simple, Elena. Your Mage Protector suspected me of tainting the wine weeks ago, of mixing feyweed into her glass to strip her of magic, and so be useless to you in her royal position." Jackson's voice rang hollow before I could answer, and I trembled inside, uncertain how this mess would end. "After all, I am a foreign mage from Spreebridge. I know how to mix the potion, as Alex watched me do five years ago for the renegade mages we captured. And do not forget," his voice dripped with sarcasm, and I was sorry I might very well lose his friendship, "I have mage talent identical to hers."

Elena narrowed her dark blue eyes, fury overtaking reason at the insult to her lover. "How dare you, Alex?" she hissed. "How can you sleep at night, suspecting innocent people, destroying their reputation—"

All at once, Jackson's whole demeanor changed, and I prayed to the lords of the sea for a sign. "Her suspicions saved your throne and your life once before, even at the high cost of your friendship." Speaking with quiet intensity to override her anger, Jackson knelt beside Elena and took her white-knuckled hand in his. "And if she had to brave your anger once more, and a hundred times more, she would, and should. Not simply because she is the queen's sworn Mage Protector but more so because she is your trusted friend." Jackson's smile, when he met my gaze across the space between us, was sad, though his words were genuine.

"I didn't want you to be guilty," I admitted, not daring to look at Elena, who hadn't moved an inch. "It would have broken my heart if you had been."

"And I am glad, too, Alex, that I am innocent."

With a resigned sigh as dramatic as mine, Elena reached over and plucked the twin pendants from beneath my tunic, the copper one she'd designed expressly for me, merging all four mage symbols into one, and the identical wooden pendant Gwynn carved five years earlier. "Even without any magic, you're still protecting me, aren't you?"

"Sure. I don't want to give up my life-long supply of Marain Valley wine." Relieved she seemed to easily forgive me, very likely because her lover in this case was innocent and easily forgave me himself, I said, "Thanks to an unlikely source, we now have connections in Derbarry. We're not sure, but we think the attacks are part of a plan to eradicate what some Spreebridge mages, led by Derek, consider a perversion of magic."

"Which means what?"

"Anything that's not like Spreebridge or Glynnswood magic, where one element changes to another. That explains the attack on me and Jackson, as well as why Frontish was so pleased the three renegades lost their magic. They're freaks, too. No offense." I grinned at Jackson, whose smile was considerably more relaxed. "And if our theory is correct," —I sipped my wine, feeling my throat dry, more from tension than thirst— "then all mages, with the exception of Glynnswood mages, are at risk."

"But someone gave your father and Emmy feyweed, too. That's what Jules wrote to me," she admitted sheepishly, when I raised one eyebrow. "I'd known about your father, but not your poor child. Not until Jules sent word. But they share Glynnswood blood, though Emmy is a mix of Glynnswood and Tuldamoran bloodlines."

"I think, at least in my father's case, the feyweed had more to do with revenge for creating an oddity like me. As for Emmy—" I realized that although Jules told Elena that Emmy had been attacked, he hadn't known everything and couldn't reveal the entire truth. "My daughter is a miracle child, Elena. The little glimpse of power we saw her perform was amazing. We think her magic combines what I can do with what Anders can do. Once she regains her talent," I forced optimism into my voice, "and then asserts control over it, Emmy will be able to manipulate all four elements within themselves and change them into each other."

"Alex, that means—"

"She's an entirely new breed of mage." *If she gets her talent back—* Anders read my mind, and squeezed my fingers. "I don't know if the Ardenna Crown Council of Mages are involved in all this trouble, but we've had word that—"

"Alex—" Jackson sank down onto the pillows again in one enviable graceful movement and refilled my glass, warning me his next words would be significant. "I think they must be innocent."

"Why?"

"They, too, have been given feyweed."

My mouth opened and shut without a sound emerging as I contemplated the implications, in light of what Corey discovered earlier. "What do they think? Does the Crown Council believe we're responsible? You and me?" I asked Jackson. "Or me alone? Do they even know about you and me losing our magic?"

"They know about me," Jackson said, "but not you. We thought it best to wait until you were back from your journey."

"Do you think they're telling the truth?" Anders broke his long silence, eying me as he tossed this new element into the mix. "It's possible to disguise the loss of magic. Look how long I fooled Alex into thinking I was a mere seamage, not the Crownmage."

"Good point," Jackson agreed, before I could take offense, "but I recognized the look in their eyes, Anders. It was the same horror on your wife's face, and on mine, when we drank the feyweed. No," —he shook his head— "I do not believe they were lying."

"Then we need to speak with them before the feyweed shipment arrives for a number of reasons."

"Shipment? Here in Ardenna?" Elena set aside her own glass, ready to call out the guard, judging from her alarmed expression.

"No. Calm down. Port Alain. They're smart, Elena," I explained, smothering another yawn, "thinking to send the feyweed with the first trade shipment of gems and ores from Spreebridge, the shipment Brendan is supposed to meet."

"Right under our unsuspecting noses."

"Yes. But my father, who feels Glynnswood bears some responsibility whenever Spreebridge trouble erupts—"

"So that's where you get your ridiculous sense of responsibility and guilt," Elena teased, nudging my bare foot with her own. "I always wondered."

"Hush. My father offered to have some of his best scouts keep watch along the Jendlan River in case the ship leaves early and catches us unawares."

"That's a help. I'll send word to him and coordinate our efforts. But who told you about the shipment being smuggled into Port Alain?" Elena asked, not realizing she'd given me the perfect opportunity for an introduction to yet another sibling of mine. "Let me guess. Your new connection in Derbarry?"

"Ah, well, yes." I couldn't keep a grin off my face, anticipating her reaction. "Kimmer Frehan's son, actually. Her other son," I added, when Jackson appeared confused, knowing now that Sloane was dead.

"Corey, right? Nice young man. A schoolmaster, I understand. Kimmer's pride and joy," Jackson informed Elena, both of them oblivious.

"Yes, and yes, to all of that. In fact—" Biting my lip hard to avoid laughing outright, I said, "Be right back. Corey's waiting outside, probably napping. Elena needs to meet him herself."

"I do? Why? Not that I mind, but why?"

"You'll see. And besides, he has some unsettling news for you about the Crown Council of Mages." Struggling to my feet, I exchanged a bemused glance with Anders before heading out into the corridor, where Corey was bright-eyed and wide awake with nervous anxiety, looking about as old as my daughter. "Ready?"

"Alex, I have never met a queen. Shall I bow? Kneel? Prostrate myself on the ground before her?"

"None of the above. Just bow your head."

"But—"

"Trust me. She's not your usual monarch. Just go in there and be polite. And when she asks you questions, be honest."

Which is exactly what Corey did. Disregarding my advice, whether from the expectation that I was teasing or fear of insulting the queen of Tuldamoran, Corey knelt before Elena, head bowed low, but not before she caught a good long look at his features. One eye on me, she placed a hand under his smooth-shaven chin and raised his handsome face for a better view. Blue eyes darted between our faces, comparing notes, until one black eyebrow inched skyward in anticipation.

"Alex?"

"Hmm?"

"Is there something you want to tell me?"

"Apparently" —I coughed with exaggerated delicacy into my hand— "Elder Keltie did a bit of traveling in his youth after he became a widower."

"Oh my." When Corey's fair skin blushed as acutely as Gwynn's always did, Elena laughed in open delight, dropping her hand. "Welcome to Ardenna, Master Frehan. Tell me, are there any more Kelties around?"

"No, your majesty. I—"

"You need to be at ease and relax. Jackson, a glass of wine might help Corey get comfortable." Elena sank back onto the cushions, her smile impish. "Honestly, Alex, you're always bringing surprises. Now, then—" She urged my poor nervous brother to taste the wine. "Alex said you had some disturbing news about the Crown Council of Mages. What exactly is going on?"

When Corey glanced at me, ostensibly for permission to speak, I smiled encouragement. "She won't bite, I promise. She saves her irritation for me."

Dazed by the informality and irreverence, Corey took another sip and then set the glass aside on the low table beside him. "I came to Ardenna to find out why Elder Frontish was traveling to your city in secret," he explained, oblivious to the silent exchange between Jackson and me. "We have a—" Corey's face grew heated as he paused. "Your majesty, I mean no disrespect, I assure you, but there have been, ah, visitors to your city who have been keeping watch to be sure that certain Spreebridge individuals, like Elder Frontish, do no harm to your people."

Elena met my gaze, an impish twinkle in her eyes as she studied my brother's face. "You have spies in my city?"

"That's such an ugly word," I murmured.

"They are not—" Corey took heart from the smile that escaped Elena's stern expression. "Yes, they are spies, your majesty, but for a good cause."

"Well, that's a new angle. Go on."

Relieved she wasn't going to chop off his head, Corey hurried on with his news. "Derek Frontish," at the name, Corey's voice grew steadier, "came here unannounced a week ago to meet in secret with the Ardenna Crown Council of Mages."

Elena leaned forward. "You know this for certain?"

"Yes, your majesty. He was seen meeting with them by one of our, ah, spies. One other point we have confirmed is significant. Derek was traveling with another man, though his identity is unknown. When they arrived in Ardenna, they split up, and the other man vanished into the crowd during a street fair. We do not know where he went. I am sorry, because I do not know what trouble they are brewing in Tuldamoran."

"It could mean several things," I said, thinking out loud. "Derek might have wanted to persuade the Crown Council of Mages to join his little party because he knows they're not very thrilled with me or Jackson, simply because our magic, when it existed, threatened them. Or he may very well have told them a tall tale, wanting only to slip them feyweed and have them suspicious of me and Jackson. As for his companion, it's possible he was making other contacts here." Unable to stifle the next yawn, I shrugged. "Sorry. I don't know. And it's too late to think clearly." I grabbed my boots and held them in my hand, prepared to walk barefoot through the corridors. "So, your majesty, if you don't mind, I'd love a nice soft bed. Nothing fancy, just plain, clean, and comfortable."

"You'll actually stay in Ardenna overnight? Willingly?"

"Sure, but it'll cost you."

* * * *

Snuggled like a newborn piglet beside Anders in a lush guest chamber down the corridor from the royal apartment, I yawned and slipped deeper into the warm blankets, prepared to sleep like the dead. But the queen, as I might have expected, had other ideas, judging from the loud persistent knocking that wouldn't go away.

"It's always your fault, Alex," Anders grumbled as he threw back the blankets in disgust and grabbed the silk robes her majesty's servants left for us. He put one on, and tossed the other to me. "First you upset Elena, and then she can't sleep."

"Not my fault this time. I had no choice about Jackson." Belting the scarlet robe around my waist, I sat cross-legged on the bed, rubbing my eyes to stay awake, as Anders went to open the door.

As expected, Elena stood in the doorway, contrite. "Sorry, Anders."

"No, you're not, your majesty. I've had four years of uninterrupted sleep, with the exception of my wife's snoring, and now, I see, we're back to your old tricks." Anders stepped aside to let her in, arms folded across his chest in mock annoyance.

"Only because Emmy isn't here. I'd never risk waking that angelic child."

"Don't believe her," I warned Anders, who decided to sit at the far end of the huge bed. "After the chat we had in Rosanna's garden some weeks ago, when Elena made absolutely no sense, I figured she'd come to her senses sooner or later," I said, delighted to twist the facts around and further upset my friend. "We always talk better at night. Have a seat, your majesty." With a chagrined smile, Elena sank into a velvet armchair, and I started the conversation, catching her off guard. "I'm sorry about Jackson, about investigating him."

"If Jackson had been guilty, and you'd done nothing—"

"Doesn't matter. I'm still sorry."

"I had no right to snap at you, as though you were deliberately searching for trouble," she admitted, though, under the circumstances, I didn't agree with her reasoning.

"For the second time in five years, I was suspicious of the man you love. You had every right to yell and scream. However," — I leaned over the edge of the bed and poked her silk-covered arm— "if you had stayed angry for, what was it last time, three months, four— Well, I might have grown impatient this time and not let you continue your little temper tantrum."

"Is that what it was? Anyway, unlike you, I do learn some lessons." Too late to cover a yawn, Elena shut her eyes for a moment. "I did have another reason for coming here. Three, actually, if Anders doesn't mind waiting another minute before getting back to sleep."

"Sleep? I don't know the meaning of the word when I'm in your fortress," Anders grumbled, lying across the foot of the bed, his chin propped up on one hand.

"Let me guess the first reason," I cut in, before the two of them continued bantering. "You want to know if I'm ready to strangle my father for having another secret child." At the flush in her cheeks, I reassured my friend, "No. I'm fine about Corey, believe it or not, particularly since the old man didn't know about him, either. But I refused to let Father off the seahook and pretended to be furious, just to give him a hard time."

"Why am I not surprised?" Elena laughed, though her eyes were somber. "Poor man, though you've come a long way, old friend."

"Well, yes. I do learn some lessons, too. Besides, I didn't get to this incredible level of maturity on my own." Studying her face, it was easy to see the sleepless nights. "Jackson has you worried, which is your second reason for this uncivilized visit."

"I'm worried about you, too. Seeing you both dealing with this loss, I feel helpless." Elena glanced at Anders, who nodded. "I don't know how to make either of you feel better or ease your pain."

"You're not alone in that," Anders reassured her. "All we can do is give comfort where we can and never give up the search for an antidote."

"More for Emmy's sake than mine," I told them both. "The poor child had only a glimpse of her magic, took such joy and pride in it, right before it was stolen." Shutting my eyes tight, grieving for my daughter's pain, I fought back tears of rage. "When I lost my magic as a child, it was because I forced it away, denied it from fear. What happened to Emmy— She was so distraught when we returned to Glynnswood, so distressed that it was gone. I don't ever want to see that sorrow on her face again."

"You can't shield her from all pain, Mage Protector, even as you can't shield me, either. You can only do what's in your power to do. And knowing both you and Jackson, even without mage talent, you're both quite resourceful." Elena leaned over to kiss my forehead. "Try and get some sleep."

"You, too. But what about the last reason for your visit?"

"I must be getting old. I nearly forgot." Standing beside the bed, she kept her eyes fixed on mine. "Before you bite off my head—"

"Now I can't wait to hear what you have to say."

"Just giving you fair warning. Listen, Brendan has come back to the capital. I was so caught up in all those mixed emotions before, I forgot to tell you. Jackson and I were talking after you left, Alex. In light of the news Corey brought, I'd like to summon the Crown Council, test the waters a little. If you can bear to stay another day in Ardenna, I think you both should attend the meeting."

"You always manage to find a somewhat-legitimate excuse for me to stay in this hateful city," I whined. "Why is that?"

Slanting a sidelong glance at my husband, Elena said, "Because I know you despise being here."

Chapter Twelve

"Ready for this meeting, Mage Protector?" Elena's murmur was solely for my hearing, with both our backs turned toward the others seated around the huge oak table in her less-formal council chamber.

"Hmm."

I knew, without turning around, that Brendan, Elena's heir and younger brother, sat between Anders and Jackson at the near end of the table, the friendlier end. Farthest from their monarch and her impotent Mage Protector were the four members of the Ardenna Crown Council: Seamage Jenny Bretan, the voice of the Mage Council, as Charlton Ravess had been five years earlier. Kiran Frase, firemage, Colin Revers, earthmage, and Chase Matten, windmage, all here at the polite request of their queen, though none of them dared refuse to make an appearance.

"Is that a yes or no?" Elena's voice sounded a trifle impatient, though she tried to disguise it by adding, "Not that I'm pushing you, mind, but they've been quite patient while you've been sightseeing outside my window."

"It's not a yes or a no. I'm— Well, I'm not entirely sure." Sliding Elena a glance from beneath hooded lids, I bit back a smile. It wouldn't do for the already-uneasy Crown Council of Mages to suspect their queen of plotting right before their very eyes with her Mage Protector. Heaving a huge sigh that felt as though my chest would burst, I turned to face the expectant and hostile council members, all of whom were recently stripped of their magic.

Elena said nothing, though her eyes watched everyone and everything, a skill she'd learned from her father before his unexpected death eight years earlier. Rather than sitting at the table, Elena stood upright behind her ornate carved chair, encouraging me to start the discussion with a slight nod.

"Seamage Bretan." I bowed a respectful greeting to the older woman, whose tight blonde braid left her face ashen and devoid of emotion, and then made the same gesture toward the others. "Thank you for coming at such short notice. I would not have had the queen disturb your work unless it was a matter of grave importance."

"To you?" Jenny Bretan challenged, not daring to look at Elena, which was amusing in its way. "Or to the queen?"

"To all of us here, mages and nonmages alike." I inclined my head in Brendan's direction, and earned a sly wink for my efforts. Unruffled by the seamage's open dislike, I leaned back against the window ledge overlooking the Kieran River and the bustling city below, my face in shadow against the morning sunlight that surrounded my body and warmed my back and shoulders.

"Speaking for the council, I may say we're all quite, well, curious. After all, while the queen has summoned us to advise her in the past, though rarely often," —Jenny shot a quick glance at Elena, whose features were chiseled in stone— "she has never once done so with both you and the Crownmage in attendance."

"Ah, well, those meetings might have been a little crowded, don't you think? Besides, there hadn't been any need for all of us at those sessions, but there is now. To be honest, I never wanted the queen to force my presence on you since I'm well aware you have no great love for me, or indeed, any affection, for that matter." I smiled to take the sting from my comment, noting the seamage's open look of surprise at my direct words. "But none of that matters. Though I will say one thing more. I doubt any of you will believe my sincerity, which is genuine, but I'd hoped, as both Elena and Brendan have shared my hope, that you and I could have bridged our differences and found a way to work together for the common good of Tuldamoran."

"You give us little credit."

"You gave me little welcome," I said without hesitation, watching the fire flash and fade in her eyes. "But the past no longer matters. It seems," I added, before the seamage could make a token protest that would only serve to irritate Elena, "I've finally found the way to bridge our differences, though it brings me no joy. In fact, it was our mutual enemy who handed me the key."

Jenny Bretan narrowed her eyes and stared at me, the words "mutual enemy" hanging in the air between us as I pushed away from the window ledge and started to pace as Elena often did. In fact, I half expected both of us to be pacing, though she hadn't moved from her position behind the chair at the head of the table. When no one said a word to break the awkward silence, I stopped at the non-hostile end of the table and leaned both hands on the smooth wood, opposite Jenny Bretan, holding her gaze.

"I, too, have been given feyweed to drink."

Chaos ensued, and all four mages spoke over each other, until Seamage Bretan, not Elena as expected, raised both hands for silence. "Can you prove it?"

"Seamage Bretan—" Elena's face lost its stony composure, her cheeks scarlet with rage at the challenge. I edged closer to her chair and touched my friend's tense shoulder to stop her potential movement, afraid she'd haul off and smash her fist in the woman's face. When Elena glared at me in open annoyance, I shot her a silent warning, relieved when her dangerous anger subsided.

"It's a fair question, your majesty," I said calmly, having doubted Jackson only weeks earlier, but not wanting to bring up that nasty reminder in front of the Crown Council. "But one I can't prove any easier than Seamage Bretan can prove to you, except to say the loss inside me, the empty ache that never ceases to go away, is a pain no mage should ever feel. However," —I met and held Anders's quiet gaze and smiled— "I could always place myself in dire peril and prove I can't save myself. But before I did something so patently foolish," I added, more to reassure Elena and Brendan, who looked horrified, "I'd ask the Crown Council to do the same. And since we haven't yet reached that level of trust, though I still hope someday we might, it seems we have to accept on faith that I, as well as Jackson Tunney, and the entire Crown Council, have been stripped of magic by a mutual, as yet unknown, enemy."

Smoothing the soft leather of my white vest, the Mage Protector symbol embroidered on the chest, I glanced at Elena and smiled. Though her face had lost its brilliant angry hue, she didn't smile back.

"It also occurred to me during the night, when I should have been resting peacefully beside my husband, that you all may have thought I gave the order for feyweed to be mixed into your wine."

Jenny Bretan's smile was predatory. "It occurred to me, too."

"I'll bet. Here's a question to consider. Did it occur to you on your own, Seamage Bretan? Or did someone whisper that treasonous thought in your ear?" Holding the woman's gaze across the polished table, I wanted her to squirm and blurt out the fact Derek Frontish of Spreebridge had poisoned their minds even further against me. Though I was likely doomed to disappointment, I needed indisputable proof that after they had lost their mage talent, possibly at the hands of Elder Frontish, that same gentleman offered them comfort in the form of providing a possible suspect, namely me.

"No one said any such thing, Mage Protector. I am" —her smile was chilly, though I caught the merest hint of doubt— "perfectly capable of independent thought."

"That's good to know. And yes, well, let me reassure you the mere act of watching three renegade mages from Spreebridge take the potion and lose their magic turned my stomach. Not that I wouldn't do it," I hastened to add, lest the Crown Council think me weak, even though I still refused to learn the ingredients for the feyweed mixture, "if I had good reason. But not one I would do on a whim. I may be vicious, but I'm not often needlessly cruel."

"So you say. But your actions prove otherwise," she challenged, and I braced for the attack I knew was coming, had indeed expected. "I, for one, though not a member of the Crown Council of Mages who served beneath Charlton Ravess at the time, was present at Tucker's Meadow for the Mage Challenge." Her eyes searched my face, as she added, "Cruelty was quite evident in that duel."

Along with the hostility and smugness on Jenny Bretan's face was fear, though why she should fear me now, without mage power, made no sense, unless she really believed I was lying about my loss. All the more reason to keep Anders safe at my side, with his formidable mage power intact.

Before I could reply, the seamage added, "You made spectacular use of your mage talent that morning."

"I was defending my life and my queen."

"Yes, thus the title of Mage Protector. Very apt, though the abuse you piled on Charlton Ravess was, shall we say, excessive? Not that I minded. The man was, after all, a traitor." Seamage Bretan chuckled, though there wasn't a hint of humor in the sound. "And so, our beloved queen names you Mage Protector," she repeated my title as though it were an insult, and maybe, considering her next comment, it was. "As I said, quite fitting. Until now, anyway, since you're powerless to wield any magic." *Or so you say,* her steady gaze implied. "You think our enemy is mutual?"

"I like to think we have some things in common," I said, amused as Elena rolled her eyes behind the mage's back at my bright smile. "Mutual, yes, but not for reasons you might find flattering. I have a theory regarding the potential parties, but nothing solid, not yet. And until I do, I'll keep that theory close to my chest."

"You're not very discreet in your mistrust of us."

"Think of it instead," I suggested, "as not wanting to smear a person's good name unless one has definite proof. One other thing has made me curious," I said, keeping my tone very casual. "No one's told me how you came to drink the feyweed? Were you all gathered together? Sharing a bottle of wine? A pitcher of water or ale? Was it crushed and mixed in with your meat gravy?"

"I don't see why that fact should make a difference, but we were sharing a bottle of wine. Your favorite, in fact," —the seamage shot me a crafty look— "which is why I did wonder about your involvement."

"Logical." Scratching the tip of my nose, I asked, "Do you usually enjoy wine at your council meetings or was this a special event?"

"Why all the questions, Mage Keltie? Aren't we entitled to privacy?"

"Absolutely." Which meant they were likely sharing a bottle of wine Derek Frontish had somehow delivered in secret, if what I suspected were true. How else to explain that he, as a mage from Spreebridge, remained unaffected if he shared that same bottle? "My apologies, Seamage Bretan. I was simply curious. My own experience came with Marain Valley wine, too. In any case, I have a favor to ask of you all." Not missing the open suspicion and resentment in the woman's expression, I laughed, taking not the slightest insult. "Yes, I know. I'd be pretty suspicious, too, but believe me, it's important, and more than that, it's definitely not a trick."

"Again, so you say."

"Yes, again, so I say." It was difficult not to smash my fist in her face, or even call upon magic simply to frighten the wits from her brain. But I'd reached for what wasn't there too often in past weeks, and the pain simply wasn't worth it. "I need your help. The mages in Tuldamoran need your help. You must spread the word, discreetly and swiftly, through the local Mage Councils in each Duchy, warning them of strangers from Spreebridge, warning them of feyweed and its distinctive odor, sometimes easily masked, I'm afraid. And—"

"Spreebridge is what you fear?" Surprised, Seamage Bretan glanced at Elena for confirmation. "How is this possible? We're on the brink of starting a new trade relationship with their merchants, an endeavor based on trust and good will. Yet by allowing their ships to enter our ports, we make ourselves vulnerable if we let strangers into our kingdom."

"They are not all suspected of dealing in feyweed, I assure you. The trade agreement will greatly benefit our own merchants years into the future, long after this danger has passed. Think of how beneficial our commerce has been with Meravan, despite our earlier misgivings," Elena slipped that little dig into the conversation, reminding the seamage of the protests made against interaction with our southern neighbor when Elena first ascended the throne. "Besides, we are not fools, Seamage Bretan. Trust that we will take precautions," she added quietly. "For the good of both our countries, we need to go forward with the agreement. But that doesn't mean that we will blindly welcome any stranger from Spreebridge, not until this matter is settled. Nor that we will hesitate to take whatever action is required to keep our people safe."

Considering Elena's somber words, Jenny Bretan glanced around the table at her colleagues, all of whom looked as though they'd swallowed something distasteful. If I'd managed to make them wary of

Derek Frontish, without openly accusing them of duplicity, I'd be satisfied. "You forget one other group, Mage Keltie. What about the renegade mages in Tuldamoran?" Seamage Bretan demanded, her expression a mockery as her unvoiced words resounded in my head.

"Ah, yes, the more independent mages, like me. In fact, like my mother, is what you really meant to say, I'd guess, if I were a woman who delighted in wagering," I challenged back, not daring to look at Elena and give her an excuse to haul off and put the entire council in chains. "I hope in future those independent mages will be able to trust their local councils and go to them for training and guidance. But until the old corruption is washed away—" I shrugged. "I myself, with the help of the Crownmage, will spread that particular word."

"A very good reason why there is so little trust between us, Mage Protector," Jenny Bretan took careful aim and shot a verbal arrow at my heart. "Apparently, you hold far more allegiance to renegade mages who travel freely without guidance or rules."

"Not true. They have guidance and rules, ones set down by my own mother before I was even a flicker of thought in her heart. As such," — I smiled at Anders, knowing how hard he'd worked to spread my mother's word— "I place a lot of trust in those renegades, who would indeed join the local councils if they respected them. We all have much work to do before we reach that point, Seamage Bretan, including me." I set one hip on the table, my profile to the mage. "One other favor, I'd ask, if you're willing—" Taking her silence for assent, which was certainly doubtful, I said, "In time, I'd appreciate your help in purging the local councils of corruption and greed. Though some changes have been made, trouble spots remain. And if you agree to cooperate, maybe at that point you'll begin to believe that we're on the same side."

"Ah." Jenny Bretan smiled, showing even white teeth. "But you can't prove that, either, can you, Mage Protector?"

"Not at the moment, no."

"How shall I then take that comment? You ask us to purge the local councils, in time, of course. But do you consider us, the Crown Council, free of corruption and greed?"

"I should hope so," I said without hesitation, "or else the queen would not have kept you on the council for the past five years. Although you haven't been very friendly, I can forgive that oversight" —my smile matched hers— "when you consider that our roles are different. Yours is more demanding, in my opinion, because you're charged with guiding and directing the work of all the Duchy councils, who, in turn, guide and direct all our mages. The only responsibility I have is to my queen."

"Have we no responsibility to our queen?"

"Yes, of course, to advise her if she seeks your counsel. And if not, then it is up to the Crownmage and myself to advise her. The Crownmage" —who'd sat so silent I thought he might have taken a nap— "supports me in my role of Mage Protector, as I support him."

"And the queen," Elena added her own opinion, eying each one at the table, one by one, including me, "depends only on those mages she can trust, with or without magic."

* * * *

"A very pretty speech, so I heard." Without invitation, Seamage Neal Brandt, the head of the local Mage Council back home in Port Alain, sat at our table in the Seaman's Berth where Anders and I stopped for a quick ale and gossip before returning home from our trek. He slung his cloak over the back of an empty chair. "Though there were sufficient insults traded back and forth to keep everyone happy."

"News travels fast." Anders sipped his ale, eying Chester, the proprietor and our friend, to stay away. "Though in this case, I wonder," —he slanted a grin in my direction, as I stole the mug from his hand— "is it good news or bad?"

"Depends on your perspective," I chimed in, sipping the foam from Anders's ale before touching my own, ignoring the pitcher of cold water on the table. Ale, at the moment, was a better quencher of my thirst from the dusty road. And next to Marain Valley wine, I loved ale, and its bright white foam, best. "What do you think, Seamage Brandt? I'm quite certain you have an opinion."

"Indeed. Sad news, that the queen's Mage Protector has lost her magic, though I'd heard that rumored weeks ago. Be careful whom you trust with ill news, Mage Keltie." With that warning, the older mage, whom my grandmother and mother had both so despised, rested his hands on the table and steepled his fingers together. "Sad news, indeed, when you'd denied your talent for so long as a little girl and now that you hold it precious, find it missing."

"Your concern for my welfare is overwhelming."

"Now, now, Mage Keltie, we need not be at opposite sides, as you yourself informed the Ardenna Crown Council. Speaking of whom, it is worrisome that they, too, have fallen victim to this treachery." Brandt's eyes shifted to Anders, a question in them he daren't ask. "Thank the lords of the sea your husband still has his potency."

"Potency in all things, yes, indeed." I grinned, elbowing Anders before he could smash his fist in the seamage's face. "And for that, I take delight each and every night," I added, since he once accused me of being the village whore for no other reason than to provoke my temper. Not to mention he considered my mother a whore, too, a shared insult in which I took a certain perverse pride. "But I can assure you, Seamage Brandt, that as far as my husband's mage potency, I don't need Anders to protect me, even though my own magic is gone. Temporarily," I added, wondering if he'd send word of hope to the Crown Council. I'd not mentioned an antidote, not seeing the point in offering hope where I held so little. My kindness and the resulting omission had another, less humane reason, which was that Seamage Bretan had irritated me. Besides, Jackson knew enough to fend off any of their questions, though their suspicions would never entirely fade.

"Ah. So there is an antidote."

"Perhaps." If the lords of the sea were merciful. But perhaps not, and if that were the case, I had best get on with my life. "Now tell me, Seamage Brandt, why you're inside a noisy establishment on such a fine sunny day as this?"

"A simple matter, Mage Keltie. I saw you and your husband arrive in town and wished to offer my condolences in person. The Crown Council sent word to all the duchies, and I wondered that the news arrived before you did. In fact, I was deeply concerned you'd met trouble along the way." His grave expression was admirably sorrowful, and I had to bite back a laugh.

"Not at all. We took our time, making a leisurely detour to Glynnswood." So my new-found brother could spend some time with his new-found father.

"Ah, yes, to visit your family." His emphasis on the word "family" was almost an insult that I might not have chosen to ignore had my mood been different. However, I'd learned over the years to pick my battles with the seamage. "Well, I hope your father and stepmother are in good health. But to answer your question, I also wished to reassure you I'd spread the word to our mages, especially the proprietor's daughter—" He indicated Chester's young daughter, who was serving tables at the far end of the common room. The child, now eleven and a firemage in her own right, had, thankfully, avoided becoming arrogant because of her father's constant guidance and my own interference during the years she spent under Brandt's tutelage. "If strangers do show up in Port Alain, it's bound to be in an establishment such as an inn."

"I'm sure Duke Barlow will appreciate your good faith."

"Do send him my regards. I always prefer that the duke and his mother think kindly of me. And your daughter?" Beneath the table, I stepped hard on Anders's foot to keep him quiet as the seamage rose to leave, his polite query hanging in the air between us. "Is little Emila well? I haven't seen the child in some time."

"Very well, thanks. Off visiting her grandparents for a time, and now back at the manor, with Lady Barlow, who must have heard news by now that we're home. We'd best be going ourselves." I stood opposite the table from the seamage, knowing he'd been eying Emmy from the day she was born, waiting to spread word of her powers, as he'd kept close watch on me, particularly after my mother's odd death. "Anders? Are you coming?"

"You're rushing my ale."

"Sorry."

"And you've hardly touched your own."

"Hmm, you're right." I grabbed the mug of ale and took a sip, not willing to sit down, instinct warning me of something imminent, something dangerous.

"My fault, Crownmage," Seamage Brandt apologized, grabbing his cloak from the empty chair. "Your wife was standing up so that I would surely take the hint and leave. In fact— Ah, sorry, indeed— How clumsy of me." Slinging his cloak over his shoulders, the older mage reached for the pitcher of water that had caught onto the heavy material, spilling the contents in my direction.

Jumping back to avoid ice cold water on my travel-stained trousers, and instead sloshing ale all over my tunic, an ugly thought occurred to me. Grabbing an extra cloth from Chester's outstretched hand as he hastened to my side I began to mop up the spill on the table, ignoring my ale-drenched tunic, locking my eyes on the seamage's face.

"Mage Keltie, I am so very sorry."

"That I didn't change the water in the pitcher to air and avoid a mess for poor Chester to clean up? Assuming that I still had mage talent," I spat the bitter words out one by one, "I'd never use it for such a wasteful purpose."

"If you're implying I'd trick you to see whether you had indeed lost your mage powers, you insult me." Puffing out his chest, the seamage looked wounded, so sincerely hurt I wondered if my old prejudice had led me astray this one time. But the glint in his eye when I spun on my heels to face Anders brought me back to my senses.

"I'm afraid, Seamage Brandt, that it is our fate to insult each other. Good day." I turned my back to him in a direct insult and winked at Chester, whose face had gone ashen with fear. "Sorry about the mess, Chester. You might think about being more selective with your customers." Studying the proprietor's wrinkled features I could tell when the seamage had departed the inn.

"Alex Keltie," Chester hissed, throwing another rag in my face, ostensibly for use on my soiled tunic, "you are going to make me grayer than I already am." Annoyance transformed to concern as he added, "Is it true what he said?"

"About my magic?" At the genuine regret on the proprietor's face, I patted his grizzly cheek. "Unfortunately, yes. I've lost it, and do sincerely hope it's temporary. That's for the lords of the sea to determine. In the meantime, old friend, beware of anything mixed in one of your glasses that has an odd smell, something foul, like a carcass gone bad."

"Ugh."

"Well, yes, but it can be very nearly disguised so be careful what you serve your guests, who may not even admit they're mages. Not everyone wears a pendant openly."

"Most do, now, Alex, thanks to you."

"You're just looking for a good tip. Listen," —I drained the remainder of my glass of ale, refusing his offer of a refill, and delicately covered a burp— "keep watch for strangers, too. Especially when that ship from Spreebridge, the Stoutheart, arrives in a few weeks. I know you can't stop anyone from doing anything, but watch to see if your customers do or say anything unusual. By that time, I'll have my own eyes down at the dock."

"If you're talking about those sneaky Glynnswood folk of yours, they'll do a job better than any of us could. Your brother's already told me about the ship. But you know I'll do what I can."

"We depend on you. Oh, and listen, in a few days, you'll see a young man in my brother's company, or mine, who looks a little like Gwynn and—"

"Don't tell me." A wide grin creased the old man's face. "A little like you?"

"You devil. How'd you know?"

Chester laughed aloud, and then lowered his voice when curious heads turned in our direction. "Because your brother and his pretty young woman warned me the other day, over a glass or two of ale, to be on the watch for a strange young man looking like the Kelties. Where is the lad?"

"Spending a little time getting to know my father, which in itself is dangerous. But that's Sernyn's problem. For me, right now, I've got to get up to the manor and see my daughter, whom I miss terribly."

"That seamage has his eyes on Emmy."

"That's more than he'll ever get."

Chester took the rags from my hand. "He couldn't touch your grandmother, or your mother, or you. And we'll never let him touch that precious little girl."

Chapter Thirteen

"Trading insults" —Rosanna sighed, heaving her wool-clad bosom for dramatic effect, which did nothing to faze me— "is one of the things you do best. In a perverse way, I can understand the fascination for insulting people you love, Alex, but surely, with adversaries like the Crown Council of Mages, ridiculing them in front of their queen, and then Seamage Brandt, and—"

"Hold on. I didn't insult any other enemies."

Having lost my frothy ale due to Seamage Brandt's mock ineptness, I was enjoying a glass of Marain Valley wine. I dismissed Anders to go find my brother while I caught up with the senior Lady Barlow. No sense wasting time while Emmy and the other children were in the schoolroom with their temporary schoolmistress, the junior Lady Barlow. What would I have possibly done without Lauryn's help these past few years, often covering for me at the last minute when an emergency reared its ugly head?

"I'm sure if they were available, you would have."

"Hmm. Do you mind very much if I lean against these pillows instead of sitting upright?" I asked, getting stiff from my awkward position.

Rosanna narrowed her eyes. "Is this a trick question?"

"Now, see, here I am being polite because I haven't yet changed out of my travel-stained trousers and tunic—"

"Definitely a trick question. I never expect politeness from you. Go on." She waved airily in my direction. "Just be sure to lean against the dark brown pillows, not the yellow or rose ones with all that fancy embroidery."

"That was my intention." Stretching out on the deep chocolate-hued pillows, I grinned and smothered a yawn. "Anyway, back to my major talent for insulting people. I have to admit it was fun. And besides, the seamage was testing me, to see whether I'd really lost my mage talent." Without worrying Rosanna, I reached inside that hollow space in my gut to find nothing, no magic lying anxiously in wait for my notice.

"Alex?"

Did nothing slip by that woman? "Well, that's all my news. What's been happening here in Port Alain? Why is it so quiet? Where are the twins?"

"Aha. You noticed."

"They're the only ones who make noise."

"Yes, well, Jules decided they're old enough to start earning their right to their future Duchy. He's visiting the local merchants and dragged the boys along." She laughed, sipping her own wine. "Well, dragged Carey, who'd rather go fishing. Hunter, naturally, couldn't wait."

"Thank the lords of the sea for that boy. How's Linsey?"

"You mean, is she safe? Or has she shown any latent mage power?"

"I know she's safe, or Chester would have sent me flying up the Hill without taking time for an ale."

"I didn't think of that, but you're right. Maylen has been safeguarding both Linsey and Emmy, while your brother skulks around the docks, looking for signs of trouble." Rosanna smiled at the sound of light running footsteps coming nearer the sun parlor. "Maylen's a wonder, really. It's not only Gwynn who's lucky to have her around. But no, Alex, my granddaughter has still shown no mage talent, not since the day she was born. Poor Khrista's half hoping Linsey will turn out to be a seamage, like herself, while the other half hopes for more. But having that 'more,' unfortunately, will always be a reminder of the child's father."

"We learn to live with the truth about our fathers, don't we?" I said, more to earn a raised eyebrow at my unexpected mature comment, than for any other reason. Over the years, I'd bested the old witch every once in awhile. Regardless, Rosanna's tart answer was lost in joyous squealing as the doors to the sun parlor flew open and Emmy ran straight for me, Maylen right behind in case the child was intruding on a very private conversation. "Hold on. Emmy, wait—" Instinctively, Rosanna grabbed the wine glass from my hands as the child halted within a few inches of me, her eyes wide with uncertainty. "I'm all dusty and dirty, sweetling, and—"

"I don't care." Bouncing into my lap, the child threw her arms around my neck and hugged me tight. "Papa was dusty and dirty, too. And I hugged him tight."

"You little minx. I don't know why," —I returned the embrace and held on for a second longer— "but I missed you, too. Hey, who combed your hair like that?" Holding Emmy at arm's length, I studied the neat coiled braid of dark brown hair wrapped around her tiny head. "Hmm. Let's see. Carey did it, right?"

"Mama, Carey's a boy."

"Then it couldn't be Uncle Jules. How about—" Peeking over her shoulder, I winked at Maylen, who waited with characteristic patience at the door until Rosanna waved her inside. "I know. It was your Uncle Gwynn, pretending to be a girl, wearing a dress."

"Mama, stop being silly. It was Maylen."

"Ah, of course." Planting a kiss on her lips, I set the child on my lap and wrapped my arms around her, both of us content. "Did she tell you why she made your hair look so pretty?"

"So Carey wouldn't pull my braids."

"Like Uncle Gwynn pulled hers when they were little, right?"

"Uh uh."

Maylen accepted a small glass of wine from Rosanna and joined us on the floor, another creature like me who preferred the softness of a good plush carpet. "Your uncle," she informed Emmy, "was always a pest."

"Still is. Thank you for keeping watch on the girls." Though she'd become so much a part of my family, I didn't want Maylen to think I'd ever take her presence and aid for granted. "I didn't plan on your babysitting the children."

"Gwynn and I thought it best to divide ourselves this way." She smiled as Khrista and Lauryn came in, with Linsey in tow. "These two are well-behaved. But even so, with Gwynn watching them, he would have taught them all sorts of mischief." Her eyes met mine, and I knew, without asking, Gwynn hadn't trusted himself to watch my daughter, not after his supposed failure to prevent the attack on Emmy weeks ago. "Besides, had it been the twin boys in my care, your pardon, Lady Barlow," —she grinned impishly at Lauryn, who nodded in agreement— "my experience would have been quite different. How on earth did Prince Brendan manage to keep them in line and out of too much trouble?"

"With Alex's help." Lauryn matched her smile, brushing loose strands of light brown hair behind one ear. "Our fierce schoolmistress was always the last resort when the twins were abominable. That is, when Carey was misbehaving. Hunter, like Emmy and Linsey, doesn't know the meaning of the word."

"You're selling yourself short," I told Maylen, who blinked in confusion. "After all, you grew up with Gwynn."

"You're insulting people again," Rosanna chided, as the ladies poured wine for themselves and Linsey sat beside me, quietly content to receive my hug of welcome.

"It's a gift from the lords of the sea," I said breezily. "You said so yourself only moments ago."

"I said no such thing."

"You're such a poor example, telling lies in front of these innocent children. And speaking of poor examples, has my brother really been skulking around the harbor?" I asked Maylen, who didn't have a chance to answer because Gwynn and Anders chose that moment to appear. "Ah, my beloved brother and husband. By the way, Anders," —I winked over Emmy's head— "your daughter said you were much dirtier than me."

"Mama, no—"

Which, of course, prompted a tickling session that could have gone on forever if Maylen hadn't stopped Gwynn from joining in.

"Poor examples," Rosanna huffed, "all of you."

"Indeed." I surrendered Emmy up to her father. "So, brother, what have you found out at the harbor? Or were you spending too much time and too many coins in the Seaman's Berth?"

Gwynn grinned, tugging at his still misbehaving lock of brown hair, "You must admit, it is the best place in town for news. You have told me so yourself. Numerous times."

"Duke Barlow told you that. Not me. Did Anders describe our little chat with Seamage Brandt?" When Gwynn nodded and sat cross-legged besides Maylen, I caught the quick glance they exchanged. "What?"

"I have not had a chance to tell Alex yet," Maylen said, her fair skin reddening. "I have not been here long."

"Tell me what?"

"That Seamage Brandt has been curious about the girls. The other day, when we were walking by your cottage—" Maylen looked at Khrista, who nodded, alerting me to the fact the Barlows knew about the incident. "Seamage Brandt suddenly appeared on the harbor side of the forest path, speaking sweetly to the girls."

"That's odd." I rubbed the tip of my nose, thinking for a moment. "He didn't mention Linsey when we saw him. He asked about Emmy and said he hadn't seen her in some time."

"I don't like him, Mama." My daughter met my pensive gaze and held it with an intense expression that was far more serious than a typical four-year-old child.

"You know I don't like to speak ill of people," I told her, touching Linsey's face to get her attention and be sure she listened, too, "but that man is a bad man. Don't ever speak to him or go with him. If he comes near you, and you're alone, run as fast as you can back home, all right? And if you can't come home, then hide and stay quiet until we find you." I looked at the girls for confirmation. "Promise?"

"Yes, Mama."

"Linsey?"

"Yes, Alex." She grabbed my hand and held on tight. "I didn't like him either. He scares me."

"Just stay away from him and you'll be fine." Trying to erase the child's fear, I leaned over to kiss Linsey's forehead and ruffle her hair. "I can't believe he told me little more than an hour ago," I informed the adults, "that he hadn't seen Emmy in quite some time. He lied to my face, which makes no sense. He had to know Maylen would have told me about his recent visit to the cottage."

"Maybe he thought I would decide not to say anything," Maylen offered, "so that you would not worry. But I can assure you, Alex, he did not see Emmy or Linsey for a very long time that day," the young woman added. "I was rude. I grabbed the girls by the hand and turned back toward the manor, though I was ready to fight him if need be. I am sorry—"

"For what?"

Maylen's blue eyes were grave. "I should not have strayed by the cottage."

"Why not? It's my home. Seamage Brandt was trespassing."

"Yes. I've asked Jules for troops to keep watch in the woods," Rosanna informed me, unflinching beneath my immediate annoyance. "I know you don't like to be guarded, but you have a child now."

Not bothering to answer with more than a sullen nod, I took up the forgotten glass of wine, its taste no more than ashes on my tongue. Though Rosanna probably hadn't meant her words in the way I interpreted them, I couldn't push aside my guilt at failing to protect Emmy's magic.

"Alex," Gwynn broke the uneasy silence, "I have heard from father. One of our scouts brought word that the Stoutheart left Derbarry as scheduled, with plans to make slow progress, stopping along the way at some of the towns. Our people will watch its movement, see if anyone or anything gets aboard or disembarks along the route." Gwynn accepted a glass of wine with thanks from Lauryn, who also poured one for Anders. "Father also sent word to the queen."

"Is the scout still here?"

"Yes, in case you wished to send back a message."

"I do. I guess Corey will want to be here when the Stoutheart arrives." Rubbing my eyes, I felt the weariness I'd tried to fend off, wondering if it was more emotional than physical. "If Father is still willing to send scouts to help out before and when the ship arrives, tell him to send Corey with them, straight here to the manor—" I glanced at Rosanna. "Is that a problem? Sorry, I should have asked permission first."

"This much politeness from you in one day is more than I can bear, Alex. It's not a problem at all," she said, gaining Lauryn's agreement. "You shouldn't even have to ask."

"Sure, I do. It's not my home." Raising a hand to halt the protest on her lips, I said, "You know what I mean, Rosanna. It's not what you think."

"It had better not be," she growled, both of us unhappily recalling the many uncomfortable discussions we'd had in the past, when I'd kept the Barlows and the rest of my little world at arm's length. "Or even Lauryn will pounce on you."

"What an image." Grinning at the duke's wife, I laughed. "Now stop sidetracking me. Gwynn, if the scouts come here with Corey, maybe they can teach him a little bit of stealth along the way. He's only a schoolmaster. What does he know about being sneaky and devious like all you Glynnswood folk?"

"Contrary to your brother's opinion," —Anders nudged my boot— "you learned pretty fast."

* * * *

Bundled up in a soft wool blanket, I leaned my head against the chilled window of the cottage and stared up at the stars, twinkling in defiance of the darkness, with the moon hidden behind a cloud. Reaching futilely for the nagging emptiness inside me, I felt my soul as black and empty as the sky. But Rosanna always said that I was stubborn, and so I perversely thought, in spite of logic and common sense, that if I tried hard enough, the magic would come back.

Childish illusion.

Unable to sleep for that and more, I didn't want to disturb Anders, who was as weary as I had been when we'd first tumbled into bed only three hours earlier. Emmy, bless the child, slept with no trouble, no nightmares, her soft, even breathing a comfort to me when I'd tiptoed into the small alcove that was her private space. In the silence, I turned as a shadow passed by the dying embers in the fireplace, sorry that I'd disturbed Anders, yet selfishly glad he'd come to find me.

Sitting on the wide ledge opposite me, seagray eyes twinkled with mischief, far more awake than I'd expected. Obviously, I'd misjudged him. "Now tell me the truth. Are you uneasy snoring beside me in our comfortable and cozy bed because your fool brother and Maylen insisted on sleeping outside the cottage on the cold hard ground?"

"Not hardly." I snorted, wrapping the blanket tighter as a shiver caught me unawares. "Although they gave the lame excuse of guarding the cottage, in spite of Jules's troops somewhere out there—" I waved a hand in the vague direction of the woods, and then swiftly covered it for warmth. "It was obvious they wanted more privacy than sleeping on our floor would allow."

"Considering they'd been staying at the manor with Emmy, I have a feeling they were feeling, somewhat, ah, deprived. Even Maylen blushed a bit when she graciously declined your offer. Can you imagine?"

"I'm impressed that you noticed."

"It was hard not to. And I notice many things, woman, even though I might not mention them to you. For one thing," —Anders rested his gray-streaked head against mine— "you've been quiet ever since Maylen told us about the children's encounter with Seamage Brandt and Rosanna mentioned setting the guard." When I sighed, he kissed my forehead, and I turned my body to lean back against him, snuggled in his arms. "Tell me what's running through that convoluted mind of yours."

"Talk about insults. Look, Anders, it's just . . ." I shrugged. "Things are different."

"Without your magic." Trust my husband to get right to the point.

"That, for one, and Emmy, for another."

"Ah. I thought that might be the more immediate troubling detail."

"Detail?" I squirmed in his arms, but the wily beast held me fast. "Anders, when it was just you and me, though I might have been afraid, even terrified, I'll admit, though I'd deny it if you ever told anyone, of what we had to face, I was more— I don't know. It's hard to explain, but things were different. But now that I made a choice to have a child, our child, and see what a wonderful mage we could create, I realize I was being selfish."

"Rosanna was right," he grumbled in my ear, nipping my lobe before I could pull away. "You have the most decidedly illogical, logical mind I've ever known."

"I'm serious."

"I know you are, Alex, which is why it's my job to try and place some of that illogic into more logical thoughts. We wanted a child, Alex. The fact that she would probably be a mage child wasn't the reason we decided to have her, was it? Or did I miss a point five years ago?"

"Of course not. That was only what scared me. But—"

"But now the idea of a child has become a real, flesh and blood, gorgeous little girl, who also happens to have amazing mage talent. And you're scared, wondering if we did the right thing to bring an innocent, gifted child into this cold, cruel world." When I didn't say anything to deny or confirm his words, Anders shook me gently. "Alex, Alex, would you rather she had never been born?"

I broke free of his grasp, incensed. "Are you mad? I love that child. I—"

"I know." He silenced my fury with a kiss and broke away with an impish grin. "Apparently, this is the perfect time to relate to you something Rosanna told me the very day we found out you were pregnant."

That caught my attention. He and the old seabeast were always having private chats. "I can't wait."

"Stop scowling. You'll get wrinkles." He placed his rough hand beneath my chin and held my gaze, compelling me to listen. "Rosanna said there'd come a day when you'd worry you couldn't protect your baby, a natural mother's concern, a father's, too, she reassured me, but one that had driven your mother nearly to distraction when she feared for her own life. Rosanna said when that day came, to remind you that parents cannot," —he held my chin motionless when I tried to look away— "cannot control all things, no matter how hard they try. You've seen it in your own life, Alex, many times."

"So what then?" I whispered, unable to stop a lonely tear from spilling onto his hand.

"You know the answer, as well as I do, Alex. You're just tired and scared and hurting. But the answer is that we'll do what we've always done. We'll do our best to keep her whole and healthy and happy and safe. And more than that, love her every single minute we live and breathe. All right?"

When I nodded, Anders wiped my cheek, picked me up, and carried me back to bed.

* * * *

Three days later, after the children had flown from the schoolroom as though pursued by a raging seabeast, I was hunted down and cornered by one of two unlikely sources. Rosanna, in my opinion, knowing how she and my husband plotted together at every possible opportunity, had been biding her time, though I'd expected her to hound me sooner or later about my daughter. But not the other woman, who should have been miles away, deep in the Glynnswood forest.

"Anessa!" Shoving back from the low table that served as my desk, I rushed to the doorway to greet my stepmother, our embrace as warm and loving as I'd ever hoped five years earlier. "Uh oh. If you're here, that means my father's here, too."

"Is that a bad thing?"

"Depends."

"Well, you be the judge. Sernyn is here with Corey, whom I like very much, by the way, and a band of our scouts to help Duke Barlow. In my husband's humble opinion, as an elder, he could not very well stay behind and miss all the planning, since it concerns Spreebridge. I told him he was denying the real reason. As a man, he could not very well keep his nose from what was happening in Port Alain." She laughed as I stared dumbfounded, her long dark brown hair, only lightly streaked with gray, hanging gracefully to her shoulders. "And as his wife, I could not very well stay in Glynnswood and do nothing, either. I knew it was my duty to be sure he stays out of trouble and not vex you."

Rosanna sighed, ushering Anessa into the schoolroom, where they both sat on two low wooden stools, "Try as I might, I have no power over the way your personality and influence on people disintegrates over time. This good and decent woman is worried about her husband vexing you rather than the reality that you would vex your father."

"When did I ever give him grief?" Trying my best to look innocent, it suddenly dawned on me that these two women, together, were on a mission.

"Your expression just changed to something fierce." Rosanna slyly eyed my stepmother. "Was it something I said?"

"Something you did. You've been avoiding me these last three days," I challenged the senior Lady Barlow, who didn't blink, not even when I added, "and I have a good idea why."

"Then you'll be a good girl and listen."

"I will not—"

"Alex." Anessa's soft entreaty and the touch of her hand on my arm bought me up short. Resigned to an unpleasant conversation, I sank to the low table between the two mothers, both of whom, I knew in my heart, had my welfare uppermost in their minds. "There are bags and shadows under your eyes. You worry about things over which you have no power or control. You lose sleep—"

"Didn't you lose sleep?" I shot back, immediately sorry for yelling at the kind woman, who'd never raised her voice to me, though she was accustomed to my fiery outbursts. "Every time Gwynn announced he was going on a dangerous adventure to save his mad sister, didn't you toss and turn in bed until he returned safely? Never mind," I reminded the woman, "that he was going after a sister he barely knew?"

"It devastated me every time he left, even now, every time he goes on a dangerous mission," Anessa admitted, her voice even, "but that does not change the fact I would not stop him. I understand I cannot save my son from all things." She smiled and squeezed my hand. "And besides, I would never keep him away from you, even when you were," she slid a glance at Rosanna, "vexing your father."

"You stay away from Lady Barlow."

"But I so enjoy her company." Anessa's chuckle was short-lived, and I knew she wasn't finished with her maternal lesson. "But Alex, do you see? It was no different for Rosanna when she watched you ride away to Tucker's Meadow to fight Charlton Ravess in the Mage Challenge. She did not know whether or not you would return safely."

I met Rosanna's eyes, held them for a second, and started to reply, but she cut me off.

"The situation was slightly different," Rosanna corrected softly. "I wasn't Alex's mother and—"

"You were the only mother I knew for my entire life. Are you saying it meant nothing to you when I rode away that day?" I challenged, knowing full well Rosanna didn't mean she didn't feel anything, didn't worry herself and Lauryn sick until there'd been good news. I knew in my heart that she, oh so foolishly, wouldn't ever want me to think she had replaced my own mother.

"Alex—" Averting her face, Rosanna started to get up but I grabbed onto the sleeve of her gown and held her down on the stool. "You don't think—"

"I do think that you and I need to have a chat right now, one that's been a long time coming." When Anessa indicated she would leave, I shook my head, needing her support if my own effort failed. "All my life, you scolded me for not feeling as though I belonged to the Barlows. That was my own insecurity playing games in my head and in my heart. No one's fault but my own, I know that. And as someone who finally woke up to the truth, I'm proud to say that I am a Barlow, that I am a Keltie, and that I have a child who belongs to both families." I stood up, towering over the older woman, whose uncertain expression broke my heart from the power I now had over her emotions.

Rosanna started to speak, shook her head instead.

"But here's where you come in." I raised my voice to compel her attention. "I never consciously thought about it until now, but since it's all very clear to me, I'm going to be very sure it's clear to you, too. All my life, Rosanna, you've never accepted you were a mother to me. Sure, you didn't give birth to me, and you were always gracious in telling me stories about my mother, keeping her alive for me. And for that,

I'll always be grateful. But answer me this— Who kept watch in the night when I had a cough or a runny nose? Who rocked me when I cried from nightmares? Who taught me right from wrong and what it means to love?"

I crossed my arms and gave her my most Rosanna-like glare.

Rosanna crossed her own arms and returned that glare, far more effective than mine. "I despise it when one of my children makes an intelligent point. But now I understand, since you've only known Alex for six years," —she turned to Anessa, a twinkle in her eyes— "why I'm so gray and you're not."

Chapter Fourteen

"What a pathetic bunch of strategists," I scoffed, glancing around the crowded formal parlor in the duke's manor as I joined the conspirators. "Lying around like a bunch of garden slugs, as though we weren't needed to save the mages of Tuldamoran from dire circumstances."

"Spoken like a true leader," Rosanna said dryly, sitting in the armchair nearest the blazing fireplace, in spite of the spring day's promise of warmth. "Words of encouragement, wisdom, and tact. Not to mention the fact you wouldn't know a garden slug if you squashed the slimy creature with one of your huge feet, since you don't know a thing about the art of gardening, unlike your husband, who continues to show the most amazing skill with my blossoms."

"I never claimed to be a gardener or, for that matter," I took more offense at her other suggestion, "a leader."

Ignoring Rosanna's tsk-tsk of indignation at my offhanded dismissal of responsibility, I joined Maylen and Gwynn on the floor, lounging on a bunch of soft pillows, and took mental headcount of the others present. Jules sat beside Anders on a small velvet couch near Rosanna. My father and Corey, seemingly comfortable with each other, sat in tapestried armchairs on the other side of the fireplace. And Kerrie, the duke's steward and brother-in-law, perched on a window ledge overlooking his mother-in-law's gardens, which supposedly harbored a slimy slug or two. And my father's scouts, so Jules had reassured me the night before, were settled and working with the Duchy troops in the Port Alain barracks. There were, however, a few missing faces.

"Where's Lauryn? I thought she'd be here."

"Along with Khrista and your gracious stepmother," Jules informed me, smothering a yawn when his mother shot a chiding look his way, "my wife is keeping the girls and the twins out of harm's way."

"You mean, out of our way." Eying the teapot and mound of fresh cranberry scones on the nearby tray with interest, since I missed breakfast, I snatched a scone and lifted an eyebrow at Rosanna.

"I gather that's a request for tea," she said dryly.

"Yes, please. If I were to pour a cup of tea for myself, I'd have to get up from the floor again, and I'm far too comfortable. Thanks," I added sweetly, as she practically thrust a delicate china cup and saucer into my outstretched hand.

"Don't get crumbs on the rug."

"Then what will the mice eat?"

"Thank the lords of the sea the children, and your stepmother, aren't here to witness your disrespectful behavior toward the feeble elderly." When I snorted at that unlikely description, Rosanna looked with disdain at my father, who only smiled. "I expected better of you."

"If you could not control my willful daughter during her first twenty-five years," he said in self-defense, not a bit perturbed by words that would have had me leap at him with a knife at his throat five years earlier, "then surely I cannot. And even more important for my peace of mind, I will not even try."

"Excellent decision. Now that that's settled," I cut in, before they ripped my reputation to shreds, "any news of the Spreebridge vessel?"

"The Stoutheart will arrive in Port Alain in four days," Gwynn volunteered this information, snatching half of my cranberry scone while I was doing a quick calculation in my head.

"Sneaky thief. Four days? If we backtrack—"

"You're planning something," Anders accused, seagray eyes narrowed with suspicion that was, well, justified. "I knew it."

"Of course, I'm planning something. Someone has to," I added, uncomfortably reminded of Rosanna's earlier description of me as a leader. "All right, hush, don't look so insulted. If the Stoutheart arrives in the harbor in four days, that means it would take roughly two days to get from the mouth of the river, across Shad's Bay, then to the port, right?" My rambling question was directed to Jules, who nodded. "In roughly two days' time, we can catch sight of the ship as she passes by and maybe identify some of the passengers on board, if the weather holds and they're tired of being cooped up below deck."

That last comment brought Anders and Jules and Rosanna to complete rapt attention, all of them knowing the best spot possible for that opportunity to happen was the worst possible spot for me. The look on Jules's face told me in no uncertain terms he was thinking back on how I'd traveled that road in the dark to find him and Elena when the twins went missing.

"Alex—" It was my father, however, knowing nothing of the local terrain, who broke the awkward silence. "Is something wrong?"

"Not at all," I lied through gritted teeth, disbelieving I was actually going to propose out loud what occurred to me during the night. "There's only one perfect spot along the Jendlan River where the shore and the ship come close enough to see clearly with a spyglass."

"By Jendlan Falls," Maylen said, her eyes widening as she caught the implication, too, knowing all about my personal nightmares.

"You must be a scout," I teased, trying to erase the disbelief on her pretty face. "It's where the river splits, half going west toward the falls, the other half east toward open water," I explained to my father, as though I hadn't a care in the world. "There's a stone bridge across the falls, and the far side is the optimal spot for us to take a look at the ship without being seen."

"How is that possible?" My father asked, perplexed. "If you are on the bridge, then surely you must be visible?"

"Ah, well, not exactly. When we were children," Jules admitted, flushing bright scarlet at the memory, "Elena and I would occasionally race onto the bridge and lie flat along the low wall so Alex couldn't find us. We weren't being cruel, or so we didn't think at the time. But now, well—" He dared a glance at me, reassured when I grinned. "Anyway, there are slits all along the wall for decorative purposes, but Elena and I learned to avoid them."

"Ah." My father's single word answer told me he realized the truth as well, along with Gwynn. Poor Corey was the only one lost at sea.

"I'm terrified of bridges," I admitted to my new brother, "so I would never think to look for my friends on the bridge, even though I suspected that's where they were hiding."

"Well, then, you will not be one of the party who spies on the ship," Corey said so matter-of-factly it seemed he'd been part of the family for years. "There are enough of us who know the people involved and—"

"And I intend to go along, anyway, but thanks." I smiled, catching my husband and Jules off guard, but not Rosanna.

"Is this a personal test?"

"Yes and no. No," I explained, taking a sip of tea and setting the delicate cup aside, "because I was in Spreebridge recently, so I know some of the players who might make an appearance. Besides, an extra pair of eyes can't hurt. What several pairs of eyes might miss, the last pair might catch."

"Assuming they stay open."

Knowing full well there was the very real temptation to crawl on the bridge with my eyes shut tight and keep them closed, I bit back the curse when I saw Corey's wide-eyed expression. "They will certainly remain open. And yes, thanks to my father, who didn't warn me about Lunatics' Crossing into and out of Spreebridge," I said dryly, enjoying his flush of shame, "the bridge by Jendlan Falls represents practically no threat to me," I said confidently, more to convince myself than anyone else.

And they all knew it.

"Alex, wait. Wait—" Corey was so flustered he waved both hands in the air. "You are terrified of bridges, yes?"

"Yes."

"Yet you went into and out of Spreebridge by way of Lunatics' Crossing?"

"Yes, to both questions. Not happily or willingly," I added, "but yes." When my new brother said nothing, trying, I assumed, to digest the implication of my answers, I was intrigued. "You have such a perplexed look on your face. Why?"

Corey glanced at my father, and then at me. "You make light of many things, Alex. I know that about you because Gwynn and Father, and even you, have told me so. But that feat alone, for I know that crossing," he said, looking no happier at the thought than I did, making me think I wasn't foolish for being so frightened, "proves how very brave you are. I cannot imagine the terror you must have felt."

"I don't ever wish that terror on anyone," I said, "but believe me other people have done far braver things."

"Modesty, Mage Protector?" This quip from Rosanna earned a scowl.

"Honesty, Lady Barlow."

"Good, then I did manage to get a few noble thoughts into your head when you were a little pest," she replied, sipping daintily at her tea.

"One or two, so don't be smug. All right, that's settled. We can spy on the ship in a few days, but here's the next problem. We need to get on board the Stoutheart two times when she docks in Port Alain. One to find the crates and measure them, though how we'll do that, I've not the slightest clue," I admitted. "The second time to switch them with our own crates."

"You might need some sneaky, underhanded Glynnswood folk," my father said, tongue in cheek.

"I didn't say a word."

"You were thinking so loud, Alex, my head hurt," —he grinned— "so I said it aloud for you." Unfazed by my snarl, Sernyn leaned over and helped himself to a scone from the tray. Whenever my father openly mocked me, I couldn't help thinking how far we'd come. Something in my eyes must have warned him, because his grin transformed into a sweet smile.

"I doubt you will have to measure the crates," Maylen said, catching the silent exchange and sidestepping it. She did, however, follow my father's example and broke a scone into neat pieces. "When we were in Derbarry, I took a good look at the dock before you made Anders set that fire to test Jackson. All the crates were the same size, regardless of the ship. No offense," —she grinned at Corey— "but Spreebridge shipmasters have no individuality."

"None taken." Corey matched her smile. "In fact, that is the problem we are trying to fight. The old order is trying to preserve the traditional way of doing everything, even down to the ridiculous matter of storage crates. My mother and some of the other elders wish to loosen some of the restrictions and narrow-mindedness that pervades our society. I confess," —he smiled at his own admission— "when I first came to Ardenna, and then here, I was nearly overwhelmed by the diversity I saw in all things, no matter where I looked."

"And here I thought it was just the Keltie lunacy that bowled you over," I teased, before turning to Maylen. "You really noticed that?"

"Yes. Is there something wrong?" she asked, as though I were seeking to trap her by my question.

"No. It's just impressive, that's all."

"That—" Gwynn elbowed me, grabbing the forgotten half of scone from my fingers, "is what scouts are trained to do. Watch and remember and report."

"Hey—" Sighing as he popped the scone into his mouth, I thumped his knee. "You're a terrible model for Corey."

"Yes, I am, and shall continue to be," Gwynn said with smug pride, though he quickly returned to the matter at hand. "Still, we need to know where the crates are stashed on board the ship and how many there are. I wish your mother had sent word," he said to Corey, no accusation in his voice, simply regret. "If she could have gotten a closer look at the Stoutheart before the ship sailed from Derbarry, it would have been helpful."

"To be honest, it troubles me that there has been no word at all."

"Do you wish to return north?" Sernyn asked, seeing the worry on Corey's face. "We would all surely understand and—"

"No, but thank you. Mother is quite capable of taking care of herself. My fear," Corey's anxiety transformed into a mischievous smile, "is that she is too busy nosing around where she should not."

"Well, then, she's no different than any of us, is she? We still have some time before the ship arrives. If we're lucky," I added, snatching another scone from the tray and guarding it from my brother, "Kimmer will send word. Until then, the only other thing I can think to do is to figure out how to create a diversion so we can search the ship while the sailors are busy doing something else. Since they're not military vessels but merchant traders," — I shrugged, thinking aloud— "seems to me they'd be less inclined to strict behavior, unless the captain is afraid of reprisal from Elder Frontish. But how we'll get their attention, I'm at a loss."

"Maybe the Crown will pay for whores to keep the sailors occupied." When we all turned at the unexpected female voice, rich with sarcasm, that drifted through the open doorway, Elena rolled her eyes. "Well? Isn't that a good idea?" She tossed her light wool cloak onto an armchair, as Jackson did the same, both of them coming into the room. "You know how easily men are distracted, no offense to the gentlemen present. A bare leg here, a bare arm there—" She shrugged, quite pleased with herself.

"Why are you here?" I demanded, rescuing my scone barely in time from my brother's imminent sneak attack.

"You didn't answer my question."

"Answer mine first."

"Because," —dark blue eyes laughed at me, and then glanced at Sernyn, an impish smile on Elena's face that reminded me of a thousand summer days when we were children— "I couldn't resist joining in the fun any more than your father could. I left a very disappointed and pouting heir back in Ardenna, burdened with boring administrative tasks. And here's another reason, Mage Protector," she added, accepting a chair Kerrie graciously pulled closer to the fire for her, while Jackson joined the steward on the window ledge. "Elder Frontish won't be expecting me in Port Alain. And you know how I like to keep my enemies, and my friends, on their toes. Particularly my Mage Protector, who doesn't always tell me her plans either." Sliding a glance at the senior Lady Barlow, whose face remained neutral, Elena purred sweetly, "Does that satisfy you, Alex?"

"So, your majesty," —I bit into a piece of scone and chewed for a moment— "how many prostitutes are you willing to pay for?"

* * * *

"Why are you really going on that bridge?"

The real question should have been, why was I so surprised Lauryn would corner me after my history lesson with the children? "In response to that insulting innuendo—"

"Why insulting?"

"Because you implied I wasn't telling the truth."

"Not at all," Lauryn countered, brushing an annoying strand of light brown hair from eyes that watched me like a seahawk. "However, I implied you weren't telling the whole truth. That's a different matter."

"Hmmm. So, I could say in response to that busybody question," I drawled, stretching my legs across the wooden floor, scraped by tiny boots over the past twelve years, "I'm doing it because the bridge is there, but that would be snide. All right, two reasons." I grinned, once I'd earned a well-deserved scowl. "One, Rosanna is partially right. It is a personal test of sorts. For the lords' sake, Lauryn," —I crossed my legs at the ankle and waved her onto a stool beside me— "I did manage to make my way across the bridge and back at Edgecliff when we were searching for, and then pursuing, those renegades, and even worse, I—"

"Made it through Lunatics' Crossing into Spreebridge, yes, I know," she finished. "But you had to go that way or risk being recognized. The difference now is you don't have to go to Jendlan Falls. There are plenty of others who can go in your stead."

"Because they're braver than me."

"It has nothing to do with bravery. Everyone has fears. There's nothing wrong with that. You face them now and again, and manage to get past them, and even if you can't," —Lauryn shrugged in dismissal, as though it didn't matter one whit— "No one will think any less of you. So—" Staring me down, she shot me a pretty decent rendition of her mother-in-law's expression of maternal disdain, one I hadn't quite mastered with my own daughter and probably never would. "Tell me the real reason why you're going on that bridge."

I sighed, knowing Lauryn was merciless when it came to interrogation, particularly when she sensed the person she was hounding was holding back something essential. "It's like this—" Which is as far as I got because my tongue decided to tie itself into knots.

"I'm listening."

"You're a pain in my butt."

"Now, Alex— Sweet names have no effect."

"You've been living in the same house as your mother-in-law for far too long. You sound just like her," I grumbled, "and I resent it."

"Stop trying to get me off the track. I know you, Alexandra Keltie. Now be honest and answer the question."

I found it difficult to lie to Lauryn, though I had once or twice, for the sake of decency and, more important, to avoid heartache for my friend. I got to my feet in slow motion, as though I were sixty years old instead of thirty, and toyed with the pile of crude maps on the far end of the table while I thought about my answer.

"If this ridiculous notion of bravado has anything to do with your loss of magic and the fact you feel you have to do something, or have a hand in everything, just so you can do something so ridiculous because you feel you have to prove your worth—"

My fingers tensed on the maps at her all-too-relevant words.

"Alex—" Lauryn got to her feet and turned me around forcibly by the shoulders to face her. "You don't have to prove anything to anyone. Not now, not ever. You do more than enough even when you do very little."

"When do I do very little?" I demanded, prompting a relieved grin from my friend. "All right, Lauryn, lords of the sea, but you're a pest sometimes. You've made your point. But what if I just said I want to be on that bridge because I've lived here all my life, and maybe it's time? Visitors always go up there to look at the scenery."

"True, but I wouldn't believe that was the reason. Not for you. But tell me," —blue eyes were curious— "have you never really gone on that bridge? Not even as a child? Didn't you ever feel tempted?"

"No. Not once. Not in the least."

My voice was firm, my expression natural, while inside me, a whirlwind raged. I wasn't the best liar in the world, but there were some things Lauryn didn't need to know. And one of those ugly truths was that I had made the passage across the bridge, alone, in the dark, twice, to find her husband when Jules accompanied his queen, the woman he'd always loved before Lauryn ever entered his life, into mourning for her treacherous lover.

"Pity," Lauryn broke into my dangerous thoughts. "The sight's quite impressive. Just make sure you keep your eyes open." Chuckling at my indignant pout, she turned to leave, saw Elena hesitantly standing in the doorway, and waved her inside.

"Sorry. Didn't mean to interrupt."

"You're not." Lauryn's smile was warm, an amazing fact since her husband would always love this woman. But to her credit, Lauryn never held Elena to blame, for Elena had gently rejected Jules as anything more than a dear friend many years ago, a fact that haunted all of us. "I was just on my way into Port Alain with Khrista and Corey."

"Why?"

"You don't know?" Judging the blank look on my face, Lauryn chuckled and winked at Elena. "She doesn't know." When Elena tried hard to bite back a laugh, and lost control, Lauryn patted my arm. "Maybe you should sit down. The truth may be a little unnerving."

Intrigued, more than alarmed, I leaned one hip on the schoolroom table and crossed my arms. "I'm sitting. Now tell me what's going on."

"We're going to introduce Corey to Chester at the Seaman's Berth."

"I'm surprised he hasn't already been down there with Gwynn or my husband," I said, trying to figure out what they were planning. "Is there a new ale on tap? Something that needs a few thirsty people to test? Maybe I should go along, too."

"Um, actually, no."

Glancing from one woman to the other, I shut my eyes. "Go on."

There was definite amusement in Lauryn's voice when she explained, "The pub owner is going to introduce your brother to some of the more, um, well-endowed working girls in Port Alain." When my eyes popped open, she broke out into giggles. "Your expression is priceless, Alex. Close your mouth."

I obeyed, and then pleaded, "Not Corey. Please tell me not Corey."

"He volunteered. I'm not lying, Alex." Lauryn backed away, toward the door, when I stood up, looking ready to bolt from the schoolroom. "There were plenty of witnesses."

"But why Corey?"

"Because of his accent."

"What's his accent got to do with meeting whores?"

"You're not even thinking clearly."

"I have too many disturbing images in my brain."

"Well, get rid of them. Corey's from Spreebridge and everyone in town is aware there's a ship coming down the river with trade goods for the first time in decades." Lauryn tried to keep her expression serious, but was having a difficult time. "And Corey said he'd convince the ladies he had some mates coming down he hadn't seen in awhile and wanted to, um, see that they were properly and warmly welcomed to Port Alain."

"He can't do it. The boy blushes like a child of ten."

"The boy is not a boy. And though he may very well blush in front of us, your new brother reassured us, in private, mind, that—Elena, for the lords' sake, stop," Lauryn chided, when Elena couldn't stop laughing, "well, that he's not, um, as innocent as you might like to believe."

"I'm sure he's not, but— Oh, I can't deal with this. Not Corey." I covered my face with my hands and moaned. "When was all this decided?"

"I believe it was while you were teaching your history lesson. Not very long ago, in fact. And Alex, it wasn't decided just because you weren't there," Lauryn said quickly, when I narrowed my eyes in suspicion. "The topic just sort of came up and, well, Corey volunteered. So," —she squinted out the window, stifling another giggle— "it's getting late. I'd better be going."

"Lauryn—"

"Want to come along?"

"I want nothing to do with it."

"Too bad. It could be quite entertaining."

"Yes, well, I'm sure. You just tell that fool for me I intend to send his mother a letter and—What?" I demanded, when Lauryn starting chuckling again.

"No offense to Kimmer Frehan, Alex," Lauryn tossed over her shoulder as she headed for the door, safely past Elena and out of my reach, "but she did give birth to a son out of wedlock. I doubt she'd be too strict with him. No wonder she's all for, um, easing the conservative traditions of her country folk."

I stared after Jules's wife in disbelief as she vanished out the door.

"Lauryn's wonderful, isn't she?" Elena shook her head, long black hair catching the early afternoon sunlight shining through the window. "Sure you don't want to go along?"

"Absolutely not. And don't encourage her. She knew I didn't know, and—"

"Shh. Don't be so cranky. I have something to say to you."

"Not you, too?"

Elena didn't laugh, as I'd expected, which immediately gave me cause for concern. "Yes, me, too. A few things, as a matter of fact, so be quiet for a minute and just listen."

"Your wish is my command, my queen."

"I'll have you put in chains."

"I'm terrified."

"Alex—"

At the somber plea in her eyes, I subsided. "Sorry. Go on. I just don't want to be scolded again."

"That's not my intention, though it's tempting. First of all, I didn't plan to eavesdrop just now, but the door was open, and I heard you and Lauryn discussing our plan. I want to thank you for not telling her the truth about the bridge." Elena flushed at the memory that was uncomfortable for all of us.

"No need to tell Lauryn, though I detest lying to her. Even Rosanna doesn't know where I went that night." I sighed, not sure if Elena knew this part of the recent story. "In fact, I refused to hide Emmy at the lodge weeks ago, not willing to reveal Jules's secret, and instead sent her to Glynnswood, where I assumed she'd be safe. That's why I feel somewhat responsible for my daughter's loss of mage talent."

Elena blinked, shook her head as though to digest what I'd just revealed. "Does Jules know this?"

"Of course not. I—"

"Fool. Flameblasted fool, Alex. Honestly. Jules would have gladly sheltered your child there. But I've wondered about something. Though Jules has behaved very well these past few years, do you think he keeps the lodge secret from Lauryn because he still thinks there's hope that some day—" Elena didn't finish the thought, didn't need to.

"I've wondered myself, but haven't had the courage to ask. My philosophy these days is to consider the hunting lodge in the same way I consider the tunnel from Blane Woods into your fortress. Something to keep in mind in case it's needed. And with regards to Emmy," —I shrugged at the irony of what I'd just admitted— "I would have only gone to the lodge by myself. But without magic, I didn't feel capable of protecting my daughter."

"Jules would have wanted Anders there, too."

"I know. I knew it then, too, in my heart, but I couldn't take the next step." I recalled the conversation. "In fact, Rosanna and Anders both agreed it would have been reasonable, without knowing where I'd gone that night, but I couldn't betray Jules."

"After all the grief we put you through six years ago, pushing you to uncover your mage talent, I'm humbled you feel so loyal." Dark blue eyes studied me intently for a heartbeat. "By the way, that's not sarcasm," she added, as I started to speak. "Just simple honesty."

"And very old history. Look, just don't tell Jules about my dilemma, all right?" When her expression turned argumentative, I stood up and grabbed her shoulders. "Promise me."

"Talk about pests. I should go ahead and tell Jules, just to make you feel foolish, but not guilty. Wherever Emmy would have been, they would have gotten to the poor child. No, don't argue. I know I'm right, Alex," she insisted, pacing as she always did when disturbed. "Anyone filled with such bottomless hatred wouldn't stop until they were satisfied they'd accomplished their mission. If they hadn't succeeded in Glynnswood, they'd have tried again weeks from now, wherever Emmy would be."

"I wish I could be so sure."

"You can't be. You're her mother. Now about the other matter," Elena briskly changed topics as she paused to stare out the window. "I find it hard to deal with Jackson's loss of magic. You know how helpless I feel. Same as Anders does." She started pacing again, making me dizzy. "But I find it even more difficult when it comes to you."

"Me?" Perplexed, I asked, "Why?"

"Because I was the one who urged you years ago to stop denying your talent and let it emerge. If you hadn't, you wouldn't miss it so now." Her eyes, deeply sad, stared at me with such regret, I reached out to stop her pacing.

"You didn't force me."

"I nagged and nagged and nagged you, Alex."

"Yes." I smiled suddenly, catching her off guard. "But it was the sight of Anders using what I thought was simple seamage talent for the children at Jendlan Falls that made me jealous, made me want to rediscover whatever power I had."

"You never said anything."

"Yes, I did," —my smile changed to a smug grin— "to Lauryn, because I was furious with you. I made that decision, Elena, to let the talent show itself if it was still there. And it was. So even though I've lost it now, in a different manner, I was lucky enough to have it back, if only for a few years. I've felt the joy, the power, and, unfortunately, the dangerous seduction of abusing it. So I've no regrets," I reassured my friend. "Not for me. But I do for Emmy."

"I know." Elena squeezed my arm. "But children are resilient. And she has two very strong parents for role models. So if the magic never returns, I believe Emmy will accept its loss without too much trouble."

"Let's hope you're right."

"Queens," she intoned imperiously, "are always right. Anyway," —she grinned, looking no older than my daughter— "that's what Anders tells me."

"And you believed that liar?"

Chapter Fifteen

"Alex, wait!"

At the sound of Jackson's entreating voice, I stopped my brisk stride up the path toward the manor and waited for him to catch up. He pulled abreast of me slightly out of breath. "You all right?"

"Yes." He placed a hand on his chest in mock distress. "Getting old."

"Getting too much energetic exercise in the dark." I grinned, enjoying the flash of his indecent green eyes. "You're going to have to ask the queen to give you a night off every now and then. What did you want, anyway?" I asked, before he said something that would get him into trouble.

The grin subsided. "To see if you were all right."

"All things considered, I'm handling the loss of magic better than expected. No more tantrums or crying spells or foul moods. Well, no more than usual," I added, taking his arm and leading him toward the colorful garden for more privacy. "Actually, I was wondering the same about you and" —I slid a glance at his profile— "wanted to discuss something with you in private, by which I mean, out of Elena's hearing."

"Well, then," —he quickened his pace toward the shrubs, bushes, whatever they were— "first things first. I suppose I am handling the loss as well as you. I work at hiding my grief from Elena when I can, which, as you know, is an impossible feat sometimes." When I nodded and gestured him to a seat beside me on one of Rosanna's stone benches, he went on. "What more can we do, anyway? Until we rid ourselves of the threat of feyweed spread throughout Tuldamoran, we cannot focus on an antidote. And so, every day, several times a day, I push the troublesome problem to the back of my mind, though it intrudes too often for comfort. Not to mention the many times I try to pull the magic from the depths of my soul, only to find emptiness, a void."

"I know. I do the same. Jackson—" I tangled my fingers with each other, not surprised to find his larger hands covering mine.

"Rosanna and Elena both have warned me when you do that with your fingers, it means you are uncomfortable with whatever it is you wish to say." His smile was kind. "So say it, Alex. By now, we are almost old friends. Or," his tone hinted of formality, "are you acting as the queen's Mage Protector?"

I shook my head, choosing my words with care and purposely untangling my fingers, though my cheeks betrayed me by flushing hot. "No, Jackson, only as a close and dear friend. One of the reasons we suspected you weeks ago of being involved with this whole trouble was because you and Elena are so wild about each other, but—" Unhappy with the conversation, but knowing it to be necessary, for my peace of mind, I was relieved when Jackson found the words to complete my invasive question.

"But why have we not wed?"

"Well, yes."

"Elena and I do not speak of this situation very often, not from reluctance on her part, Alex, but mine." Jackson's sigh was so deep, I patted his arm instinctively. "I am from Spreebridge, a foreigner, an ambassador from my country with all that responsibility entails. To wed Elena Dunneal, tradition demands I become Prince of Tuldamoran. I do not wish that task, nor feel entitled to it."

Green eyes met mine, seemingly expecting judgment and disapproval. Instead, I smiled. "There's another possible solution, you know."

"One Elena has proposed?"

"One Elena doesn't know." I leaned closer, our heads together, catching him up in the possibility and cheering myself up at the same time. "I know what tradition demands, but Elena isn't one to hold on to meaningless tradition. If she believes something else is possible and necessary to change tradition, without hurting her people, then she'll do it. That's one of the main differences between Tuldamoran and Spreebridge."

"True," he said thoughtfully, chewing on his lower lip. "What has she done? Give me an example."

"Me." At his blank look, I said earnestly, "She created my position of Mage Champion, and then changed the title to Mage Protector, for spite, I might add, despite the fact the Ardenna Crown Council of Mages existed. So, I figure, she could create a new position for you."

"But listen to what you have just said, Alex. Elena has a Mage Protector, who advises her side-by-side with the Crownmage." Perplexed, Jackson pulled away and shrugged. "What more is necessary?"

"A liaison between the queen and the Ardenna Crown Council of Mages." I watched Jackson's mouth open and shut, knowing what he would say, and beating him to it. "Anders and I operate out in the countryside, beating the bushes to find trouble and stop it. But you'd be in Ardenna. And just because you have no magic doesn't mean she'll let you off the hook. She's kept me on, hasn't she?" Before he could counter my reasoning, I chattered on, "So I'm hoping that by the end of this trouble, we'll convince the Crown Council we can cooperate a little bit better and, to make it easier for them since they sometimes find her intimidating, you can act as liaison since you have her ear and her heart."

Jackson crossed his arms and eyed me in silence. "You have been thinking about this for a while now."

"Ever since this whole thing started, yes."

"It might work."

Delighted that I'd given him hope, I got to my feet, planted my hands on my hips, and chided the queen's lover. "Did you think I'd propose something stupid?" He stared dumbfounded, not sure whether or not I was seriously insulted. "Come on, I'm starving." Grabbing his arm, I was relieved when he started laughing and instead raced me to the manor gate where we simultaneously stopped dead in our tracks.

Anders was crouched beyond the gate by a bucket of water, Corey beside him, not only explaining how he could manipulate the liquid to steam, but physically making the transformation happen. When he heard the clatter of our boots and then an abrupt silence, Anders turned his head to face us. His expressive eyes filled with remorse that Jackson and I had been unlucky enough to watch magic being performed, a simple feat compared to what we both used to be able to accomplish.

"Anders," I said, keeping my voice astonishingly even as I crossed my arms and stared him down, "don't you think it makes more sense to do the reverse?"

"What do you mean?" he asked carefully.

"Turn steam to cold water and dump it over Corey's head. After all, he did go on a rather, um, provocative mission in town this afternoon that likely had his blood running hot."

As expected, Corey flushed beet red, and Anders smiled in relief, though I knew he knew I was putting on an act. But in truth, I had no right to ask my husband to stop practicing magic simply because I grieved for my own. That would have been an ironic twist to what my father had asked of my mother.

"Oh, and Corey," I threw over my shoulder as I led Jackson to the side entrance of the manor, "I still plan to tell your mother how you spent the afternoon."

* * * *

Not Anders, or Maylen, or Corey, or Jackson, or, most impressively, not Elena, who insisted at the last moment that she join our little scouting party, said a single word to me about reconsidering my decision the morning we left for Jendlan Falls. Not a glance of worry or concern, nor pride or disbelief.

Not a clue, in fact, as to what was going on inside their all-too-devious minds.

After a leisurely breakfast on the Hill, where we'd enjoyed omelets with cheese, spiced sausages, and sugared rolls with cinnamon tea, our little band of spies headed up the road to Jendlan Falls. The four of them, maddeningly, skirted around my presence and tiptoed around my fears as though we were going on a family outing. By the time the roar of the falls came within hearing, I'd had quite enough.

Pulling hard on the reins of my borrowed horse, I brought the poor bewildered animal to an abrupt halt, nearly unseating Elena, who was riding close behind. Her eyes, for one fleeting moment, shone with genuine worry before vanishing beneath a cautious bland mask.

"Problem?" Anders brought his horse alongside mine, keeping his voice amiable and innocent.

"You bet."

"Saddle slipping? Saddlebag loose? Backside hurting?" While my husband kept his features neutral at my unladylike grumble, Corey flushed bright scarlet from his neck to the roots of his dark hair, Elena bit her bottom lip hard to keep from laughing, and Jackson at least had the decency to look away. Maylen, may the lords of the sea forever bless her life, shot my husband and the queen a very disapproving scowl. "Please tell us, precious wife, why you brought your poor stupefied horse to a heart-stopping halt."

Ignoring his insulting endearment, I snarled. "You're all avoiding the topic. The topic," I repeated for emphasis, in case none of them had any real clue as to why I was furious.

"Ah." The wind lifted Anders's gray-streaked hair, which he paid no mind until it fell into his eyes. "The breeze? Is that the topic to which you're referring?"

"You know what topic I'm referring to." I gathered the reins into a jumble of leather and held them in my fist, safer than bringing that fist anywhere near Anders's rugged features. "It's a conspiracy, that's what it is."

"Alex—" Elena tapped my arm, though whether to get my attention or stop me from changing my mind and smashing my fist into Anders's face. "While it may be a conspiracy, it's not an evil one. We thought for certain you'd rather we didn't mention the, ah, topic. In fact, we all concluded that you wouldn't want us to coddle you."

"I don't want you to coddle me," I said hotly, feeling blood creep up my neck beneath my skin, "but—" When I realized what I nearly admitted, my skin flushed even deeper. I started to untangle the reins, ready to move up the road. "Forget it," I murmured.

"No." Anders blocked my path with his stallion, while Elena grabbed the reins of my horse. "Tell us."

I shook my head, wishing the wind would lift my own curls and cover my face. "It's stupid and selfish."

"You thought we were ignoring you," Elena said quietly to my averted face. "All we meant to do was not make an issue of the bridge, simply because we thought it would only make matters worse. Obviously, we misjudged how you might feel." She squeezed my fingers, white-knuckled from gripping the reins. "Sorry."

"Please, no. I'm being ridiculous. It wasn't that I was ignored, but rather—" I inhaled deeply and shook my head. "Let's just go. It's getting late. I don't want to risk missing the ship."

"We have time." Anders's smile was sad as he cupped my chin, forcing me to look at him. "You thought we weren't taking you seriously. Alex—" He stopped my protest by covering my lips with his finger. "If you ever think I'd forget that ferocious slap at Edgecliff when you thought I was playing with your fears, and worse, the cost of my error in judgment to your affection,"—he raised my face and kissed me gently on the brow—"then you're daft. I took you very seriously at Lunatics' Crossing, too, though I did leave you behind hoping you'd follow."

"True, but you'd planned to make the bridge more secure," I reminded him, knowing his heart had been in the right place.

"Thank you for remembering," he murmured. "All right, let's get this straight so all of us understand what's what." He turned to the others, a smile tugging at his lips, before asking me, "Do you still plan to join us on the bridge?"

"Yes." My voice sounded very young and unsure, so I cleared my throat and sat upright in the saddle. "Absolutely. My choice. I promise not to make a scene."

As it turned out, to everyone's relief, though none of them would ever admit the truth, I didn't make a scene. Caught by the spectacular beauty of the falls, a sight I didn't enjoy nearly often enough, I felt its wonder somehow gave me courage. Though I had to admit, the sight of all that crashing water was scarier at night, much like the open sea and rough waves crashing onto shore, particularly with a storm on its way inland.

We hid our horses in a thicket a short walk from the road that led to the bridge, with enough oats to keep them well-satisfied and quiet.

In single file, we neared the narrow bridge, its short but high span daunting, though less so than when I was a child. I darted a brave grin in Anders's direction and followed first Jackson and then Elena onto the sturdy structure built of stone and wood. Anders trailed behind me, with Corey and Maylen last. As swiftly as I could manage without being too obvious, I crouched to the hard ground between two of the narrow slits in the structure. Out of sight of all that free flowing water beneath me, I fooled myself into feeling a little safer, though I was no less protected from the cold spray.

"Shouldn't be long," Jackson reassured me, "if she keeps to her schedule."

I smiled my thanks and let the others keep watch, my back to the wall behind me, my face curved upward toward the sun, letting the warmth of its rays soothe my rattled soul.

A sharp elbow nudged me in the ribs. "Didn't you promise Rosanna you'd keep your eyes open?"

"Is there a Spreebridge ship in sight, your majesty?"

"Not yet."

"A mast?"

Humor crept into Elena's tone. "Not a one in sight."

"Then let me enjoy the sunshine in peace."

"Ah. The lazy slug is emerging. I knew it was there all along." Elena nudged me again, sharper this time. "And you had the nerve to accuse the rest of us as being lazy slugs the other day." Another nudge nearly toppled me into my husband's lap. "What insolence."

"I'm not being lazy. What I am is resting my eyes, or trying to, if you'd keep your pointy elbow to yourself, so that when the Stoutheart does arrive, my eyesight will be sharp," I explained through narrowed eyes, wary of the royal arm. "Consequently, I'll be the one to catch all those important details the rest of you miss. In fact," I suggested, being practical, "you might take turns doing the same."

"That's so Alex won't be the only one looking like a lazy slug," Anders pointed out to Elena, who smothered a grin when I snarled.

"Suit yourself."

"You know," Elena drawled, as I shut my eyes again, "she might actually be right. And since I have the highest authority here—"

"As though we listen to you."

Elena ignored my insult. "I'm designating Jackson and Corey, the two most likely to spot anything or anyone of significance, to take first watch. By the time they're rested and back on lookout, the ship should be arriving. Hmm, let's see. Maylen might need to take first watch, too, along with Anders and me. She's probably got the sharpest trained eyes, thanks to her Glynnswood training. Too bad" —Elena elbowed me again when I forgot to keep an eye on that dangerous weapon— "your heritage never made an impression on you."

"Lords of the sea." I groaned, shuffling closer to Anders and away from Elena. "Are you finished chattering? I'm trying to get some peace and quiet."

"Actually," Anders purred in my ear, "I'm not. I have one more comment to make, even though Elena might be finished. I was just remembering the happy day you suggested I jump from the top of the falls."

"Leap."

"Ah, you remember, too." When he nibbled at my ear, I brushed him away. "Aren't you glad I didn't?"

"No comment."

Anders turned a bright grin to my newest brother. "See that, Corey? That's a clear sign that Alex loves me."

And with that, we all fell quiet for a short time, the crash of Jendlan Falls in the background shutting out all other sound. I felt calm, which I hadn't expected. And surrounded by friends and family, my heart beat just a little slower.

* * * *

"There she is, rounding the bend." Maylen's voice hinted at excitement, so rare an event that I eyed her curiously from beneath lowered lids. The young woman's cheeks were flushed from the sun as she focused her spyglass through the narrow slit. "I win the wager, as expected."

"What wager?" I demanded, pulling my own spyglass from the inside pocket of my spray-misted cloak. "And if you won, then who lost?"

"Gwynn set me against Corey," the scout explained without turning away from the spyglass, "to see who had sharper eyes. A farfetched bet." She flashed a bright grin at Corey for one quick second as she cheerfully slapped him on the back. "No offense, Master Frehan."

"You know, Maylen," —I stared at the young woman in disgust— "I think you've been spending too much time with Gwynn." Getting to my knees, I slipped the spyglass into the slit, suddenly queasy at the sight of all that rushing water within what seemed like touching distance when I peered through the spyglass. Swallowing my fear, I focused to the east, where the river split, one half heading away from the falls and toward the open sea. Just beyond the bend, Stoutheart came into glorious sight, three tall masts and full sails helping her fly across the water. The crew on deck and on the rigging scurried like ants, heeding the captain's commands to avoid the treacherous current that would bring the ship dangerously near the falls and beckoning disaster.

"There is Elder Frontish, standing on the bridge with the captain." Corey squinted through his own spyglass. "And with him, maybe—" His voice fell silent as Jackson gasped.

"What? Who?" Following Corey's focus, I scanned the ship's deck and stopped when I reached the bridge, where Derek Frontish had turned his face away from the captain to speak with another gentleman. My heart sank, and I glanced past Elena. "Jackson—"

"Who is it?" Elena demanded, worried not only by my reaction but Jackson's expression of dismay as he met my gaze. Before either of us could answer, she guessed. "It's Westin Harlowe, isn't it?"

"Yes."

At Jackson's terse reply, Elena said, "Well, he's an elder, too, isn't he? Can't the simple answer be that Westin is coming here as another representative?" Though Elena's tone was demanding, her voice betrayed concern. Even Jackson, judging by his sad smile, knew that his lover was trying to make things right. "Westin knows Jackson lives in Tuldamoran—"

"Yes, but in Ardenna," Jackson said softly, turning his handsome face away from her. "Not here in Port Alain. Your brother and heir," he murmured, "whom Westin does not know, was supposed to be here to welcome the ship. Not you or me." Anger suddenly transformed his handsome face as he peered through the spyglass again.

When Elena would say something more, I signaled her quiet for the moment, to leave him be. Stoutheart was reaching its closest point to where we crouched on the stone bridge. After only a few more moments, she'd move farther away and eventually fade from sight, sailing south to the mouth of the river. "What in— Lords of the sea." I sat up on my knees, cursed as cold stone bit through my trousers, and focused on the water, watching in horror. "That sailor just fell from the rigging. I don't see him, but I saw the splash." Searching the river, I spotted his head as he resurfaced. "There. See. Moving toward the edge of the falls by the shallow pool. Anders, do you see? He's drifting to the spot where you taught the children. If he's lucky, the current won't drag him toward the falls."

"I see him."

Remaining out of sight beneath the wall, I half stood up and found Anders blocking my path, eyes focused in concentration as he peered through the spyglass. Suspicious, I followed his steady gaze, not surprised, when the water nearest the shallow pool transformed to fog, neatly cutting off the sailor from his shipmates' view. "Anders—"

"Sh—" Elena chided, as she crouched beside me. "Let's go rescue the poor sailor before he drowns."

"But Anders—"

"If we rescue the sailor, Alex," —Elena brushed damp strands of black hair from her eyes— "it means we can get off the bridge."

"Right." Needing no further encouragement, I stepped over my husband's rigid body, and flew past Corey and Maylen toward solid ground. The shallow pool was a heartbeat away, and we found the drenched sailor clinging precariously to a slippery rock. Corey caught up to me, just as I reached out a hand, but stopped in mid-crouch, my jaw falling open in shock. Beside me, Corey mimicked my reaction, both of us staring like mindless idiots.

"A fine pair of rescuers, Alex Keltie. And you, Corey Frehan," the soaking sailor chided both of us in a familiar female voice, "are a disgrace and no better. Can someone please help me?" When neither Corey nor I moved a muscle, still bewildered, Maylen stepped up and stretched out a hand. With Jackson's help, she pulled the sea-soaked woman from the river. Her long white-blonde braid dripping with water, Kimmer Frehan nodded her thanks as Maylen had the good sense to offer the shivering woman her dry cloak. Kimmer shook her head at

Corey and me before studying Elena's face in silence. "Your majesty, I presume?"

"Yes." Puzzled, Elena looked to Jackson for an explanation, but he grinned, enjoying the show. "And you are?"

"Corey Frehan's mother, for which I have some regret at the moment."

* * * *

"So there they stood, Corey and Alex." Kimmer was tattling to Rosanna and Anessa, both of whom enjoyed her indignant tale at our expense a short time later, as the Spreebridge elder took smug satisfaction from their expressions of disbelief, disapproval, and horror. "As though neither of them had an intelligent brain in their heads. And both of them, to my amazement, are responsible for tutoring our impressionable children. Whose idea was the fog?"

Anders replaced her wet cloak with a plush towel. "Mine."

"I should have known. Thanks."

"Don't encourage him," I grumbled, not pleased with the day's events. "I still can't believe you intentionally dove off that rigging into the river. My heart almost stopped, and that was before I knew it was you. For the lords' sake, you could have been smashed against the rocks if the current had carried you any nearer the falls."

"That wasn't in my plan."

"Your—"

"Alex—" Rosanna's manners had reached their breaking point. "Let the poor woman get out of those wet clothes and take a hot bath." She put a hand on Kimmer's drenched shoulder and guided the woman toward the main staircase. "You'd think I didn't teach her common sense and courtesy."

"Hold on one minute more." Crossing my arms, I blocked their passage by reaching the first step before they did and slid a grin at Corey. "When you come downstairs, Elder Frehan," —I beamed— "remind me to tell you how your son spent his afternoon yesterday."

"Alex . . ." Corey groaned and cast a pleading glance to Rosanna and Anessa, neither of whom seemed inclined to help him.

Studying the dynamics with interest, and her son's flushed skin even more, Kimmer smiled at Corey in apology. "I certainly shall. Now— Oh, wait." Stopping Rosanna from pushing me out of the way, her expression grew serious. "Forgive me, Lady Barlow, but there is a matter that cannot wait for my hot bath, though it will be most welcome." She reached beneath her soggy tunic and unstrapped a water flask, carefully wrapped in oilskin to keep it dry. Handing it to me as I stepped down from the step, Kimmer smiled with warmth. "A present from Spreebridge. One long sip for you, one for Jackson, and one for your father. Not yet, I think," she said to me, "for little Emila. Not until the danger is past."

Speechless, I held the flask, afraid to believe what I so desperately wanted to believe was in that flask, carried miles downriver from Derbarry.

"Keep it safe, Alex. And this, too." Kimmer pulled a folded note from inside another oilskin packet. "Directions for its making, with notes on the required herbs and dosage."

"No." Surprising the older woman, I stepped back, refusing to accept the paper. "I can't. I don't know the ingredients for feyweed, either. I'm a mage. It might—" I took a deep breath before admitting my fear. "It might tempt me to abuse my power."

"But you wouldn't," Kimmer was swift to reassure me.

"I might." Shutting my eyes, I raised my hand to keep the note at a distance. "I've already used my mage talent in ways that have shamed me. I—"

"In my defense," Elena came to my rescue, reading my mind.

"I know." The Mage Challenge, in which I'd defended her throne and my life, had left its emotional scars on my soul. Anger that day at my adversary, as well as my father, unleashed power and arrogance I never knew I possessed, and it wasn't something of which I was proud. "But still, it's not a memory that makes me feel good about myself." I opened my eyes to find Rosanna studying my face, pity and love so evident I nearly wept. With that encouragement, I turned back to Elena. "You hang on to it. Give it to Anders if you like. I'd just feel better, all right? Just do it for my sake, as a favor."

"On one condition," she said, surprising me with a grin. "Shut up and take a sip of that precious liquid."

I laughed, unnerved at hearing the shakiness in my voice. Opening the flask, I looked at Anders, took comfort in his smile, and breathed deeply. I sipped from the flask, found the liquid cool and not unpleasant, compared with feyweed's rank odor. Slightly tart, it had a grainy feel as it slid down my throat. Eyes shut tight, I waited afraid nothing would happen, nothing would change. With an abruptness that took my breath away, fire and ice came alive. I merged them swiftly and easily to cool warmth, opened my eyes, found a target in the top log by the hall fireplace, and transformed the wood to air, happily watching it vanish with childish satisfaction.

Anders grabbed my face in both hands and planted a noisy kiss on my lips. I handed the flask to Jackson, who mimicked my movement. Watching his face, and the joy in his eyes that must have mirrored mine, I smiled when he transformed the air above the pile of logs to another log.

My father took the flask he offered, once Elena freed Jackson from a very passionate embrace. He met my gaze across the space between us and smiled sadly. Though he drank from the flask, and felt the mage talent come alive again, I knew he wouldn't use it, as he never had but for that one near-fatal time when he almost killed his best friend. And not knowing that he was a mage, my mother never had a chance when she gave birth to me, fighting an infant child with unexpected wild magic. Ironic that my own childhood experience had so closely followed my father's, but I'd found the courage to embrace my mage gift. I only wished he would, too, in time. In the back of my mind, an idea was forming, but it needed care and cautious words and perfect timing.

"Thank you." I hugged Kimmer, brushing aside her polite concerns about getting me wet. "Thank you. For all of us."

"My pleasure, Alex." The Spreebridge woman touched my cheek and smiled, though her eyes were serious. "Keep it well hidden, and keep your recovery a secret." Shivering, she smiled as Rosanna reasserted control and guided her firmly up the stairs. "When I'm warm and dry, there is much I have to tell you."

Chapter Sixteen

By the time Kimmer banished the chill of the river and donned a dry tunic and trousers borrowed from Rosanna's gardening clothes, Jules and his wife, Lauryn, along with my brother, Gwynn, had joined us.

Lauryn scooted to the window ledge, where I sat, one leg swinging back and forth, and whispered, "I heard you were fabulous on the bridge."

"Sure." The leg swung with a little more vigor. "But did they tell you I fled to solid ground the very moment I could?"

Laughing at my wry expression, Lauryn rapped me on the side of the head before sitting beside me. Anessa took the Spreebridge woman in hand while Rosanna busied herself making sure Kimmer was supplied with steaming tea, warmed by a generous dollop of Marain Valley wine, and fresh-baked walnut bread with raspberry jam. With Kimmer seated by the fireplace, and Rosanna absent to find some cheese, Anessa made polite introductions all around, but pointed her finger at Lauryn.

"You will have to ask Lady Barlow," Anessa said smoothly, though I detected a twinkle of mischief in her deep brown eyes. "She knows all about that."

"All about what?" Lauryn asked, though she rapped my head again when I snickered, guessing correctly Kimmer was referring to her son's adventure in town. "Alex, really, must you be so childish?"

"Leave her be," Jules scolded his wife, whose blue eyes held challenge. "For once, Alex is in an agreeable mood," he added, keeping a safe distance, "though I don't know why."

"You really don't?" Sitting up straight, I narrowed my eyes and focused on the chair he was sitting on, just as Rosanna re-entered the parlor, with a serving girl carrying a tray of assorted cheese and cold meats.

"Alexandra Daine Keltie," Rosanna warned, hands on her hips, "if you so much as think evil thoughts about that chair, I will banish you from the house for eternity."

"Spoilsport." Though I was grumbling for appearance sake, I kept my eyes on Jules's face, watching, with delight, as his expression transformed from befuddlement to understanding and then joy.

"Is it true?" he whispered, jumping up from his chair to hug me close. "Thank the lords of the sea, Alex. What about Jackson?" He turned to the queen's lover, whose bright smile matched mine. "I'm so very glad for both of you."

And I was so very touched. Though Jules and I often teased each other in our lifetime of friendship, and taunted each other without mercy most of the time, there were rare moments when we shared genuine emotion. And if I had to be honest, I couldn't fault Jules for the lack of open affection, but rather myself.

"Thanks," I said quietly, squeezing his hand. "And what's more, I can threaten you again. But Jules," I warned, since he hadn't been there when Kimmer had given us the antidote, "we're keeping it secret."

"Of course. You'd be stupid not to. You're many things, Alex, and crazy is one of them." He grinned, stepping deftly out of reach. "But you're not stupid. And neither is Jackson." Returning to his seat, he clapped Jackson on the back and shot Elena a huge smile of relief.

"You'd think he was the one who gave us the antidote," I whispered to Lauryn before turning back to Kimmer, who'd been watching our antics with open amusement. "By the way, how did you find out what ingredients were necessary?"

"That was easy. I stole the directions from Derek Frontish." When my mouth opened and shut, the woman laughed and took pity on me.

"Before I boarded the Stoutheart, I crept into Derek's house while he was busy elsewhere."

"I knew it," Corey exploded, breaking his polite silence with a look of profound disapproval. "I told you so, Alex. She was snooping where she did not belong, and it does not surprise me in the least."

"Well, how else was I to search his home without being caught? I do not have magic to help me. And after Sloane was murdered—" Kimmer's defiant voice faded for a heartbeat, her smile sorrowful as we murmured condolences for the tragedy that had slipped our minds in all the confusion. "I knew I had to do something more. When I asked Derek about the antidote weeks ago, I suspected he was lying when he said it did not exist. I was as sneaky as—" Her smile turned mischievous as she glanced at my father, who'd been stunned, but not completely surprised, by Kimmer's appearance. I suppose he knew a bit more of her adventurous nature than any of us. "Well, as a Glynnswood scout. I searched every room in his huge house and found the directions, of all places, beneath his feather-filled mattress. Can you imagine my disappointment? I expected a more creative hiding place."

While everyone laughed at her comical expression, Jackson and I, apparently sharing the same thought, exchanged a puzzled look.

Kimmer caught our silent exchange. "You are wondering how I knew it was genuine." When I nodded, hugging my knees to my chest, she said, "Well, I confess, Alex, I did not, not at first. But before I tell you how I knew, it occurred to me earlier while I was enjoying my hot bath that neither you nor Jackson nor Sernyn" —she eyed us in turn— "questioned the flask. It might have been poison."

"It might have been," I agreed, "but I'm a good judge of character, with the exception of certain mistakes." I inclined my head in Anders's direction, prompting a wounded look from my husband.

"Thank you, Alex," Kimmer murmured in embarrassment. She took comfort in sipping tea, her expression sad again. "I verified it was a genuine antidote with the help of an old and dear friend who is dying. I—" her voice faltered and she sipped at the tea again, though I wasn't sure she even tasted it. "I asked him a favor. A very big favor."

"He was a mage?" I asked, my heart breaking for this woman.

"Yes. To prove the antidote was not a fake, he first drank feyweed and then the antidote. He—" Sadness changed to regret as she added, "He passed on soon after, right before the ship sailed south. But he told me, in no uncertain terms," her voice gathered strength as she met my gaze with pride, "that he was glad to help because he felt it very important."

"I'm so sorry."

"Thank you. There has been too much sorrow and trouble these past few weeks, and I would see them end." She accepted a piece of walnut bread, slathered with raspberry jam, from Rosanna, who couldn't bear to see people go hungry for very long. "Thank the lords of the sea." She sighed, enjoying the bread. "No more ship food. And speaking of ships, the feyweed is housed in ten crates right beneath the captain's quarters." When Kimmer began to detail the exact measurements, Maylen glanced at me, a smile in her eyes. "I see you know something of this," Kimmer said, again catching the silent exchange.

"Believe it or not," Jules replied, "our carpenters have ten crates waiting to make the switch. All we need to do is match the markings. Maylen" —he grinned at the smug scout— "reassured us that crates used in Spreebridge for everything from food to fabrics to gems are all the same size."

"Boring, you mean."

Jules reddened at Kimmer's dry remark. "That's not what I meant. It's—"

But Corey's mother laughed merrily. "Of course not, but it is true, which is one of the reasons I wish to see some of the liveliness I find so refreshing in Tuldamoran cross the border into Spreebridge. Well, as for the crates, that is an unexpected surprise. But considering the young woman was trained in Glynnswood," —she smiled at my father and Anessa— "I should have anticipated you would be steps ahead of me. When do you plan to make the switch and remove the feyweed from the Stoutheart?"

"The town has been planning a festival to celebrate the ship's arrival. That first night, we're hosting our guests here," Jules explained, looking to Lauryn for confirmation. When she nodded, indicating that nothing had changed, he added, "Mother is hosting a formal dinner. With the captain and the elder passengers entertained in our home, it should make things easier for those involved in switching the crates."

"Excellent. But I must warn you, Duke Barlow," Kimmer said, breaking off a small piece of walnut bread. "The switch will have to be done during that affair because Derek and his companions are staying on board the Stoutheart."

"But they've been invited to stay here," Lauryn exclaimed, worrying all our plans would go astray.

"Yes, they have," Kimmer agreed, glancing apologetically at Jackson, "but Derek and the other elder on board, Westin Harlowe, plan to refuse your hospitality."

"Should I be insulted?" Jules asked, uncertain how best to play out this change in our strategy.

"You could, my lord. And more than that," Kimmer suggested, an impish twinkle appearing in her eyes when she looked at Elena, "you might make Derek feel very ill-at-ease, your majesty, by being insulted on behalf of the Duke and Lady Barlow. Both Lady Barlows, in fact. Yet I wager Derek will still refuse your hospitality, though expressing utmost courtesy and offering an acceptable excuse." Kimmer brought the walnut bread to her mouth and paused before eating it, to add, "Particularly, if you and Jackson are here. He will not expect either of you."

"Well, you know him better than me," Elena said, glancing my way for an opinion and getting a shrug in reply. "I imagine you're right, though that would mean insulting the monarch of a kingdom with whom you're trying to encourage profitable trade. That would seem to be at odds with his purpose in coming to Tuldamoran."

"Normally I'd agree with you," I told Elena, resting my chin on my knees, "but in this case, Derek Frontish, though representing Spreebridge, isn't so much interested in trade profits, though that's a nice little advantage. His focus is on one objective only. Destroying magic that's different than his magic. The man's got a bad case of jealousy and fear."

"Yes, definitely fear," Kimmer said softly. "Derek Frontish, in his narrow-minded world, is afraid of you and Jackson and Anders, and" —her eyes sent a clear warning— "your daughter, who may yet prove more terrifying, when one considers the child's heritage." She nodded, satisfied at the determination she read in my eyes. "You will need a distraction at the dock."

I couldn't help myself. I started to laugh, unable to dodge another of Lauryn's scolding smacks to the side of my head. "Your son," I tried but failed to look serious, "made all the arrangements. Everything is taken care of, Kimmer, nothing to worry about."

"It was Elena's idea," Lauryn defended my newest half-brother, who shut his eyes in resigned embarrassment, every inch of exposed skin sporting a brilliant shade of crimson.

"Yes, but he volunteered. You told me so."

"Alex—"

"What did my son volunteer to do?" Kimmer met the laughter in my eyes, trying without success to be somber as she realized this was the matter I'd mentioned earlier. "Corey?" she demanded, sounding no less maternal than Rosanna or Lauryn in a snit.

"I made a necessary arrangement." Corey met his mother's stern gaze. "For the sailors to, um . . ." He glanced sheepishly to Lauryn for help. When she started to speak, I elbowed her sharply, and Corey shook his head in despair. "The crew of the Stoutheart will have a very warm welcome upon their arrival," he blurted, adding with an embarrassed grin, "compliments of the local, um, ladies in town."

"I see. Excellent diversion, your majesty." Kimmer nodded at Elena before turning steely eyes in her son's direction again. "Tell me, Corey," she drawled, "did you interview the ladies yourself?"

"Every one, mother. I would not want the queen's most excellent plan to fail because I had been remiss."

"I wonder" —Anders shot a glance my way, tapping his chin in thought— "just where Corey learned such slippery diplomacy. You've been accusing him of spending too much time with Gwynn, but I wonder if he might be spending too much time with you."

Before I could defend myself, Lauryn nudged me in the ribs. "He's right."

"Why," Rosanna broke into my tart reply, speaking to the so-called adults in the room, "are all children fools?"

"Speaking of fools," I cut in before she launched an attack on the younger generation, "are we really the fools, no offense intended, Jackson," I said, knowing how deeply disappointed he was about his mentor's recent behavior, "to trust Westin Harlowe?"

"I do not know." Kimmer stared for a heartbeat at Jackson. "But I will tell you two things of importance. Only recently, when Corey came south to find out what Derek was planning with his unannounced visit to Ardenna, I learned Westin had accompanied him."

"That explains the unidentified man the scout noticed in Ardenna," I murmured, remembering what Corey had told Elena and Jackson days ago, "though no one was able to discover his destination."

"That is what worries me." Kimmer sighed, draining her teacup. "I fear Westin was making contacts in Tuldamoran. The other troublesome point you must understand is that on our journey downriver, the two men spoke often and in private. I had to take extra caution so as not to be caught, but I did manage to hear a thing or two of significance."

"Mother—"

"Hush," she chided Corey with gentle dismissal. "I am here. I am fine. Did you think adventure was only for the young?"

Watching the fond amusement on my father's face, I could easily understand how he'd taken solace with this woman after my mother died in childbirth. Anessa had been quietly studying his face, too. Catching my eye, she winked, looking not the least bit ill-at-ease.

"Their plan is wicked, I fear." Kimmer snagged our attention again. "Once the Stoutheart arrives in port, they intend to spread the feyweed by way of the local Mage Councils throughout Tuldamoran, proclaiming it not only a cure for feyweed if ingested, but also a preventive potion. So you can be sure that alarmed and nervous mages will be crowding the local council halls to get their hands on a dose."

"Lords of the sea, but Kimmer, wait— Westin told you in Derbarry that there was no antidote, didn't he?" I asked, struggling to understand Westin's role and whose side he was really on.

"Yes, but Westin still thinks I am safe at home in Spreebridge," she said, a bemused smile on her face. "And it does not really matter. Westin will only say that he knew nothing of the antidote, that he and Derek are not responsible for the poison or the cure. How could they know feyweed was carried on board and smuggled into port? Besides, who would dare dispute such honored visitors to your kingdom?"

"But—"

"Listen to me!" Kimmer's sharp tone became grave with warning. "Both men will say to any fool who will listen that the malicious distribution of feyweed to all mages is a plot by you, Alex, the queen's Mage Protector, with the help of the Ardenna Crown Council of Mages. Your joint goal is to have only an elite handful of mages that includes yourself, the Crown Council, and perhaps a few other favored mages of your choosing. Your plan is to strip all other mages in your kingdom of their magic so they will never be a threat to you. But it is you, Alex, in your bid for supremacy, who will take the brunt of the blame."

Stunned, I could only stare at the Spreebridge elder in silence.

"They will say you intend to create an elite corps of mages, but, in truth, Alex," she continued, holding my gaze, "they will say you intend to rob all mages, including the Crown Council, of mage talent. You and Anders and Jackson, of course, will be the sole survivors with magic." Absently sipping from the delicate teacup Rosanna had refilled, she added in the heavy silence, "Derek's goal is to destabilize Tuldamoran by spreading feyweed, along with fear and distrust. And with uncertainty in your kingdom, he will take the opportunity to eradicate mage talent."

"I have to warn the Crown Council," Elena said quietly, a shadow of anxiety passing over her face. "If they did meet in secret with Derek, they should know they're stepping into danger. They—"

"No." When Elena stared at me in disbelief, raising one black eyebrow in imperious query, I shrugged. "Not yet. I may have warned them when we met in Ardenna. Jenny Bretan isn't a fool. She could easily read between the lines. But the truth is that I won't feel safe until we have the feyweed locked away and hidden. Only then."

"You don't trust the Crown Council."

"No more" —I shrugged, owing her an honest answer— "than they trust me."

Chapter Seventeen

Elena found me later that day, closeted in the schoolroom, poring over the notes I'd prepared for the lesson on Spreebridge, in honor of the arriving Stoutheart and our new trade partners. My daughter sat on a stool opposite me, concentrating intently on a picture she was drawing. Emmy's head was bent low, her tiny nose almost touching the paper, long brown curls hiding much of her pretty face.

"Come to scold me for my attitude toward the Ardenna Crown Council?" I asked the queen, who sat cozily beside my daughter on a low stool, smiling in delight as the imp smothered her in a tight hug.

"Not me." Elena laughed, coming up for air. "You made a valid point."

"Surprised to hear you admit that."

"I'm wounded." Looking anything but, Elena studied the picture in progress. "Lovely," she murmured to Emmy, who grinned at the regal approval and went back to work. "What is she drawing?" Elena had the decency to mouth over my child's head so poor Emmy wouldn't be insulted.

"No idea," I mouthed back, saying aloud, "So, your majesty, if you didn't come to reprimand me, should I assume this call is social?"

"No. It's anything but social." Reaching across the table, Elena plucked the twin pendants from beneath my tunic, the copper one she'd given me and the wooden one Gwynn had carved, both secured on a thin leather thong at my neck. "I have a valid point to make, too."

Uncertainty gathered in my gut. "Am I going to like it?"

"Let's just say, you won't dislike it." Elena shot me a crooked grin. "And maybe you'll even agree. Imagine that. My Mage Protector, agreeing with something I've said."

Intrigued rather than annoyed, I set aside my writing implements. Resting my chin in one hand, I waved her to explain.

"You must know how pleased and relieved I am for you and Jackson." Elena waited for my nod before continuing, "But it doesn't change anything." At the immediate fire in my eyes, she chided, "Hush and listen." When Emmy glanced up, curious for the simple fact her mother was being scolded, Elena whispered, "She always talks and never listens."

"Hey, hey—"

"See what I mean?"

When Emmy bent her head to hide a smile, I tugged at a curl. "Don't you dare agree with Elena, young lady," I said sternly, "or I'll send you to bed with no supper."

"As though you ever would," Elena scoffed, pretending to shield the little minx, now giggling openly at the absurdity of my statement. When she was certain the child had returned to her artwork, Elena turned serious. "I told you before the Mage Challenge that although it—" Reaching across the table again, she tapped the pendants. "Although it was helpful, quite helpful, I won't deny it, so don't give me that nasty look, Alex. I made a point of informing you that your friendship was far more important. You didn't believe me then." Elena sat back, deep blue eyes flashing with challenge and a hint of six-year-old residual annoyance. "I hope you've grown a little smarter and believe it now."

"You know why I didn't."

"You were being a fool."

Seagray eyes peeked at me, judging my mood, before returning to the drawing.

"I was—"

What had I been? Angry. Confused. Disappointed. Heartbroken. Betrayed.

"All of those," Elena said softly, reading the emotions flashing across my face. "But that's in the past, Mage Protector."

"Was it necessary to say all that?"

"Absolutely." Elena rested her chin in one hand, the diamond and sapphire ring of office glittering on her finger. "I know you thought yourself useless these past few weeks, which was enough to drive me to distraction. But as Jules said earlier, you're many things, including crazy, but you're not useless."

"Two thinly disguised insults from my dearest friends in one day are much more than I can bear."

"One other thing." Ignoring me, Elena pulled two folded sheets of paper from the pocket of her silk tunic and handed them to me, though I hesitated. "I know you refused this earlier and why. But I don't agree." When I started to protest, pulling my hand back, she grabbed my fingers and shoved the papers inside. "I'd feel better if you had a copy of the ingredients for both potions. No, Alex," —she brushed strands of black hair from her face with an impatient gesture— "don't argue. For the lords' sake, what are you afraid of? What do you really think you're going to do? Give the mixture to anyone who annoys you, and then dangle the antidote in their face?" She didn't give me a chance to sneak a word in. "Of course not. So hush and take them. Hide them away."

Before I could protest, Emmy stopped drawing and studied the paper, snagging our attention. The illustration appeared to be a somewhat circular shape on the left, a bunch of dots in the center, and another somewhat circular shape, with wavy lines inside, on the right.

"Are you finished?" I asked, though whether the question was meant for Elena or my daughter, I wasn't quite certain. Judging from Elena's raised eyebrow, neither was she.

Emmy's nod was grave as she pointed to the shape on the left. "That's a rock, Mama. Can you see it?"

"Yes. It certainly looks like a rock."

"And this" —she pointed to the bunch of scattered dots— "is what happens when the rock is crushed, like sand. And this" —Emmy tapped the circle on the right, her seagray eyes meeting mine— "is water. See?"

"Yes, of course. But I can't tell whether it's a puddle or a pond."

Taking my question seriously, as I'd meant her to, Emmy thought for a moment. "Puddle."

"That's lovely," Elena said, while I frantically tried to think how to answer, not sure why my daughter was so serious. "Why did you draw a rock and sand and a puddle of water? Was it something you saw in the garden?"

Emmy looked at Elena, the child's expression so much older and wiser than it should have been, prompting a shiver down my spine. "If my magic doesn't come back," she said, "I'll always remember what I did that day with Papa and Uncle Gwynn. Remember the magic I showed you, Mama?"

When all I could do was nod, catching back the threat of tears at her unexpected words, Elena took pity and came to my rescue, gathering Emmy on her lap and hugging her close. "Want to know what I think?" When Emmy nodded, she said, "I believe your magic will certainly come back. You know why? No? Then I'll tell you." Elena's voice had certainty and authority. If I hadn't known that an antidote existed, I might have believed her, too. "You look just like your mama, only you have your papa's eyes. That means they both had a part in making you. And even better, they both have magic, don't they? And don't forget," she reminded my daughter, "your mama lost her magic when she was a little girl, too. I remember because I was her friend and came to stay in Port Alain all summer long." Elena's smile was tinged with sorrow for the pain that age-old incident had caused us all. "And since her magic came back, that's how I know yours will, too. All right?"

Smiling now, Emmy reached up to hug Elena, and then turned her head toward the doorway when she caught sight of a visitor. "Uncle Corey—"

"Forgive me, your majesty. I am interrupting."

"Why are you apologizing to her and not me?" I demanded, enjoying his deep flush immensely.

"Leave your brother alone. Honestly, Alex." Elena rolled her eyes and stood up to leave. "I've had quite enough of her, Corey. She's all yours. Let her drive you mad instead of me." The curse was out of my mouth before I could stop it. Emmy's eyes went wide in amazement, and Elena covered the child's ears, whispering, "Don't forget to tell Grandma Rosanna that Mama said a very bad word."

"Go away."

"And she was rude."

"I'm going to turn you into a squealing pig."

"You can't, and you know it." Shooting me one last smug grin, Elena patted my brother's shoulder in sympathy as she left the schoolroom.

I stared long and hard at Corey, who couldn't hide a smile. In fact, he didn't even bother to try, which meant he was getting far too comfortable with my brother and husband and friends. "No gloating?"

"Absolutely not, Alex, though it is tempting. If I tell the queen you were rude again, she will tattle on you to Lady Barlow as you tattled on me to my mother and will probably tattle on me again about something else."

"That's the spirit."

"I am learning. In fact, I am learning from the best." With that, his cocky grin faded. "Alex, Mother told me how lucky I was to be so welcome here and in Glynnswood."

Curious at his mood, I studied his somber eyes and wondered what was wrong. "You know," I said after a moment, "if you were the least bit wicked, we'd have kept you at arm's length. But you're a good man, Corey, and we were right to welcome you with open hearts. But surely that's not troubling you, is it?"

"No." Beneath Emmy's serious scrutiny, he said, "Mother asked whether I wished to stay here, in Tuldamoran."

Surprised, I sat back, never having considered the possibility. "Do you? It would mean a lot to us to have you near." Saying that, I mocked myself in the privacy of my heart, that I, who for so long had kept family and friends at bay, should feel so different now, only a few years later.

"You see? You make it seem so possible, even welcoming my mother. But—"

"Ah." I saw his dilemma. "Your mother wouldn't come here."

Corey shook his head. "She is an elder in Spreebridge and has much work to do when this trouble is finally over, setting things to right again."

"And I have full confidence that she'll succeed," I reassured him, believing Kimmer would single-handedly revolutionize Spreebridge society. "Look, Corey, it's not something you need to decide now. Or ever, for that matter. You know you're always welcome here, in Glynnswood, even Ardenna. And if you stay in Derbarry, we'll visit you there."

"I would be hurt if you did not."

"Then put it aside for now. I need you sharp and alert in two days." Suddenly, I grinned, gathering my notes into a neat pile. "You know, when you close the deal with all those, um," —I caught Emmy's curious expression— "women in Port Alain."

* * * *

Knocking on the door of the sun parlor where Father was absorbed in writing a letter to someone back in Glynnswood, or so I assumed, I waited until he looked up.

A smile lit his eyes when he saw me. "Alex, come in." He set aside the papers and waved me to join him by the cluttered desk beneath the window.

"If you're busy—"

"I am never too busy for you." Every once in a long while these days, the old familiar heartache of his abandonment of me to Rosanna's care resurfaced. My father read the swiftly banished pain on my face, as easily as I read his heartfelt regret. "Alex—"

"Don't you dare say a word, Elder Keltie. You know what it's like, an old wound that aches with the coming of a summer storm from the bay. Over. Done. Useless. And a colossal waste of time." I towered over my father's chair, daring him to argue with my logic.

He started to speak, reconsidered, and waved me to a footstool near his feet. Running rough hands through his thick brown hair, he sighed. "You have a right to feel those emotions," he said quietly.

"Not anymore."

"So say our heads, but our hearts know better."

"Wrong, wrong, wrong. That's what forgiveness means. It's over. Besides," —I gave him a cocky smile— "if I haven't forgiven you, then it means you have a right to not forgive me for being an obnoxious, contentious, arrogant— What else was I six years ago when I met you for the first time?"

"My loving, frightened, heartsick, furious, beautiful daughter." Sernyn touched my cheek with a gentle caress and smiled. "So what mischief has Gwynn done to you now?"

"Gwynn?" Befuddled by his abrupt change of topic, I scratched my head, wondering what he could possibly mean. "Nothing."

My father's laugh was warm, a sound I'd missed during the first twenty-five years of my life. "I assumed you came to complain about your pest of a brother, as usual."

"Ah, well, I can certainly make up some story. Even Anessa would believe it, too." I sighed in mock resignation. "However, you must like him better than me, or you'd let me tell lies about him."

"Did I ever tell you, young lady," —his eyes laughed at me, the mischief eerily reminiscent of Anessa when she introduced Kimmer to Lauryn— "that Lady Barlow related many key details of your behavior growing up. You know this, yes, but did you know that her letters never spared me."

"Meaning what?" I challenged, narrowing my eyes in suspicion.

"I learned about many of your more precocious incidents and cheeky replies, even when you were no older than Emmy." The mischief turned smug. "Indeed, it amazes me Emmy is so unlike you. That child is well-behaved, polite, loving, funny, respectful of her elders, and she is also—"

"That's what you think," I said in self-defense. "She laughed at me only a little while ago when the queen insulted, scolded, and annoyed me."

"Surely you deserved it."

"Why am I wasting my breath?" I said in disgust, rolling my eyes. "I'm speaking with an adoring grandfather, who thinks the world revolves around his precious little Emmy."

"As well as his precious Alex and Anessa and Gwynn and Maylen and Anders and now Corey," my father said, suddenly serious. "I am very blessed, Alex, to be surrounded by those whom I love, particularly you, when I never thought to ever have your affection or acceptance or forgiveness."

"I thought something similar a little while ago about my own fortune. Corey came to see me, a bit troubled. He said Kimmer asked him whether he wanted to stay in Tuldamoran when this affair is over. Corey said he was lucky to be so warmly welcomed. And I—" Tangling my fingers together, I searched for the right words until my father's larger hands covered mine. "I said it would mean a lot to us if he did stay, either with you in Glynnswood or with us here in Port Alain, but that we'd visit him in Derbarry if he didn't."

"So what is wrong with that?" he asked, brushing a strand of hair from my eyes as I looked up. "It is a wonderful, loving thought, Alex."

"Yes, I know. But when I said that, it struck me how I'd spent so many years keeping my distance from people who loved me."

"Ah." Bending to kiss my cheek, my father smiled. "But you forget one important fact. You may have kept your distance from family and friends, but it was not because you did not love them. You inherited your mother's need for independence. And as for me, you did not even know I was alive." He placed a finger over my lips as I started to speak. "And though you took your time in letting me into your life, you have made up for our mutual loss five thousand times over."

"Think you're so smart, do you?"

"Indeed. Now," —he sat back, proud of himself— "was there a specific reason you came to visit me? Or simply to brighten my day?"

"Flattery will get you nowhere, old man. But yes, I had a reason. Two, actually." I bit my lip, wondering if I could actually go through with the second part. "All right, don't look at me like that. I'm not sure if I even have a right to ask you such a dicey question, but I will, anyway." Under his serene scrutiny, I felt about three years old. "Are you comfortable with Kimmer here in Port Alain? I mean, her arrival was quite a surprise. And, well, is Anessa?"

"Yes, of course. Both of us are delighted." Judging from his smile, it occurred to me the old fox might have expected that question. "You know we have remained friends, and I have hidden nothing from Anessa about our time together. Except my son," he hastened to add before I did, "about whom I had no idea. But I have not seen Kimmer, face-to-face, since the time I spent with her years ago."

After mother died giving birth to me. Sernyn read that thought in my eyes, too, and I cut him off. "That's good. Even though you're both very mature adults, I was a little worried it might cause problems." I grinned, enjoying his indignant expression. "So what do you think of Corey, now that I've already gone and told him he could stay here."

"I am glad you had the decency to admit that little fact. Had I done so, you would have cried foul," he teased. "But truly, I think he is a fine young man. After all, he did inherit some of my better qualities."

"Don't be smug. You had very little to do with it. Well, I like him, too, but I have one complaint." Keeping my expression grave, though Sernyn wasn't fooled, I said, "We have to get him into a little more mischief. I might have to ask Gwynn to help out."

"Alex, please, I will be all gray by the time this trouble has ended."

"Thank you."

"For what?" Suspicious, Sernyn crossed his arms, looking a bit like Rosanna when she knew I was keeping something from her or plotting something villainous.

"For bringing me right to the next point I wanted to make. I have something I'd like you to think about." I got up from the stool and paced away from the desk and my father's questioning eyes, halfway across the cozy chamber, and then back. "It's more dicey than my earlier question."

"So I gathered from your trek across the carpet. Go on."

"It's about—" I couldn't easily ask, though I'd practiced the conversation in my head several times.

"Alex, you can ask me anything."

"I know. It's just hard, sometimes, to intrude in a person's private life. Even for me," I added, forcing a grin to my face that felt false.

"Is it about Anessa? No, then Kimmer?" My father studied my face, at a loss. "Your mother?" he asked softly, nodding when a flush betrayed me.

"Not directly," I said. "Not really. But it's about your mage talent."

Getting to his feet, Sernyn mimicked my pacing, and then came to stand before me, so that we were inches away. "Go on."

"I know you never use it, and why, though I've never told you I know the reason. You always assumed I linked it to my mother's death, didn't you?" Catching the surprise on his face as he nodded, I explained, "Anders told me about your friend when he was teaching me to use my own mage talent. Your fear was the same as mine, that you had nearly killed or seriously hurt a very dear friend."

Old sorrow filled his eyes. "You were stronger than me, Alex, and for that, I am glad. You found the courage and the strength to overcome your fears and do what needed to be done for Elena and, maybe even more importantly, for yourself." His smile was full with a father's pride, and then he shrugged. "But I have no reason to use the gift."

"Sure, you do."

My tone was so matter of fact it stopped his protest. "I do not understand. What reason do I have?"

"An adored and adoring imp who has shown amazing mage talent."

"And that precious child has a mother and father who can teach her. And if they fall short of the task," he argued quietly, "Emmy is surrounded by many loving family and friends who could step in. Besides—"

"Calm down." My turn to place a hand over his lips. "I'm not making any demands. I just think it would be wonderful if you and Emmy could share your magic."

Bowing his head, so that it rested against mine, my father whispered, "I do not know if I can, Alex. I am sorry. But your mother—" His sigh held the weight of a lifetime of regret. "If I had overcome my childhood fear and used my talent before she gave birth to you, I might have saved her. Your mother might still be alive, and you would have your own memories of Emila, rather than someone else's."

"And if you use your mage talent now," I said just as softly, "my mother might very well approve."

Chapter Eighteen

"Alex, hurry! The ship is in sight, and I have just—" Gwynn flashed a bright grin, full of mischief and affection, at Maylen, who scowled, "won the wager."

"Only because you pretended you lost some coins on the ground," Maylen asserted with loud indignation, her cheeks rosy from racing into the Seaman's Berth.

Glancing from one young face to the other, and then to Chester, the amused owner of the inn, I demanded, "Didn't I warn you to keep these troublemakers out of your establishment? What will your clientele think?"

"Yes, you did, but these two, in particular, are your troublemakers," Chester defended himself as my husband and Corey strolled into the cool interior of the inn as though they didn't have a care in the world. "Your responsibility."

"Hmm. Well, in that case," —I pointed a finger at Gwynn, the quintessential troublemaker— "you are a disgrace to the Keltie name. And you," I scolded Maylen, who looked surprised when I turned that finger in her direction, "should know better than to believe anything, anything, that he says, particularly when there's a wager involved." Before the flustered young woman could defend herself, I sighed. "Why did you believe him, anyway?"

Framed by blonde hair pulled back into a neat braid, Maylen's thin face flushed a deeper scarlet than the shade her wild chase had brought to her skin. "The pest looked so distraught, Alex, and said the money belonged to Lady Barlow, who asked him, entrusted him, so he said, to purchase something for the duke." Her flush faded as she smiled, warning me. "You remember when we brought Gwynn back to Port Alain, wounded by the renegade mages, and he pretended to be angry with you for— What was it that he said to you?"

"For not bothering to stay behind and see whether he lived or died," I growled, remembering all too clearly the hurt and betrayal on his young face. And I'd fallen right into his trap. "All right, so I was gullible enough to fall for his act, too. I forgive you, though I should thank you for reminding me I never did kick his butt for that little incident." Edging closer to Gwynn, I snorted when he fled past Corey into the cloud-dimmed sunshine. "And you," —I prodded Corey's chest— "should never use that poor excuse for a man as a role model."

"Never, Alex. I promise."

"You lie as prettily as every other man around me." Ignoring my husband's wounded expression as he placed a hand over his heart, I headed for the door. "Let's go, children. Chester, thank you for breakfast. The sausages were perfect."

"My pleasure, Alex. And you be careful," he warned, catching my eye before I left the inn. "There are more troublemakers in Port Alain these days than even you can handle."

"That's why I have a little bit of help from my own troublemakers." I grinned, though Chester, who'd known me as a child, easily saw through my bravado. "Don't worry, old friend. I'll be careful."

With that assurance, I left the inn, my companions trailing behind. The weather had been unstable all morning, with clouds shifting across the sky, bringing the promise of sun and threat of rain. On the horizon, far off to the south, darker clouds were gathering. If the lords of the sea had any influence over the weather, I hoped the storm would hold off until morning and not interfere with our smuggling plans, as that little maneuver was worrisome enough for me to lose sleep. The streets were crowded with vendors selling sausage rolls, fresh muffins of cranberry and walnut and summer berries, bunches of flowers whose names I'd never learn to remember, wooden carvings, crafted jewelry, tunics of wool and cotton and silk, rugs and oil lamps, everything one could possibly want. The duke had declared the day a holiday, and the local merchants were delighted to set up their wares, though more than one glanced with anxiety at the sky.

Down at the harbor, several ships from Meravan had sailed into port earlier in the week, and the crews were lined up, idle, watching the sleek arrival of the Stoutheart, no doubt wondering about the competition the fledgling trade might bring. By the time we'd made our way through the crowds, the Stoutheart had neared land. Her crew, minus Kimmer, were bringing her dockside between two three-masted Meravan ships.

A lane, kept open by Port Alain troops, led from the main street to the dock. As we waited for the arrival of the duke's carriage from the Hill, I scanned the festive crowd, and noticed, interspersed here and there, a number of my father's scouts. At the end of the open lane, at the juncture where it met the main road, Seamage Neal Brandt waited, his copper mage pendant blazing beneath the occasional ray of sun that fought its way through the overcast sky. Beside him were arrayed his complement of mages, waiting with dutiful expressions to match their leader. Though Brandt's face was set in a pleasant half-smile, his eyes roamed the crowd without stopping, and came to rest on mine. Nodding with a smile that brought a shiver to my spine, he regarded my companions with interest before turning his attention back to the bustling activity aboard the Stoutheart.

Rosanna had chosen to remain at the manor with Khrista and Kerrie, overseeing preparations for the formal dinner she was hosting that evening. Though Jules's twin boys would accompany their parents to greet the ship, Anders and I decided to leave Emmy, along with Linsey, safe in the care of Sernyn and Anessa. With too many strangers in town, and Seamage Brandt shooting a malicious eye my way now and again, I wanted the girls out of sight and temptation.

The crew of the Stoutheart scurried to obey the captain's barked orders, securing the ship in her assigned berth. On deck, out of the captain's way, Westin Harlowe and Derek Frontish watched the organized chaos, as well as the crowd. Anders and I elbowed our way through the throng of curious folk until we reached the Port Alain trooper nearest the dock, who, on recognizing us, allowed us to pass through. I spied Maylen, Gwynn, and Corey, a heartbeat before they melted into the crowd.

By the time the gangplank hit the creaking dock, the clatter of hooves on the cobblestones was clear and strong, approaching along the main port road, rounding the corner just beyond Seamage Brandt. Shiny and polished for the occasion, Jules's carriage came to a smooth halt beside the seamage and his entourage at the beginning of the open lane. With the assistance of his coachman, who opened the door, Jules stepped onto the cobblestones and smiled a greeting at the gathered mages from the local council. Jules offered a hand to Lauryn, who stepped from the carriage, followed by the twins. I turned and watched Derek Frontish, as he stood waiting at the foot of the gangplank, Westin beside him, for the duke's party to arrive. I knew the very moment Elena and Jackson emerged from the carriage because all color drained from the elder's face.

When Anders pinched my backside, I hissed, "Stop that," thinking, of course, that my frivolous husband was trying to smear my reputation with the people of Port Alain.

"Did you see?"

Apparently, it was his way of sending me a message. "Yes. Come on." Elbowing Anders, I nodded to the new arrivals as they strolled down the open lane, greeting some of the folk along the way. I sent

Jackson a sympathetic smile of encouragement and joined the little procession that halted at the foot of the gangplank.

"Welcome to Port Alain, Elder Frontish." Elena smiled with gracious warmth, taking immediate control of the situation, as planned, even though the harbor was the central part of Jules's domain. "We thought you'd never arrive. And, truly, we were worried about the threatening weather."

"Your majesty." Bowing low, the elder forced a smile to his face. "We are honored you would leave your onerous duties in Ardenna and travel all this way to greet us on our maiden voyage to Tuldamoran. I trust there has been no trouble for your heir, whom we were expecting in your stead."

"Brendan was needed elsewhere," Elena reassured the Spreebridge man. "He was very disappointed" —blue eyes danced with mischief, and I had the distinct impression my friend was enjoying herself— "when I admitted that I preferred to welcome you myself. He grumbled for days about the privileges of rank and overbearing sisters. But I won the argument and banished him off to do my bidding."

"Well, then, we are truly honored by your presence, as by the gracious welcome Duke and Lady Barlow have bestowed on us. Mage Protector, Crownmage," he greeted us with another forced smile, and turned his attention to the boys before either Anders or I could say a word. "Your sons, my lord?"

"Indeed. Carey, here, is the most likely to get into a scrape, as their schoolmistress knows all too well, but for the calming influence of Hunter, his twin." Jules laughed with genuine affection at his sons, who made their polite bows, though Carey shot his father an evil look for that comment, followed by a sly grin in my direction.

"They are handsome young men, and evidence the good looks and honorable character of both their parents." Derek gestured to the captain, as though to invite us aboard, determined, I thought, to ignore Westin Harlowe's presence. However, the royal minx wouldn't let him so easily off the fishhook.

"And your companion, Elder Frontish?" Although Elena's query was polite, her tone made it clear she wouldn't be deterred. "Your pardon, but we haven't yet been introduced."

"No fear, your majesty. He is very well known to me," Jackson cut in with a warm smile for his mentor. "Elena, this is Westin Harlowe, the gentleman I have spoken so much about with such praise and gratitude."

"Ah, of course. What a wonderful surprise." Elena beamed at the man, who looked much like a mouse about to be devoured by a hungry cat. "Any fond friend of Jackson is welcome here, Elder Harlowe." Acknowledging his uneasy gratitude, she turned back to Derek. "We'll transfer your baggage to the manor so you can rest awhile before the affair tonight."

As Elena turned to give the command to the nearest trooper, Derek Frontish swiftly intervened. "My apologies, your majesty, but there is no need. We will stay aboard the Stoutheart. We would not intrude on the privacy of the duke and his family."

"Oh, but you don't understand." Elena leaned close to the two men as though to whisper a secret, which was laughable, since any of the townsfolk lucky enough to be standing this close could hear every word. "If Jules doesn't bring you and your baggage up to the manor, Lady Barlow, the senior Lady Barlow, that is, will be livid. The duke is not very fond of getting into trouble with his formidable mother. And I can assure you" —she smiled at the Spreebridge elder— "that I, as well as my Mage Protector, can attest to that fact, having been under that woman's strict thumb for many years as a child. I may be queen of

Tuldamoran, but the senior Lady Barlow is queen of the manor on the Hill."

"Without a doubt," Lauryn said, blue eyes smiling at the bewildered foreign gentlemen. "And I, for one, my lords, would never think to depose that particular queen."

Without a doubt, my friends were all mad. I bit my lip to keep from scolding Lauryn and Elena as they improvised this little melodrama right before my disbelieving eyes.

"I beg your pardon, my lord and my lady," —Derek Frontish bowed so low I thought his aristocratic nose would hit the ground— "but we will dine at the manor tonight, which I hope will placate your mother, as well as please you. But, truly, we cannot take the risk of staying too long away from Stoutheart. We have too much work to do these next few days, and we would be remiss were we to leave it unattended." He smiled at the man, listening above us. "Not that I have any doubts of the captain's abilities, but we have placed great store on the success of this first trade endeavor between our nations."

Elena sighed, bit her lip as though in grave mental debate, and turned to Jules and Lauryn, who shrugged, leaving the decision to their queen. "Very well, gentlemen, I won't force you to leave the ship, though I daresay, the accommodations on the Hill are much finer than aboard the Stoutheart. No offense intended, captain." She smiled to the man, who waved away her concern. "However, I will leave you to your own defense in the matter of the senior Lady Barlow." She laughed then, as though trying to convince them that it was a jest all along. "Now, shall we come aboard and have a tour of this graceful ship? I wish" —she winked at Derek, who hadn't a clue how to handle her— "to see the quality of the fine accommodations you are both so reluctant to leave behind."

Tongue-tied, Derek offered Elena his arm and led her up the gangplank, the rest of us following along like stupid sheep. The captain brought us fore and aft, onto the bridge, explaining particulars about the ship's design, while Elena listened intently and graced every crewman with her brightest smile. When the captain led her to the snug passenger accommodations, she merely lifted an eyebrow in Derek's direction. At least the man had the decency to blush.

"May we go farther below the passenger deck?" Elena inquired, all innocence. "Though I have spent my summers sailing on these waters here in Port Alain with the duke and his family, I have never been on a commercial trading ship. I would love to see how one manages to store provisions for the crew, all those extra masts and sails, living space for everyone aboard— And all that before the addition of cargo even comes under consideration. I must confess," —she smiled to the captain— "my own rooms in Ardenna are overcrowded with my things. If I can learn a lesson in neatness and efficiency, I will be indebted to you, as will my maid."

Either narrow-minded, conservative Spreebridge men were unaccustomed to the likes of Elena, or it was simply this group who hadn't the slightest idea of what Elena was about. She twirled them around her slender finger like strips of silk. Before I could say "royal witch," Elena had us all trailing along behind her, down to the lowest deck of the ship. Thank the lords of the sea, I'd grown up in Port Alain and was accustomed to the narrow, treacherous stairs between decks. There was barely room for the crates to pass when we made the switch later that night, but we'd have to make do. Judging our location beneath the captain's quarters, I spied the ten crates of feyweed, marked no different than any other except they were kept apart. But there were markings that indicated their origin in Spreebridge, and those needed to be reproduced on our own crates that were already filled with sand.

Elena took her time looking around, shaking her head in amazement at the hammocks that provided sleeping quarters for the crew, attached here and there wherever open space was available. "I would never make a sailor, I fear."

"Then it's a good thing you were born a Dunneal in Ardenna" — Jackson laughed, taking her hand and raising it to his lips— "and, therefore, royal."

"Have I just been insulted, ambassador?"

"Of course not." Jackson winked at me in full view of the two elders. "Well, my love, I think you've taken enough of the captain's time. Shall we leave the gentleman to his duties?"

"Of course, forgive me. But I did learn much. Though not enough" —she laughed gaily in the direction of the Spreebridge elders— "to offer a better trade deal than what we've already negotiated. Thank you, gentlemen, all. And now— Ah, this wonderful tour has driven the thought from my head about something you said earlier, Elder Frontish." When he waited for her to go on, and hopefully leave his ship, Elena asked, "Would it be to your benefit for the duke to post guards around the Stoutheart to protect your cargo? Though our folk here in Port Alain are very well bred, we do occasionally find greedy fingers."

"No need, your majesty," Derek hastened to say, as anticipated, "though we do very much appreciate the duke's generosity. Our crew has been told to keep watch, so never fear. We, too, have greedy fingers in Derbarry." Dismissing the topic, Derek led our party up the narrow steps to the main deck, where I breathed a lungful of fresh air beneath the still overcast sky.

Before disembarking, Elena stopped at the head of the gangplank. "One more thing, Elder Frontish. Could I have a word in private?"

"Of course," he said, flashing a swift look at Westin before joining Elena at the rail, away from eavesdroppers.

"Alex? You, too." When I obeyed, Elena's expression lost all gaiety and became grave. "Elder Frontish, on behalf of my Mage Protector, I wish to ask, and greatly hope to hear good news, whether there has been an antidote found for feyweed. I confess, and beg you to keep this admission private, but I am lost without her magic."

The elder's expression was somber, but the glint in his eyes betrayed the depth of his true feeling. "I am grieved to say that I cannot offer good news. I have asked my colleagues in Spreebridge, but no one can tell me anything more than that rumor and myth say there is a cure. Still, no one can give me solid proof that it exists." The serious expression turned sly. "But, I wonder, your majesty, why you have asked me on behalf of your Mage Protector and not Jackson Tunney?"

"You know of his trouble?" Raising a hand to her lips, Elena pretended horror, turning her back so that Jackson couldn't see her face.

"His trouble, and loss of magic, so like the Mage Protector's," he said, bowing his head to me, "is common news in Derbarry, your majesty."

Which meant that Westin, a man whom Jackson trusted and admired, told Derek, because I doubted Kimmer would offer harmful knowledge to a man she considered an adversary.

"What else," Elena asked sharply, "is common knowledge in Derbarry?"

Taking careful note of her speed to anger, the elder whispered, "That your majesty should be wary of her lover."

"How dare you—" I stopped my immediate protest, lowering my voice, genuinely stunned at the blatant accusation. I had, after all, expected more subtlety. "What are you saying?" I hissed, knowing that although part of my anger was feigned, a large part was genuine.

Elena placed a restraining hand on my arm. "We are in public, Mage Protector." She used my title to enforce her authority, but her eyes were locked on the foreigner's face. "Perhaps Elder Frontish can explain his words better."

"I am sorry to say, your majesty, Jackson was a rogue mage in Spreebridge before ever coming to Tuldamoran. His eye is set on one thing only, your throne, and—"

"If that's true—"

"Let him speak, Alex," Elena said, edging closer to me. "Let our guest say what I expect he will say."

Elder Frontish smiled as though Elena were a star pupil. "Your majesty is wise indeed. To answer the Mage Protector's query, my words are simply this—If it is true, then why has Jackson not pressed you for marriage? I can assure you, his reluctance is no more than an act. The word in Spreebridge" —he looked with apology at Elena— "is that he is playing you for a fool. Westin took Jackson under his wing as a protégé. He dare not reveal his vast disappointment, not yet. Jackson seeks to undermine your throne, but he is biding his time, knowing how cautious you would be after your hurtful betrayal by Erich Harwoode. Though he may be treacherous, your majesty, Jackson is no fool."

I was incensed, and didn't need to play act. "This news is how you greet the queen of Tuldamoran? With poisonous words and—"

"Alex." Elena's smile was full of sorrow as she met my gaze. If I didn't know better, I would have believed her emotion was true. "Elder Frontish brings warning of something I have suspected for some time. And you, my fierce and devoted Mage Protector, missed the signs. I don't blame you. I blame the feyweed that poisoned your mage talent and took your mind away from matters around you, locking you inside the prison of your own sorrow. So you see, Elder Frontish," Elena entreated the man, "why I am desperate for an antidote. I am vulnerable, as is my crown. But not" —she slid a glance at Jackson, who was chatting with Westin— "without resources. My thanks, Elder Frontish. I am in your debt, and I promise you, that debt shall be repaid."

* * * *

"Of all the things he might have said," I growled, too busy pacing the length and breadth of the parlor to pay attention to my friends' silent exchange, "that was certainly not it."

"I must thank you for defending me." Jackson smiled, trying to deflect my still-hot anger at the elder. "I understand you were fierce."

"I could have strangled him."

"That was clear. Thank you for superb playacting, Alex, in light of the fact Derek tossed us that new little element of surprise. If you'll hold still for just a moment, I might be able to hand you a glass of wine." Elena grinned as I stopped in my tracks and turned around, grabbing the glass from her outstretched hand. "In fact, I think we all did rather well. Though I'm sorry about Westin." She went to Jackson's side and caressed his cheek. "Suspicion is one thing, knowledge a very different matter, as I've come to know firsthand. Alex, do we still intend to switch the crates tonight?"

"I don't see why not. The sooner we get our hands on the feyweed, the safer I'll feel." I sipped the wine, staring out the window, where my father was tossing a ball with Emmy and Linsey in the garden.

"Under the circumstances, now Derek has accused Jackson of betrayal, would it help if I pretend to have an argument with him? It would allow Jackson to give you a hand tonight and explain his absence at the dinner," she explained when I turned back to face her.

"Sure. In fact, it would explain my absence, too."

"How?"

"Well, since I don't believe a word Elder Frontish said, I want to keep an eye on Jackson myself. Right?"

"Excellent, yes." Elena brushed a strand of hair from her eyes that now held a bright glimmer of impish plotting. "Anders will be more agreeable than you, anyway."

"Not fair. He gets all the easy jobs."

"That's because" —Elena shrugged— "Anders isn't my Mage Protector."

Chapter Nineteen

With one last lingering look at the glowing lamplight within the manor on the Hill, I turned my back on the festivities and gathered Maylen, Gwynn, and Jackson in the darkening shadows. We headed down the path that cut through the forest past my cottage, walking in companionable silence, until we reached the outskirts of Port Alain. Maylen ducked into the bushes and returned a few moments later with a handful of my father's scouts, woven rope coiled around their shoulders beneath their dark cloaks. Still silent, we split into pairs, Gwynn with me, and Maylen with Jackson, dividing our magic. Reaching the Seaman's Berth, Jackson and Maylen went inside.

Watching from a short distance away beside the seawall, I waited with my brother until Maylen signaled us from the roof of the building, where the two had a clear view of the Stoutheart, rocking in its berth with a soothing motion. The young woman's job was to protect Jackson while he wielded his magic, as Gwynn would protect me, should either of us be discovered. I spied Corey a block away, with his well-chosen whores paid in advance from the queen's treasury, some of them carrying a bonus of ale and wine with which to entertain the sailors and keep their senses fully occupied. When the small group passed within earshot of our position, I was barely able to keep a straight face when my pest of a brother nudged me at a choice comment that had to have poor Corey's skin flaming.

"Stop that."

"I just wished to be sure you heard it," Gwynn whispered in my ear, "so that you can tattle to his mother."

"I'm going to tattle to your mother if you don't behave."

We watched in silence as they approached the ship. Breaking away from the group, a bosomy blonde, whose chest was not securely contained within her half-laced tunic, glanced up at the wide-eyed sailor on watch. "Welcome to Port Alain, my handsome lad. Care to come down and join us for a little fun and excitement? A special gift from your hosts here in town."

"Who coached her?" I murmured to Gwynn. "Do whores really talk like that? About fun and excitement?"

"I would not know." Gwynn's handsome face was neutral, though he couldn't resist allowing a tiny smile to escape. "Though Corey might."

"I cannot leave my post," the sailor answered, regret evident on his weathered face. "But—" He glanced over his shoulder as a fellow crewman came by and whispered in his ear. "As our captain and his honored passengers are off visiting with the nobility up at the manor for a few hours, if you and your lady friends would care to come aboard—"

"I thought you'd never ask." The blonde smiled, leading her girls briskly up the gangplank as though she were an experienced seaman, and guided the sailors aft, away from the bridge. Once they'd all boarded, Corey disappeared into the shadows to wait for us.

"Men," I pronounced, keeping my voice low, knowing how it carried near water, "are so simple and easily led."

"And women are not?" Gwynn whispered back. "Look how Maylen believed me about the coins I lost."

"She's in love with you, though I don't see why." I elbowed him in the ribs. "But this— I'm not talking about love. I'm talking about lust. And besides, wait until Father hears about your deception. You didn't win that wager fairly."

"Alex, please. That man scolds me like a child, even when I am innocent."

"You're never innocent. Hush—" I raised my hand to stop our banter and listen to the festivities on board and watch the unfolding drama. "Those women are good, I must say. Look at them, leading the sailors all aft like stupid sheep. Ah, there. The blonde just waved to Corey that she has things under control. That's our signal."

Gwynn dogged my muffled footsteps as we approached the Stoutheart, a light fog drifting along with us, compliments of Jackson, who changed the moist air to cloud. As my father's scouts emerged from their hiding places, Corey stepped into view. I craned my neck upward to be sure Jackson had created the light barrier on board the ship, transforming air to a thin layer of earth, hidden in the fog, blocking the view of the bridge from where the sailors were carrying on with their visitors.

Gwynn tossed a padded hook over the side of the ship and swung aboard like a monkey, motioning me to follow, while Corey remained on the wharf as lookout. All the girls had to do was keep the men entertained, drunk, and away from the bridge area, so that we could smuggle the crates of feyweed out from below and transfer the crates of sand waiting in Chester's storeroom a block away.

One by one the scouts slipped aboard, silent as the proverbial grave, putting me to shame. Gwynn went below deck first, an argument I'd lost earlier when he pointed out that if he was there to protect me, what good would it do if there were sailors below waiting to clobber me over the head, or worse. When my brother waved me down the narrow steps, signaling that it was safe, his face wore a peculiar expression. I took the steps with care and stopped abruptly on the bottom, a blistering curse on my lips.

The ten crates of feyweed were gone.

"How?" Gwynn whispered, as I signaled to the scouts to wait.

"I don't know." Scanning the cargo hold, I noted everything in its place as I'd seen earlier, all but the feyweed. "Either they know our plan, though I've no idea how that would have happened," I whispered back, "or they didn't want to take a chance keeping the feyweed crates on board."

"But our scouts kept watch on the ship all day. That is not to say that they are perfect," my brother added, "but—"

"It's not their fault." Furious, and resigned to failure, I pointed to a barely visible trap door cut into the port side. "They snuck the crates out right under our noses, with the Meravan ships blocking our view." I turned to the patient scout behind me, who looked as chagrined as Gwynn. "Can your people watch the ship tonight and tomorrow? See if anyone comes or goes?"

"Of course, Mage Protector. I am sorry that—"

All too familiar with misplaced guilt, I placed a hand on his arm. "It's not your fault. Besides, I have every intention of catching them at their game. I refuse to let that arrogant man best me."

* * * *

Keeping in character with our little charade, I didn't bother to change into formal attire to attend the dinner because I had no intention of staying. My sudden appearance at the door to the manor's formal, brightly lit dining room, dressed in dark tunic and trousers, my dusty cloak still clasped at the throat, and the dual pendants of office clearly visible on my chest, stopped the pre-dinner conversation for a brief moment. Across the room, Rosanna, deep in conversation with the captain of the Stoutheart and Jules, glanced up and frowned, making me wonder whether she guessed my tight-lipped expression was genuine. Without signaling to her, I scanned the crowded room, caught Elena's alert eye, and bade her, silently, to leave off her discussion with Seamage Brandt, of all people, and follow me. Waiting just outside the chamber, I remained visible, on purpose, to the residents of the manor, merchants, community leaders, the Port Alain Mage Council, and, most important, our Spreebridge visitors.

"You're back far too soon, Mage Protector," Elena murmured, smoothing the silk of her royal blue gown as she studied the restrained emotion on my face. "You're angry, and I have a feeling that the fury is real instead of the fake emotion we planned to prove that yet another lover has indeed betrayed me."

Cautious, I covered my words with a feigned cough. "The crates are gone."

"Gone? How? Where?" Blue eyes widened as her cheeks lost their rosy color. "Lords of the sea, Alex—"

"Careful," I warned, turning my face away from the door. "Here comes our guest of honor. Look furious, your majesty. That's right," I said, not needing to encourage my friend as she considered the implications of our discovery.

"Mage Protector? Your majesty?" Elder Frontish interrupted our little private conversation, as we'd hoped he would, though not under these circumstances. "Has something happened? Is there trouble?"

"Trouble?" I hissed, not bothering to hide my anger from the guests who wandered near enough to hear without seeming to listen, including Seamage Brandt. When I glanced up, staring at the mage until he felt my eyes on his back, I met his gaze with a chilly expression. If I'd had my way, he wouldn't have been on the invitation list, but Rosanna's common sense had prevailed. You couldn't host a dinner party in Port Alain without inviting the head of the local Mage Council, along with his cronies. Turning back to Frontish, I snapped an answer, taking the man by surprise. "I've spent the past few hours tailing Jackson Tunney, and, for the lords' sake, I've still no idea what he's up to."

"No good, I fear."

"You don't know that for sure," I made a fair attempt to defend Jackson, turning to Elena, as I added, "You don't. You suspect him, but you have no proof. Queen or not, what kind of justice is that? What message does that send to your subjects? You've thrown Jackson aside and— Oh, what's the use?"

While I shook my head in disgust, Derek frowned with sympathy in Elena's direction, placing his hand on her silk sleeve. "I am so very sorry, your majesty. I know the Mage Protector has doubts, for which I cannot blame her. If Jackson's treachery is true, then Mage Keltie feels she has failed you." When I started to protest, wanting instead to smash my fist in his face, he said with false compassion, "No blame to you, Mage Protector. Westin always thought highly of the young man, though, in his heart, feared the worst. If there is anything I can do to help you in this dire time, your majesty—"

"No, thank you." I cut off Elena's polite reply. "You've done quite enough."

"Alex—" Elena grabbed my cloak as I turned to leave, her expression a believable mixture of irritation and worry. "I don't have proof but what's in my heart. It's not your fault. How could you have known about Jackson's treachery?"

"It's my job, isn't it? And maybe Elder Frontish is right, though I don't have to like it. I failed to protect you. I—" My cloak flowing with a dramatic flourish around my knees, I spun on my heel, almost barreling into my husband, who'd edged near our group. Waving Anders away, I bounded for the main stairway and left him with Elena to play out the drama. I'd just reached the private parlor where Jackson hid with Kimmer while I playacted below, when my father followed me out of the dining room and caught up to me on the upper floor.

"Superb acting, Alex," he complimented my performance, though when I turned to face him, his careful appraisal of my mood changed his mind. "But you have come back too early. Something has gone wrong."

"That's an understatement." Pulling him into the parlor, I greeted the others before exploding in frustration, "The crates were missing from the ship." I saw his immediate response and squashed it. "Your scouts are not at fault. The Stoutheart has a trap door on the port side that enabled them to remove the crates under cover of the Meravan ships in broad daylight. My guess is that they rowed a far distance before unloading the crates on land and hiding them somewhere close by, though it makes me wonder if anyone along their route, land or sea, saw anything unusual. But how do we ask the local populace" —I flung my cloak over a chair in disgust— "without arousing suspicion?"

"Chester can help," my father offered, pouring a glass of Marain Valley wine from the bottle on the table and handing it to me.

"Thanks, yes. We've told him to be on the lookout. Maylen and Gwynn are down at the Seaman's Berth now with Corey." Turning to Kimmer, I gave the Spreebridge woman a tired smile. "He played his part well. If the crates had been there, it would have been easy."

"Yes, but we are back to the beginning," she said quietly. "All that information, all that planning, wasted. I am sorry, Alex."

"Don't be." Weary, I shut my eyes and savored a sip of wine. "We're on my turf now."

Chapter Twenty

Befuddled, I sat on a tree stump behind the cottage, beside the little pond that entertained a family of ducks from time to time, watching Maylen teach Emmy and Linsey how to plait daisies, or some other weed, into a crown. Weary from lack of sleep after the night's disappointing failure, I'd opted to stay with Maylen when she volunteered to watch the girls, while the rest of the manor's residents joined the townsfolk in the festivities down at the harbor. I didn't want the children in town, not until the danger was past.

Besides, I needed space and time to think.

If the Spreebridge elders had planned to unload the feyweed crates through the trap door, it implied either knowledge of the town or a local connection to someone with that knowledge. They needed a hiding place, which meant the feyweed could be anywhere, without a guarantee that it had been brought to land. For all I knew, it was still floating somewhere in Shad's Bay. It was easy enough to camouflage the crates, transport them on a small boat back upriver, or further along the east coast of Tuldamoran. Not knowing where the feyweed was stashed, not knowing when they planned to disperse it, or how, left a knot in my gut that grew larger as the day wore on, despite the existence of an antidote. The harsh memory of the absence of magic was a nightmare that still haunted my dreams.

"This flower is too big." Emmy held up the bright yellow blossom for Maylen to inspect. "Isn't it?"

"Yes," Linsey answered before Maylen drew breath to answer. The scout met my gaze over their heads and smiled, as Linsey added, "Throw it away and get another, Emmy. Just throw it away." And without apparent effort, the flower vanished from Emmy's hand, prompting my daughter to gape in shock, while Linsey's eyes glittered with tears at the unexpected appearance of her fledgling magic.

I was on my feet and by their side in a heartbeat, crouching in front of Khrista's little girl. "Linsey, sweetling, hush. It's all right."

"Mama?" Emmy tapped my arm, her voice hushed. "Did Linsey do magic?" When I nodded, my daughter knelt beside her friend who'd climbed into my lap. "It's all right, Linsey, Mama and Papa do magic, too. So does Uncle Gwynn. And so does your mama."

"And so will you," I hugged Emmy close with my free arm, kissing the top of her curls as tears threatened my own face.

"I know, Mama."

"Such an endearing scene, Mage Keltie." The cold familiar voice of Seamage Brandt startled me as he stepped from the cover of the trees beyond the cottage, eyes locked on Linsey's tearful face. "I'd heard rumors about that child's questionable parentage."

No one had ever uttered a word about Linsey's father being a renegade mage. How had he known? Was there a link, after all, between Derek Frontish and the imprisoned renegade who'd assaulted Khrista? And was there, then, a link between Frontish and Seamage Brandt? Fighting the urge to overreact, I got to my feet, careful to shove the girls behind Maylen, who'd drawn a dagger and knew all too well how to wield the sharp weapon.

"For shame. Is that how you teach your children? Be rude to their elders, especially one in authority?" Seamage Brandt stepped closer, coming near the tree stump where I'd been sitting only moments earlier. "Be hostile? There's no need for that dagger, Mistress Stockrie."

"When the elder comes uninvited and unwelcome," I snarled, eying his every move, "yes. That is precisely how I teach my children to behave."

"Pity you took after your mother. She was no less rude than you. A waste, truly." An odd expression flashed in the older man's eyes, and I could hardly believe his next words. "If she had been more hospitable, we might have been friends. I was destined to be her teacher, and she my student."

"Over her dead body, I imagine."

"Possibly over yours, too, one day."

When Maylen stepped around me at his threat, I held her back with my eyes. "He's an impotent and unimportant old man, Maylen. Don't waste your time on him."

"Impotent?" The seamage bristled with insult. "How is this for impotent, Mage Keltie?" One hand gestured to the small pond, raising the shallow water to the height of a man-high wave that frightened the children, now clinging to Maylen's legs and hampering her movement, though Emmy appeared to be reaching for Linsey to lead her into the safety of the trees. "That is power, Mage Keltie, and you no longer possess that talent or any other."

"That's crude showmanship," I spat back, refusing to respond to his latter comment about my own impotence, though he was waiting, the wall of water held in check.

Losing patience, Brandt smiled with open malice. "Ah. You're so jealous. And because of your own impotence, I can take the children from you without fear," he said, unaware Emmy had succeeded in getting Linsey's attention and pulling her slowly toward the dense forest. "You have no magic, and mine can wash your Glynnswood bodyguard to the sea before you could lift a finger to cry for help." The seamage lifted a hand, prompting a half dozen dagger-wielding thugs to emerge from the cover of the trees inches from the now-terrified children. They surrounded us, easily explaining why the seamage had been so careless of the children's movements. "Drop the Gwynnswood dagger."

"Maylen," I warned, my voice low, breathing a sigh of relief when she dropped her weapon to the ground in barely restrained fury. Coaxing fire and ice to cool warmth, I thanked the lords of the sea for Kimmer's antidote. Focusing on the ground, I swiftly transformed the air, which surrounded each filthy brigand, to a shoulder-high ring of flame, imprisoning them. Seamage Brandt, caught off guard by the showmanship of my supposedly lost magic, judging from the unsteadiness of his own water wall, I saved for last. That wall became a tempest to match the one that had hurt Anders all those years ago when my magic was raw and uncontrolled. With ease, the wind picked his heavy body from the ground and slammed him into the wall of the cottage, holding him upright.

"Believed the rumors, did you, Seamage Brandt, about my loss? You shouldn't trust everything you hear." When the wind's force knocked him unconscious, I kept careful watch on the firewalls I'd built to keep the terrified prisoners in check. "Maylen, take the children and find Jules or Anders in town."

"Alex—" Obviously torn between getting help, feeling useless, and abandoning me, Maylen didn't budge.

"I'm fine. Now go. Hurry."

Grabbing the girls by the hand, Maylen fled down the path toward Port Alain. Relieved they would soon be safe, I removed my belt and used it to tie the seamage's hands behind his back, and then used his belt on his ankles. By the time I'd secured him, the seamage regained consciousness, dark eyes on fire with bitterness and loathing.

"It's your grandmother's fault," he snarled.

Surprised, I stood back and stared at him. "What are you talking about?"

"Old history that might have changed everything. If your grandmother had only returned my affection, things would've been different." Beyond the anger, to my great surprise, lay genuine emotion.

"You loved her?"

"Yes, Alex, I loved your grandmother, but she scorned me. I could have given her the world and prestige, but she wanted none of it and married your grandfather. And then one day, when your mother exhibited mage talent and was old enough to apprentice with a tutor, your grandmother brought Emila to the Mage Council Hall." His features hardened at the memory. "When I threw your mother out of the school for willful behavior, your grandmother insulted me and defended her child, refusing to even send the girl back to apologize. Your grandmother's rejection of the Mage Council prompted your mother to become a renegade, and you," he spat at my feet, "how it galls me you have risen so high in the queen's favor with your perverted magic. You don't deserve the honor or the magic. You don't deserve to live."

My blood chilled at his hateful words, calling to mind the mission of the Spreebridge elders in their use of feyweed. Was Brandt their connection? Had Westin traveled to Port Alain to meet with Brandt, while Derek stayed in Ardenna to meet with the Crown Council of Mages? The thought had never occurred to me, though maybe it should have.

"You're placing the blame for your treachery in trying to steal my daughter on my grandmother's long-ago rejection of your love?" I asked, unable to believe what I was hearing. "Are you mad?"

"Emmy should have been my great-granddaughter, as you should have been my granddaughter," he said with such heartfelt conviction that I turned my back, unable to look at the confused emotions on his face.

"Over my dead body, Seamage Brandt."

"As I said before— Or weren't you listening? It may come to that. Watch your back, Mage Protector."

"Why?" Suddenly, I spun on my heel and knelt beside the seamage, safely out of reach. "Do you have friends in high places who can do me harm?"

"If I did," —he laughed— "surely you don't think I'd tell you."

"You—"

"Alex—Are you all right?" Jules's shout of concern interrupted my question, as the duke led a small band of troopers on horseback along the forest path, their faces incredulous at the sight of the firewalls that greeted them.

Anders and Elena had come along, too, though they were riding on horseback from the direction of the manor, which I didn't understand. I doused the flames with water to allow the Port Alain guard to take charge of my prisoners.

"I'm fine." Rubbing my eyes, I leaned against Anders when he dismounted and came to stand beside me. Still reeling from the seamage's curious words about my grandmother, I didn't know what to think. "Just caught off guard, for which I feel responsible."

"Looks like you caught him off guard." Anders nudged the seamage with his boot. "Never underestimate my wife. After all these years, you should know that by now."

"He'll never underestimate any of us, not anymore." Elena's voice was harsh as she pulled a small vial from the pocket of her violet tunic. "I can guarantee that. Trust me."

"Hold on," I cried, realizing her intention and why she'd come along the path from the Hill. When Maylen found them, Elena and Anders must have taken the main road up from the harbor, stopping at the manor first. Horrified Elena had kept a supply of feyweed on hand, I stepped in her path, blocking her view of the seamage. "What do you think you're doing?"

"Dispensing justice, as I see fit," she said softly, sliding a glance at Anders, both of them surprised, I thought, by my attitude. "Seamage Brandt violated the ethics of his profession and endangered your daughter and Khrista's child, attempting to kidnap them for his own foul use, not to mention threatening you and Maylen. I'm punishing him, Alex, as he deserves."

"Not with—" Bad enough I had nightmares of the poison, I couldn't say the word aloud. "You can't just go around punishing mages like that."

Elena started to say something, and then reconsidered. "All right. As Mage Protector of the throne of Tuldamoran, the punishment should rightfully be your responsibility." When she went to hand me the vial, I refused, placing my hands out of reach. My stomach knotted with tension as her expression underwent a transformation from compassion to ice. "If you abdicate this responsibility, then step aside and allow me to finish what I came here to do."

"Elena—"

Blue eyes bored into mine, and I knew she would win, whatever the cost. "Five years earlier, when you hunted the renegade mages in Edgecliff, you allowed Jackson to punish those mages in this same manner. Though you didn't have the stomach to do it yourself back then either," she said with such icy contempt, I stared at my friend in bewildered hurt, "I was given the impression you agreed with his action. Was I misled?"

"Those mages were mad. They—"

"Not all of them. The women were mad. The man was not. And Seamage Brandt, with all his full powers of intelligence and logic, has broken the law with full knowledge. My law, which I swore to uphold.

Now, step aside, Mage Protector," Elena snapped, losing all patience with my argument, "and bear witness to what I do."

Heartbroken, I held Elena's chilly gaze for a long time, until I acknowledged defeat. I couldn't make her see why her action was wrong. That was clear in her eyes. Without a word or signal of my intent, I stepped aside. Yet, though she had the legitimate authority as queen of Tuldamoran to punish the seamage and command my presence, I made a difficult decision, refusing to cooperate, and knew I would bear the consequences of that disobedience. Without a glance at Anders or Jules, I disappeared into the safe harbor of my cottage, braced for what I knew would come.

And when it did, when Seamage Brandt uttered his anguished cry beneath my open window, I curled into a ball and wept.

* * * *

The door to the cottage opened and shut to reveal Elena, alone, without the support of my husband or Jules. She sank heavily into the cushions of the chair opposite me, though not before reaching down, to where I sat on the floor, leaning back against the other chair, my knees hugged close to my chest. Elena's finger touched my cheek and came away wet.

"I didn't expect you to take it so hard."

"Does it matter?"

Elena's long-suffering sigh spoke with more eloquence than any words could. She got to her feet once more and went into the pantry, unstoppered a bottle of Marain Valley wine and poured me a glass, shoving it into my reluctant hand. "I had to make an example of him."

"You sure did." Seeing the fire leap into her eyes, I raised a hand to stop her protest. "I know you did. I even understand why. But I don't have to like it or feel comfortable with it."

"Yes, you do, Mage Protector. Maybe you don't have to like it, but you have to accept it. Or are you frightened I might use feyweed against you?"

Lords of the sea, was that possibility at the base of my misgiving? I set aside the wine glass, untouched.

"Good," she snapped, "maybe you should be frightened. I prefer that my advisors not take me for granted. At the least, I require you to agree with me in public, not to question my decisions about anything, including the administration of feyweed." Before I could respond to Elena's demands, she perched on the edge of the chair, leaning closer to my face. "You yourself, only days ago, told me you didn't think it right that you should have the formula for feyweed or its antidote, that as a mage, you couldn't be trusted with decisions about its use. After today's pathetic little spectacle, Mage Protector," though Elena whispered, I felt her fury like a blast of searing flame, "I completely agree you can't be trusted regarding feyweed. However, that doesn't mean I can't be trusted about the use of the poison. It's my duty as queen to see justice is done, and I will not, I repeat, I will not suffer self-doubt in upholding my law, particularly in light of your flawed judgment."

"I never thought I'd see the day," I said, furious that my voice betrayed me by trembling, "that I'd look at you as a tyrant."

"Tyrant?" Her hand, wearing the Dunneal ring of sapphires and diamonds, curled into a fist, and I braced for a blow, but Elena controlled her rage, and turned it into a mocking laugh. "I'm not a tyrant, Alex. I'm a queen whose kingdom is under silent attack. I can't afford to look the slightest bit weak or unsupported. And when my appointed Mage

Protector questions my decisions in public, weak and unsupported is exactly how I appear."

Though my head understood her words, my heart couldn't accept them. I struggled to my feet in silence and stood over her chair. Slipping the leather thong from my neck, the copper and wood pendants side by side, I tossed the symbols of my office in her lap. When I walked out the door, Elena didn't even try to stop me.

By this time, the Port Alain troops had taken the prisoners away, including, thank the lords of the sea, Seamage Brandt. Even Jules was gone. In his place, speaking with Anders, was my brother Gwynn.

Easily reading the emotion on my face, Anders touched my damp cheek. "You all right?" he said softly.

I shook my head, not wanting to discuss what had happened either outside or inside the cottage. "Shouldn't you be with Maylen?" I asked Gwynn.

"She sent me to make sure you were all right. Alex—"

"Seamage Brandt said something," I swiftly cut into my brother's concern. "He spoke of my mage talent as a perversion. He also mentioned Linsey, implied he'd heard rumors of her parentage, which means," —I brushed strands of hair from my eyes as a cool wind blew through— "that he may have heard those rumors from Elder Frontish or Westin Harlowe."

"You believe Brandt is the Port Alain connection," Anders said, correctly reading my intent in sidestepping the issue of Elena Dunneal. "If so, the crates may be sitting in the Mage Council Hall."

"My very thoughts. I'll go with Gwynn to look."

"I'll go with your brother. Why don't you go up to the manor and stay with Emmy for a while," Anders suggested, compassion and unconditional love reflected in his seagray eyes. "After what happened here, she could use her mother's presence. And vice versa."

"At the moment," I said quietly, kissing his cheek, "you'd be the better influence. Tell her I love her, and I'll see her later." Anders didn't argue, for which I secretly blessed him, when I grabbed Gwynn's arm and led him down the forest path toward the harbor. "I know it's daylight, but everyone is likely to be in the streets indulging themselves," I told my brother. "I'll be your lookout while you practice your sneaky thieving skills."

"That sounds like an insult."

"It is."

"Fine, and the plan makes sense, but I need to know something." Brown eyes slid me a glance as we walked side by side. "Where is your pendant of office?" When I refused to answer, he persisted, "You were alone in the cottage with the queen. When you emerged, your cheeks were damp from crying, and the leather thong is no longer around your neck."

"Leave it," I said, angry when my brother skipped ahead to block my path. I grabbed his cloak and held on tight. "We have work to do, and I don't want to talk about it."

Reluctance was written all over his handsome face, but he let me be, for the moment. At the outskirts of Port Alain, we slipped through the narrow corridors behind the buildings until we came to the rear of the Mage Council Hall in the center of town. The building looked deserted, and I prayed it were true. Acting as lookout, I sent Gwynn inside, which was probably a bad idea. The moment I was alone, jumbled thoughts crowded my head.

Had I just surrendered my commitment to the queen? More important, would my friend ever forgive me?

Who was right? Who was wrong? Did it even matter?

Scaring the living breath from me, Gwynn appeared at my side and led me back down the alleyways to the rear door of the Seaman's Berth.

Signaling Chester's daughter, Gwynn ordered some ale and squeezed me into the end of the very crowded bar as all the tables were taken. Thanks to the festivities, it looked as though Chester, who waved from across the room, was making a small fortune. We soon had mugs of foaming ale in front of us, and Gwynn's smile was huge as he clinked my glass.

"I gather that's good news."

"Indeed, it is, Alex. In the basement," he whispered in my ear, "hidden under a tarp in the wine cellar. It might mean the seamage acted alone."

"Maybe." I took a sip of ale and then another, not realizing how thirsty I'd been. "When you get back up the Hill, tell Jules to question his prisoner about that. And tell Anders we have to move fast and switch the crates before news of the mage's capture travels to our foreign guests."

"Would it not be better," Gwynn asked, "if you spoke to them in person?"

"No. I—" Clapping my brother on the back, I drained the mug and tossed him some coins. "Tell Anders to meet me here at midnight, with whomever he needs to help us. Oh, and Gwynn, when he has a moment of peace and quiet" —I nodded at the busy innkeeper— "let Chester know what we're doing."

Before my brother could say anything more, I moved out of earshot and blended into the noisy crowd, with nowhere to go.

Chapter Twenty-One

"Spectacular sunset."

"I hadn't noticed."

"Then you must be blind, Alex."

Turning my head from the glorious sky, where clouds were lit from behind as the setting sun lowered inch by inch on the horizon, I shot Lauryn a lopsided smile. "How were you chosen to be the lucky one to come and slay the dragon?"

Blue eyes twinkled with undisguised mischief. "Your father suggested I might be the only one who could get within a safe distance. He, um, seemed to think everyone else ran the risk of getting a fist smashed into his or her lovely face."

Sighing, though I had to admit the old fox was right, I was suddenly aware of the cold hard stone of the seawall beneath my backside. How long had I been sitting there?

"Sernyn thought you might say that."

"You all think I'm wrong."

"First of all," Lauryn assumed her maternal voice, "it doesn't matter what any of us think, and that includes Elena," she added, meeting my gaze with a stubborn look. "You're the only one whose opinion and heart should matter to you."

"And second?"

"The household is split. Don't ask me to name names." She grinned, elbowing me until I almost fell off the wall. "I'm sworn to secrecy."

"Fool." I tucked my hands beneath my rear to add a bit of cushioning. "What's your opinion?" I asked because her opinion did matter to me, and always had.

"It's not important."

"It is to me," I said, suddenly serious. Craning my neck to see the manor in the distance atop the Hill, I added, "Whenever I find myself in a dilemma, you're the only one I can count on to be objective. Rosanna, though I love her dearly, isn't always objective and, in her defense, she can't be, but don't ever tell her I said that. Considering the arguments she and I have had in the past, you can see why."

Lauryn put her arm around my shoulder and hugged me close before letting go. "You want my honest opinion?" When I nodded, she admitted, "I'm divided, too, Alex. I can see both sides in this little wrangle. In the years Jules and I have been married, I've come to appreciate how challenging it is to rule peacefully and fairly, and how even more difficult it is when times are troubled. As monarch, Elena faces more complications and has the right to demand unconditional support. Hold on, Alex, before smashing my face," she said, half in jest, "let me finish." Smiling as she saw the angry fire in my eyes fade away, Lauryn continued with her long-winded explanation. "That doesn't mean, however, that a monarch should expect her advisors to mindlessly and blindly obey her commands."

"Only in public, so it looks like they are mindlessly and blindly obeying her every wish, Lauryn."

When I would have fled, Lauryn grabbed my cloak and held on tight. "Question her in private, Alex. That's all she's really asking. In the end, it's Elena's decision to make. She's the one who has to live with it."

"So I'm wrong."

Smiling at my pouting response, as she would if either of her twins stood arguing in front of her, Lauryn said, "You're both wrong. And you're both right. And you're both sulking like spoiled children. In fact, I've never seen your own daughter with such a pout on her pretty face." Lauryn's sunny smile turned sly. "By the way, you caught Elena off guard by throwing the pendants in her lap. In my humble opinion, she didn't come after you for the simple reason she was speechless. Every once in a while," —Lauryn beamed— "people, the rest of us included, need to be reminded you have a very strong mind of your own."

"You see why I depend on you."

Lauryn laughed and got to her feet, releasing my cloak as the sun finally disappeared. "Coming home for dinner? Or is that too much to ask?"

"Too much."

"I thought so. Oh, and Alex, Elena did say to tell you that she's going to keep Elders Frontish and Harlowe busy tonight." Lauryn's smile was impish. "She intends to go down to the Stoutheart and supply a guard of Port Alain troops, courtesy of the Crown. It seems she heard a, um, credible rumor someone is planning to rob precious cargo from the ship, you know, all those gems and ore they've brought south from the Keshtang mines."

"Is that," I drawled my question, "her way of apologizing?"

Lauryn's face underwent an exquisite transformation from amused mischief to bland neutrality in the blink of an eye. "Elena also said, um, if you chose to interpret her message in that manner, you're wrong. Her plan" —Lauryn cleared her throat with great delicacy— "is intended to keep those involved in tonight's dangerous activity safe from harm. Um, Alex," —she blinked once, then again— "is there any message for the queen?"

"Tell her that—" I bit back the crude reply which leaped to mind when Lauryn stifled a laugh. "Tell her majesty I'm quite certain my father's scouts are grateful for her extra precautions. And that" —I narrowed my eyes at Lauryn, defying her to laugh aloud— "if she chooses to interpret that as my way of apologizing, she's dead wrong since I'm not a scout."

"That's for sure. You're too noisy." Lauryn laughed aloud as she scampered out of reach and back up the Hill.

* * * *

Sitting comfortably in the back of the common room of the Seaman's Berth near the kitchen, I was biding my time while Chester encouraged the remaining stragglers to go home and sleep off their excess celebrating. Finally, when he'd sent his daughter off to bed, and the common room was blessedly silent, Chester joined me at the table, a mug of ale in his hand. Wiping his brow melodramatically, he grinned, downing half the mug. "What a day."

"Stop complaining. You made a queen's ransom in business."

"That I did. Even the queen's Mage Protector honored my establishment, though she dined alone. And all day long, my good friend." He downed the rest of the ale, and belched politely. "It's been on the tip of my tongue to ask why. Trouble at home?"

"Difference of opinion."

"With your husband?"

"With my queen."

"Ah. Oh, Alex, that's not good." Chester eyed me in speculation, but correctly guessed he'd get no more from me. "Your fellow conspirators should already be in the cellar. Shall we join them?"

"Sure." I followed the innkeeper like a docile lamb to the dank cellar, where he kept his kegs of ale, racks of wine from the Marain Valley vineyards, and some of his nonperishable food supplies. Greeting the others, I nodded in turn to Gwynn, Maylen, and a handful of my father's scouts, who were almost finished marking the sand-filled containers with Spreebridge notations to duplicate what was found on the feyweed crates aboard the Stoutheart. "Anders? Is Emmy all right?" I asked, sidling over to my husband, who watched me through narrowed eyes.

"Fine, though she misses her mama."

"Well, I miss her, too."

"How will you know the difference?" Chester asked, indicating the markings on the crates before Anders could make another snide comment.

"Smell. You'll be able to tell the difference yourself up close." Anders produced a flask filled with the unmistakable appalling odor of feyweed with which to sprinkle the crates.

When he offered a sniff to the innkeeper, Chester waved him away. "Ugh. I see what you mean."

"I thought you might. Any reason not to start moving the crates upstairs?"

"None. Everyone's gone home, though you'd best post a lookout." At Chester's reply, one of the scouts signaled she'd take that responsibility and disappeared on quiet feet up the narrow staircase.

"You might let the younger folk do the heavy lifting," I teased Anders, playfully poking his firm stomach. "Otherwise, you'll be useless later on when we go home." Leaning closer, I brushed his lips with my own, reading concern in those seagray eyes. "I'm all right," I said quietly. "For the moment, anyway. And now isn't the time to discuss it."

Yielding to his desire to pull the truth from me, Anders backed away. "Later, then." When I nodded, he directed the young scouts to start bringing the crates up to the rear entrance on the main floor.

To my surprise, the switch was made without incident, from the back of one building to the other in less than two hours. No one was about, not even on the streets, which was likely the result of the day's indulgence. Added to that was the expertise of the Glynnswood scouts, whose stealth and caution were exemplary, and the presence of Port

Alain troops patrolling the docks, thanks to Elena's feigned worry for her prestigious visitors. Exhausted by the time we'd finished, though my effort was more lookout and mage, should magic be necessary, I waved the scouts into the common room for ale or whatever they desired. I wasn't surprised when they declined and melted into the night, one of them, no doubt, going up to the Hill to report their success to my father. Maylen and Gwynn stayed behind with Anders and me, along with Chester, whose eyelids were drooping. It was on the tip of my tongue to send him off to bed, when I caught his furtive glance to a table set against the wall.

A nearly empty bottle of vintage Marain Valley wine between them, Elena and Jackson sat watching, as I stopped dead in my tracks. Elena got to her feet, her face blank. With one easy, smooth movement, she tossed something my way. Catching the article in my hand, I knew before I looked what she'd thrown. Across the vast width of the space between us, physical and emotional, I met her querying gaze and slipped the leather thong over my head, letting the twin pendants settle comfortably on my chest.

"Well, now that that little bit of business is settled," Anders began, immediately raising his hands in defense when both Elena and I glared at him, identical scowls on our faces. "Ah, why don't the rest of us" — he gathered Jackson, Maylen, Gwynn, and Chester with his eyes, indicating the back of the room on the opposite side, as far from the two of us as possible— "give the ladies some privacy."

I bit my lip to restrain a laugh. When the others were safely out of earshot, Elena edged closer until we were inches away from each other. "I don't want mindless, blindly obedient, blithering fools to act as my advisors," she said quietly. "I thought you knew that."

The urge to defend my actions was nearly overwhelming, but I forced it back down and out of reach. "I did, and I do."

She started to argue, but I raised a hand to halt her words.

"I know what Seamage Brandt tried to do. And now we have the crates in the Mage Council Hall to hold over his head, his guilt is even more apparent." I shut my eyes for a moment, hoping to make her see why I might have been so adamant about giving him feyweed. "But, when you and Jules arrived, he'd just told me how he'd loved my grandmother, though she'd rejected him. And how his life might have been different if she'd given him a chance." When Elena blinked in confusion at this unexpected turn of the conversation, I added, "Look, I'm not saying it should matter or help forgive his crimes, because it shouldn't. But—" I sighed, shaking my head in defeat. "I don't know, Elena. It was hard enough to know by my own experience what he would feel when he drank the feyweed. And to experience that on top of his own bitterness— Maybe I just pitied some small part of him because under all his malice, he had the makings of a heart."

Elena studied my face for so long in silence that I wasn't at all sure what she was thinking. Finally, losing patience, I said, "What? For the lords' sake, tell me what's going on in that head of yours—"

"Only this." My friend placed her hands on my shoulders, leaned closer, and kissed my forehead, almost in blessing, surprising me completely. "Not only do people underestimate your mage talent and your intelligence, Alex, but they always underestimate the depth of your own heart." Her smile, even as it reached her blue eyes, was sad. "I'm sorry. I did what I had to do, and I've no regrets, but I am so very sorry you were caught up in it."

"I shouldn't have questioned your decision in public."

"No," —her smile was brighter now— "you shouldn't have, but you're off the hook. There weren't too many witnesses."

Chapter Twenty-Two

With barely a few hours sleep and none of them restful, I scrubbed my eyes free of grit and fatigue and headed down to the harbor, where Port Alain troops still patrolled the streets. Beyond the perimeter set around the Stoutheart, ostensibly for its protection, a brisk trade was going on aboard the ship between the captain and a group of local merchants. Apparently, the presence of the ducal military did nothing to impede the flow of commerce, for which her majesty would be relieved. Either that or she'd be hearing Jules's complaints until we were all dead and buried.

Chasing away that frivolous thought, I slipped a somber expression on my face just as I reached the foot of the gangplank. "Permission to come aboard, Captain?" I shouted, hoping to be heard above the noisy haggling.

The Spreebridge official peered over the railing, expecting another merchant, his eyes widening at sight of me. "Mage Protector, yes, of course. Come aboard. Join the crowd." He offered me a hand as I neared the top. "How can I be of service?"

"Actually, I was looking for Elder Frontish. Is he aboard?"

"Yes, below deck in his cabin. The noise was a little overwhelming," the captain added with a grin as he signaled a crew member to fetch the elder. "He will be delighted to see you."

"I wouldn't wager on that, but thanks. Go on. I don't want to impose on your time." I smiled, not wanting him to think me rude. "I'll just enjoy the sea breeze, while you conduct business. Looks brisk."

"It is indeed. Though, I confess, after all the festivities, I could use nothing more than some quiet and a few good nights' sleep. But if you are sure—" Smiling, he returned to the anxious group of merchants when I waved him on.

Watching the captain walk away, I wondered about the extent of his knowledge concerning feyweed. While my instinct judged him clueless, how could he not notice the fact that ten crates were missing?

"Mage Protector?"

Remembering to keep the somber expression on my face, I turned at the sound of my name to find the Spreebridge elder striding across the deck. "Good morning, Elder Frontish. I'm sorry to disturb you so early." Indicating the nearest Port Alain trooper on horseback, I shook my head. "Troublesome welcome, for which I must apologize on behalf of my people."

"Surely you need not take the blame," he said smoothly. "It is a wise action, as your queen graciously pointed out, to take precautions. Crime is not unknown in Derbarry, either."

"Still, it is my home. In fact, the sight of the troopers this morning made me think of something." Touching his sleeve to draw him aside for privacy away from the transactions taking place, I glanced over my shoulder to be sure no one was near enough to listen. I was gratified when he leaned closer, intrigued. "Is it possible Jackson is behind the rumors of theft the queen's heard? You know," —I intentionally touched the twin pendants hanging at my neck— "to unsettle the fledgling trade relationship between us and make things more difficult for Elena?"

"Ah, Mage Protector, I had not considered that possibility."

"After the odd and, I confess, suspicious behavior Jackson has been exhibiting, I don't know what to think. But I can assure you," I said earnestly, "I've considered his involvement." I flashed a self-conscious smile. "My defense of him the other night was selfish. Admitting he was guilty of some crime would, as you guessed correctly, make me feel I'd failed in my responsibility to the queen. But you were right, and I have no choice but to follow the trail and see where it leads. In any event, is there anything I can do to make this situation" —I waved a hand in the direction of the guard— "more tolerable?"

"Not at all," the elder reassured me. "I have no quarrel with the queen's caution and, in fact, welcome it. Especially in light of" —leaning closer to me, he glanced across the road to the Mage Council Hall— "the arrest of Seamage Brandt. The children, I trust, are unharmed?"

"Yes, thank you. The seamage underestimated me," I said quietly, thinking about Elena's words only a few hours earlier, "as well as my bodyguard, who defended and saved my life. And believe me, Elder Frontish, I was in dire need, without magic. But all ended well, the children think of it as an adventure, a criminal is now off the streets of Port Alain, and you" —I bowed low with respect— "are a very busy man. Don't let me keep you." I smiled. "Unless, of course, you've learned the art of delegation and have Elder Harlowe do all the work."

Matching my smile, he said, "Sometimes, Mage Protector, as they say, rank does have its privileges. As senior elder of Spreebridge's council—" His shrug completed the thought.

Laughing, I clapped him on the back. "It's true. The queen constantly delegates to me." Turning to leave, I stopped as though a thought just occurred to me. "Is Elder Harlowe aboard? I feel as though I've been slighting him."

"I will pass along your compliments, Mage Protector. Only last evening, Westin expressed a similar thought, that he had not had sufficient time to speak with you, particularly about Jackson. But at the moment" —the man's smile grew cagey— "he is busy running errands for me."

With a mock groan, I shook my head. "Send him my sympathy."

* * * *

Stifling a huge yawn, I almost flattened my father as he turned the corner of the upper floor of the manor, heading toward Rosanna's parlor. "Sorry."

Catching me with a graceful motion before I fell on my face, he frowned. "How much sleep have you had, Alex?" Father demanded, shaking me gently by the shoulders.

"Sleep? What's that?"

"My very point."

"Sh— You sound like a father," I scolded, trying, and failing admirably, to lessen his concern. "I promise I'll sleep for a week when this trouble is over and done. Have you had any word about Westin Harlowe?"

"How did you know we have just heard from one of my scouts?" Brushing unruly brown hair from his eyes, Sernyn steered me into the sunny parlor, where Anders and Jules were having tea with Elena and the senior Lady Barlow.

Staring at the cozy little party, I announced, "I'm the queen's Mage Protector. I know everything." When Elena snorted, and Rosanna shot me a scathing look, I ignored them both and demanded, "Well? Where has Westin been hiding? He wasn't on the ship just now."

"He visited the Mage Council Hall in town early this morning, Alex." My father took my arm and shoved me into a chair before I could even think of protesting. "Apparently, he was up earlier even than you, and then he stayed in the building for nearly an hour."

"Inspecting his cargo? Or discussing logistics with his co-conspirators?" I stifled another yawn before Rosanna could scold me about my appalling lack of manners. "You think they're all in on the deal?" I asked Jules, who interacted with the Mage Council nearly as much as I did, which is to say, as little as possible.

"Perhaps. If they are, their involvement might not be voluntary. Brandt was a bully. But I have to admit," Jules said, offering me a slice of blueberry bread, "I hope they are involved, so I have a legitimate excuse to clean house and find some new mages."

"Well, today might be your lucky day. They never struck me as being too eager to cross your path."

"Or yours."

"Hmm. Where's Jackson?"

"I thought you knew everything," Rosanna said dryly, though she did answer my question. "Taking turns with the others, keeping watch."

"Spying."

"That's such a crude word."

"But accurate." Gratefully accepting a cup of tea from my father, who stood over me until I took a sip and swallowed a piece of the blueberry bread, I waved the mother hen away. "With the arrest of Seamage Brandt, they're bound to make their move tonight or tomorrow, in case Elena decides to have the Mage Council Hall searched. I doubt they'd want to run that risk."

"Then more likely tonight, I think," my father offered. "The scouts are ready to take their positions whenever you give the word, Alex."

"Great, thanks." I broke off another small bit of blueberry bread and popped it into my mouth. "How's Linsey? I haven't had a chance to speak with her, though I'd like to."

"Yes, I'm sure she'd like that, too, Alex." Rosanna's expression was odd, unreadable, and worrisome. "Seamage Brandt scared her, as did the unexpectedness of her magic."

"Understandable. Only moments before the seamage threatened us all, the poor child made a simple suggestion to Emmy, and poof, her wish became reality. It's a frightening and powerful talent." I set the teacup aside, watching the older woman's face, and guessed there was something she wasn't telling me. "What else? Come on, Rosanna," I snapped, edgy from lack of sleep and emotional strain. "What else is going on with Linsey?"

"She—" Rosanna glanced at my father before adding, "My granddaughter was frightened of you, too, yesterday."

"Of me? I didn't mean to scare her. I had to move fast, and—"

"I know that," Rosanna defended my action. "I'm not blaming you, Alex. And I'm quite certain the child will be fine, given some time and distance to think about things. Khrista and Lauryn and I, and Emmy, too, bless that little girl's heart, have spent a lot of time with Linsey, reassuring her about her new powers. The fact her mother is a seamage will help. I have to admit, though it pains me," —her expression shifted imperceptibly, and I braced for sarcasm— "that both you and Anders have done a wonderful job raising your daughter. Emmy already understands the ethics of her magic, even though she's lost it and, in her mind, is likely never to have it again."

"That's more to Anders's credit." I raised my teacup in salute to the man, who'd been listening quietly.

"And your credit, too. Emmy kept telling Linsey, 'Mama says and Papa says,' so it's apparent she includes you among her influences." Rosanna sighed. "But what I really want to know is why I had the misfortune to deal with a brat like you?"

"Obviously," I drawled, getting up to find Linsey before heading to the cottage for a well-earned nap, "you deserved it." With a childish expression, I left the little tea party in progress and sauntered down the hall to the opposite wing of the manor to Linsey's room, where Khrista was watching the girls at play.

When I poked my head into the room, Emmy flew into my arms. "Mama—"

"Whoa, hold on." I grabbed her in mid-leap and hugged her tight. "Did you really miss me this much? Or did you do something bad and want to fool me so I won't yell at you?"

"Silly." She planted a kiss on my cheek. "I missed you a lot."

"Well, I missed you, too." Setting her down on the ground, I knelt beside Linsey and held out my arms to her. When the child hesitated, I didn't let the disappointment show, but waited until she, too, finally came to hug me. Over her head, Khrista and I exchanged a worried glance. "Linsey?" I held her at arm's length and cupped her chin. "I'm sorry I scared you."

"Mama said you were trying to save me."

"I was. I couldn't let that bad man take you away."

Smiling, Linsey kissed my cheek, and the growing knot in my gut eased just a little. "Thank you, Alex." She sat on one of my knees when I sank to the ground cross-legged, and Emmy rested on the other.

"You know how special you are, don't you? Your magic is exactly like mine, but" —I smoothed light brown bangs from her eyes— "you have to learn to control it and use it to help people. What I did yesterday—"

The little girl's eyes bore into mine, and I could hear her smart little brain thinking, *'What you did yesterday, Alex, was to help me.'* And that wasn't what I wanted her to think.

"When I created fire and wind yesterday to capture the bad men, I did it because it was necessary. When I surrounded them with fire, I didn't hurt them. I just made it impossible for them to move. I didn't hurt them," I repeated, hoping against hope she'd understand my point.

"But you hurt Seamage Brandt."

"Yes, I did," I said quietly, holding her gaze. "And I was very sad that I hurt him." Her eyes went wide in disbelief, so I hastened to add, "He was a mage, too, Linsey, and more powerful than the other bad men, so I had to be sure he wouldn't hurt you and Emmy. But I didn't have to throw him around like that. All I should have done was to knock him unconscious. I made a mistake, Linsey. I didn't have to hurt him as much as I did. Do you understand that?"

"But you saved me, Alex." Linsey's tone was defiant. "And I'm glad you threw him around like that."

"Don't be glad," I whispered, worried I'd tainted the child. "It was the wrong thing to do."

When I left a few moments later, I was more worried than before.

Chapter Twenty-Three

The night was clear and cool, a typical spring evening, though, for what we were doing, too cool in my opinion. I shivered from head to toes beneath the heavier wool cloak I'd donned earlier. Pressing closer to my father for warmth, where we sat companionably together on the roof of the Seaman's Berth, I kept watch beside him. Down the block, atop the roof of the Mage Council Hall, Jackson and Anders did the same. I squinted past the Stoutheart to see whether I could spy the small fishing boat that carried two of my father's scouts. I couldn't see it, though my father did as he peered through the spyglass. The last piece of our web flitted from shadow to shadow along the street, ready to move in a heartbeat when signaled.

"Ah." My father tapped my arm and pointed toward the bay. "The scouts are drifting eastward."

"You think the Spreebridge agents used the trapdoor on the port side again to escape notice?"

"Most likely," my father murmured, eyes locked on the water, "and lowered themselves onto a waiting boat. If they disembarked onto the wharf, they would run the risk of confronting the Port Alain troops. It will be interesting to see how far along the coast they go, but I doubt it will be too distant." Glancing at me when I remained silent, he shrugged. "They must make their way back here to take possession of the crates. They would needlessly waste time if they had to travel far into the countryside."

"Hmmm." Pulling my cloak tighter around my chilled body, I said, "But they'd have a cart and horses ready, don't you think?"

Taking the spyglass he offered, I trained my eye on the water and saw the scouts fishing along, looking innocent and natural, though it was the middle of the night. One good thing in their favor was that Port Alain folk fished any time they felt the urge, day or night. Bringing the focus closer to home, I watched a shadow blend into another just beyond the Mage Council Hall. If I hadn't been aware of their presence, I would have missed the scouts completely. Glancing back toward the water, I turned the spyglass east to find the boat we assumed our scouts were tailing.

"You're right," I admitted grudgingly, handing the spyglass back. "The Spreebridge boat is heading inland, just before the curve of seawall a half mile past the end of the harbor."

"And there," —my father grinned, showing even white teeth— "is proof that your guess was right. A cart just crossed the road to meet them by the seawall. It seems Anders was smart to refuse your wager."

"He hates to lose money to me."

"He hates to lose an argument to you, too."

"True, but that's because I'm always right. Well, not always," I amended, thinking with remorse of Linsey. When he arched one eyebrow at my serious tone, I explained, "I made an error in judgment with Khrista's little girl."

"You forget, Alex, though children are impressionable," my father said, following the progress of the foreign boat as it approached the shoreline, "most eventually listen to reason. Even you," he murmured, laughing when I elbowed his thin ribs. "And you were angry the other afternoon, not to mention afraid that Seamage Brandt would harm the children."

"No excuse." When he glanced at me in surprise, I said earnestly, "Listen, the truth is, I was furious. And in my anger, I forgot the girls were watching. I gave no heed to how my actions would affect them beyond the necessity to keep them safe. I unleashed a lifetime of rage and grief against the seamage in one ill-judged action."

"Ah."

"Ah, what?" I demanded, keeping my voice low.

"You admit to being human?"

"I admit to being serious. What if I've damaged Linsey's attitude toward her mage talent?" I said, thinking back on the child's parting words to me. "What if—" I took a deep breath and said the words I hadn't had the courage to utter aloud to anyone since we'd found out Khrista was pregnant. "What if her father's heritage has passed down? What if she's flawed?"

"Alex—" Surprised at my outburst, my father set aside the spyglass. "There are many things in that child's life which will influence her attitude toward magic. Perhaps her father's criminal behavior may one day prove troublesome. For the moment, we cannot know that. And I must confess Rosanna and I have spoken in private about that very topic. She had not wanted to worry you, but it is something we considered. And so," he went on serenely, while I digested that little fact, "what happened at the cottage with Seamage Brandt is only one of many examples you will set for Linsey as she grows. I expect the rest of your actions, or at least the majority," he amended, peering out through the spyglass again, a small smile tugging at his lips, "will be well-intentioned and to your credit. Not to mention that the child will be surrounded by other mages, including her mother, who will support her education. Ah, here comes the empty cart with its crew—"

As I listened, the far-off sound of muffled hooves and harness came closer.

"And look, Alex," —he beamed with boyish delight— "a prize awaits us."

"Please tell me Westin Harlowe is sitting in the cart."

"Not only sitting in the cart, Alex, but driving it. The lords of the sea must be generous with their favors tonight." Sernyn chuckled, as he swung the spyglass toward the Mage Council Hall. "Not only have we caught Westin in the act, but it seems Seamage Brandt's cronies are waiting in the alley for the cart to arrive. And after tonight's little adventure, Jules can happily pick and choose a new Mage Council for Port Alain."

"Perfect." Envisioning a warm bed in my not-too-distant future, I sighed with pleasure. "So all we need to do now is watch them load the cart and head back out of town on their way to distribute the fake crates of feyweed."

"Yes, and let the duke's troopers play their part. Then, Alex, we release the trap and get you into bed for a week's worth of sleep."

* * * *

Crouched knee-to-knee behind the bar with Jackson, the two of us waited with growing impatience for the Port Alain trooper, Captain Reedy, to escort Elder Frontish from the Stoutheart, where he was supposedly sound asleep, to the Seaman's Berth. Faced with the temptation of a handful of open bottles of Marain Valley wine, I reminded myself I was here on the queen's business, and that she owed me another shipment. The common room had been cleared of tables and chairs an hour earlier to make room for the prisoners, now bound and gagged, whom Captain Reedy had deposited into our care. Along one wall, the captain's men had stacked the ten sand-filled crates taken from the cart.

Anders and Elena were hidden behind the crates of feyweed-sprinkled sand. In the shadowy opposite corner of the common room, where the tables and chairs had been pushed aside, my father and Kimmer waited together. The rest of our welcoming party, my two half-brothers and Maylen, were uncomfortably squashed into the narrow pantry with Chester.

Through a chink in the wood beneath the bar, carved there years ago by the devious innkeeper, I watched Captain Reedy guide Derek Frontish inside. Although the interior of the inn was dim, the flickering lamplight provided sufficient brightness to give me smug satisfaction as the blood drained from the Spreebridge elder's skin when faced with the stacked crates and the prisoners, waiting for his inspection and identification.

"What is the meaning of this?" Elder Frontish demanded of the trooper, whose face remained impassive.

Captain Reedy indicated the remaining inhabitants of the room, gathered in a group on the floor. All but one was gagged, and his eyes were narrowed with restrained rage. "We found these men in possession of ten crates stolen from your ship, the Stoutheart. My troopers caught them on the road, heading east toward Belbridge Cliffs. The queen commanded we remain on alert, in the event of such a possibility. I assumed our actions would please you, but—" The captain suddenly appeared uncertain as he watched the elder's face undergo a number of curious transformations. "These are your goods, aren't they? The crate markings—"

"My dear captain, I have no idea whether or not these crates belong to the Stoutheart," Frontish offered with a shrug of apology, his eyes shifting away from the trooper's bewildered gaze. "You will have to ask the ship's captain to identify them. In fact, you should bring him here and let me go back to the ship. The captain is responsible for the goods we brought from Spreebridge. I know only we have merchandise to offer for sale, and nothing more as to the contents of each crate, the amount, color or cut of gem or mineral, indeed, nothing beyond what my role as trade negotiator and senior representative of my people demands of me."

"Smooth, Derek, very smooth, and almost convincing, but he is telling lies, Captain Reedy, I assure you." With those words, Westin continued to inform the captain, "Derek Frontish is not only responsible for the entire contents of these particular crates, but also behind our little thieving effort tonight. It was his plan—"

"I have no idea what you are talking about," Elder Frontish countered, telling the Port Alain captain, "This man was obviously trying to steal gems and sell them at a profit to your country folk, beginning with the people of Belbridge Cliffs. The queen warned me of a possible plot to do so. In fact," —the elder stood tall, a malicious light in his eyes, as he said— "Jackson Tunney, your queen's lover, is likely involved in the scheme, as well. Wake up the Mage Protector and ask her about him. She has been tracking his footsteps for the last few days, convinced of his guilt."

"Now that is an insult and a lie," Jackson drawled, coming out from behind the shelter of the bar and hopping nimbly over the top. "I take grave offense, Elder Frontish, at the implication and stain on my good name and reputation with the people of Tuldamoran. And Captain Reedy is a friend of mine. As for you, Master Harlowe—" Jackson ignored the elder's shock and strolled toward his former mentor. "I am deeply saddened you would involve yourself in this man's narrow-minded scheme."

"I am completely innocent. Derek duped me, I am ashamed to admit." Westin's smile was sheepish as he made the plea to his protégé. "I became involved for a very different reason than you would expect, Jackson. You must understand. Derek planned to slip these crates of feyweed, not gems, as you and your friends suspected, into Tuldamoran. If he succeeded, Derek planned to distribute the potion by means of the local Mage Councils, on the pretense it is an antidote to also be used as a precautionary measure. Do you see how dangerous he is?" Believing he had Jackson half-convinced, Westin sighed heavily and delivered his final persuasive argument. "I came here to Port Alain, Jackson, to stop Derek from carrying out his treachery."

"You came along to stop Derek by helping him smuggle it from the Mage Council Hall to the surrounding countryside?" Jackson's expression was blank, and I couldn't read it.

Did he believe his mentor? Did he want to believe him? Had we underestimated the influence Westin exerted over the queen's lover?

"Of course not. That was a ruse to get the feyweed out of Derek's hands."

When Jackson said nothing, merely held his mentor's gaze, Derek lost patience. "It is your word against mine," he snapped at Westin.

"My lord." Captain Reedy stepped into the elder's line of sight to get his attention away from Westin. "Under these dubious circumstances, the queen must be told. If you'd—"

"Captain," —the elder shoved the trooper out of his way— "you have no right to harass me or threaten me with the queen's authority. I am a diplomat, a distinguished and invited guest. You cannot touch me."

"That is true. But if I escort you back to Spreebridge, under lock and key and the influence of feyweed poured down your throat," Kimmer said wryly, emerging from her hiding place, "then the elder council can dispense further justice as they see fit. And before you get yourself into any more trouble with the good people of Port Alain, Derek, bear in mind that it is your word and Westin's, too," she informed the other man, "against the evidence that I and my colleagues gathered in Derbarry against you. Not to mention" —her face turned grim— "the notes that my son, Sloane, left for Corey. My poor misguided son died by your command, and, for that crime, I will never forgive you."

"Nonsense," Derek sputtered, though his cheeks flushed at Kimmer's unexpected appearance. "I had nothing to do with your son's death. He became involved with the wrong sort of people in Derbarry's back streets—"

"Your people. One of my allies sent word they caught the man who murdered my son." She smiled sadly at Jackson. "Not only has he confessed to the crime, but he has implicated you in that and more. I fear, Derek, your days as Senior Elder are only a fond memory."

"You are bluffing."

"I never bluff."

"It is a trap. This whole conspiracy— The Stoutheart's captain—"

"The poor man is a greedy little fool who did not dare interfere in your scheme because you offered him gold. I have his oath, too, Derek, and worse." Her smile changed to wicked, though levity never reached her eyes. "I am well acquainted with his formidable mother."

"I should have had you killed, too," Derek snarled, lunging for Kimmer and drawing a dagger from the sheath at his waist. As it sailed across the space between them, half of the blade transformed to water and dropped in an awkward plop to the hardwood floor. When I joined Jackson from behind the bar, the Elder was horrified. "You have both lost your magic. You—"

"I don't know about you," I said to Jackson, "but I'm getting a little tired of people underestimating me. As for that little trick," I drawled, as though we were having a social discussion, "I always wondered which one of us was faster. But since I didn't use magic just now, and you're usually better than that, Jackson, I have to assume the mage who transformed the dagger is a little, um, rusty and in need of practice." When my father stepped out of hiding, scarlet with embarrassment, I smiled. "I'm glad you found another reason to wield your magic."

"Apparently," —he shot Kimmer a lopsided grin— "there are many reasons."

"Good to know you can still learn something. Captain Reedy, would you kindly arrest Elder Frontish and escort him to the Stoutheart under Elder Frehan's authority? The ship leaves on the morning tide."

As the captain moved to obey my request, Derek Frontish stepped out of reach. "You have no authority, Mage Protector."

"Now, there, I have to disagree with you. As my Mage Protector, she certainly does have the authority," Elena informed the Elder, coming out from her hiding place with Anders. "But just in case you need convincing and to keep matters neat and tidy between your country and mine, Elder Frontish, I certainly have the appropriate authority. It is my regret to say you are no longer a distinguished and invited guest. The same goes for you, Elder Harlowe. As for your escort," —she turned to Kimmer and smiled at Jackson— "take care of my future husband, will you? I want him back in Ardenna in time for the wedding. With you, of course."

"It would be my pleasure, your majesty." When Kimmer was sure Derek Frontish and Westin Harlowe were out of hearing range, she laughed. "I must confess, I have not had this much fun in years."

I elbowed my father. "Was she always a little crazy?"

"Always."

His smile was fond as Kimmer reached over to kiss his cheek. "Give my love to Anessa. Tell her I will see her soon." She placed a hand on his arm and squeezed lightly. "And Sernyn, thank you for my son. It seems that Corey" —she smiled at my newest brother, who wore a bewildered look— "has decided to spend his winters in Tuldamoran and summers in Spreebridge, if that meets with your approval? Yes? Excellent. Alex? What do you think?"

"I always knew the boy had potential."

Epilogue

Jenny Bretan, head of the Ardenna Crown Council of Mages, stared at the silver flask I held outstretched in my hand as though it were poison. From her point of view, based on our history, I suppose I couldn't blame the woman. But I was disappointed. Sitting across from me at the opposite head of the long table in the semi-formal meeting chamber in the fortress, Elena lifted one black eyebrow. Her look was subject to any number of interpretations, and I wasn't sure which made the most sense, considering the awkward situation.

Holding the flask up to the window, I squinted at the sunlight in my eyes. "I don't see a drop of poison," I murmured, twirling the silver bottle in the air. With one swift motion, I slammed the flask on the polished tabletop. "Look, Seamage Bretan, I know you might— No, that's wrong, I know you find it hard to believe I'm offering you an antidote to feyweed, but it's true. Why would I poison you when I could simply whip up a tempest and hurl you and the rest of the council out the window to the ground below?" Elena winced at my choice of words, but didn't interfere. "You heard what happened to the head of the Port Alain Mage Council. I could just as easily do the same to you."

"Are you threatening us, Mage Keltie?"

"Only insofar as I wish I could force you to trust me. But you're right, if I read your expression correctly. Trust has to be earned. On both sides," I added, giving the woman credit for holding her tongue. "I can assure you without proof, but I have the sworn testimony of witnesses who you will claim to be my allies, that both Jackson and I drank the antidote and had our magic fully restored. I have no proof you would be willing to accept, though maybe this will convince you." My smile turned predatory as I lowered my voice. "The antidote is not without a price." When the older mage narrowed her eyes, I had the sudden suspicion she assumed I was finally about to come clean and admit the truth. "I have a deal to offer, if you're willing to listen."

Glancing at her fellow mages seated around the table, Seamage Bretan nodded without offering any commitment.

"Excellent." I leaned a hip on the table. "I'm tired of coming to Ardenna to respond to the queen's summons every time she sneezes. I want her to feel she has a Mage Council she can trust here in the city. A Mage Council, I might add, committed to drawing up a sensible code of behavior for the rest of the kingdom's mages to follow."

"And if we are kept busy solving the queen's summons," Jenny Bretan found her voice and challenged, "what will you be doing?"

"For one thing, I have a schoolroom full of ignorant children to teach in Port Alain. But this pendant, these actually" —I tugged on the twin symbols around my neck— "don't excuse me from responsibility. They designate me as the queen's troubleshooter wherever and whenever she needs my help. And that goes for the Crownmage, too." Not wanting to smear their faces with my title, I tucked the pendants out of sight. "Ever since the appearance of my particular brand of mage talent, and then my husband's and Jackson Tunney, of course, there's been a desperate need for some study of bloodlines. I've asked my father to start working with the local councils to gather a census of as many mages as possible in each Duchy, those registered with the council and the rogue mages who avoid them like the plague."

"To control them?"

Restraining my impatience, I bit back the urge to smack the woman. "To prevent them from going mad as the renegade mages in Spreebridge did some years ago." Elena's barely perceptible nod prompted me to add, "On his journey back to Derbarry, under house arrest, and right before he was given feyweed, Elder Frontish admitted he'd met with you in secret." The seamage was cool I had to grant her that, as her expression gave nothing away. "Believe me, he offered you nothing as honorable as what the queen and I intend to offer you now."

"We did not meet—"

"Seamage Bretan," I warned, sliding a glance in Elena's direction, "don't lie in front of the queen, please. It will only damage her present and future good will. And let me assure you, with her upcoming marriage to Mage Tunney drawing near, she would like to remain in an excellent mood. Oh, and by the way, with their marriage, Mage Tunney will become your liaison to the queen."

"Because you don't trust us?" Though Jenny Bretan's question was directed to both Elena and me, I decided to let Elena reply.

"Because we thought you might find it a more comfortable manner of dealing with me, for the moment." Elena's voice was cool as she studied the older woman. "Until, that is, you and your colleagues are more at ease with me. As Alex said earlier, trust must be earned all around, and that includes on my end. If we agree to start fresh, here and now, all of us," —she shrugged, downplaying the generosity of her offer in ignoring their clandestine meeting with the Spreebridge elder— "we'll see how matters develop."

"I honestly hope they'll prove satisfactory," I chimed in, turning my attention to Seamage Bretan. While the mage still appeared to be unconvinced, I glimpsed a hint of doubt. "I know you probably mistrusted Elena's message, warning about the capture of the crates filled with feyweed, along with details of the foreign plot, but I can only say this. I had nothing to do with his plan to incriminate both of us." I scanned the table and saw the faces with varying degrees of acceptance. "I was the one he'd slated to take the major responsibility. It would have been blamed on my bid for power. And power, though you may not believe me, is something I don't want. If you knew me well—In fact, if you knew me even a little," I said softly, heartened by Elena's smile, "you'd understand that. So," I challenged, "Will you accept the antidote?"

The woman shut her eyes for a heartbeat, and I wondered what was going through her thoughts. When she opened them again, her expression was so full of hope I nearly shouted for joy. "Why are you really doing this?" she whispered, holding my gaze with her own.

"Because I'm tired of being mistrusted. All right." I pushed off the table and leaned down, both hands on the slick surface. "Maybe this will convince you of my good faith. I'm willing to tell you a secret very few people yet know." Intrigued, but still cautious, the woman leaned closer, as did her colleagues. "My daughter, Emila, has mage talent that's a combination of my magic and my husband's. My child represents a bright new future, and I'm willing to trust you all with that knowledge."

"If this is true," Seamage Bretan said slowly, digesting the information, and very likely looking for the trap, "then why are you willing to trust us?"

"Because if anything happens to my daughter," —I grinned fiercely, pushing free of the table— "I'll know who to blame."

Matching my grin, the seamage got to her feet, snatched the flask from the table, and drank.

The End

About the Author

Virginia G. McMorrow has worked as an editor/writer for more than 30 years, after a career in human resources. In her professional capacity, Ginny has worked for business publishers as an editor of books, journals, reports, and newsletters targeted for clients, and now works as a freelance editor/writer. She has also had numerous articles on both professional and writing topics published, along with several short stories. As a playwright, Ginny has had 28 short one acts and one full-length play produced off-off Broadway by Love Creek Productions in a black box theater, as well as two short plays performed on a west coast radio show. She now lives and works in Venice, Florida.

Upcoming New Release!

VIRGINIA G. McMORROW

ON THE RIGHT TRACK

Louisa Carletta (Lou) leaves a two-year self-imposed exile in upstate New York to temporarily return home to Long Island to help her father (Rocco) with the family private eye business after his heart attack. Faced with a new client, who is worried about vandalism and apparently identified as a potential murder suspect, Lou sinks her teeth into the case to uncover the truth. But murder isn't the only crime involved—smuggling and theft are tangled in the murder, too. While investigating the murder, Lou must deal with her past, including a domineering mother, an estranged best friend, a ex-addict brother, a busybody minister, and an adversarial homicide detective…

For more information visit: www.SpeakingVolumes.us

Now Available!

VIRGINIA G. MCMORROW

The Mage Trilogy
Book One – Book Two

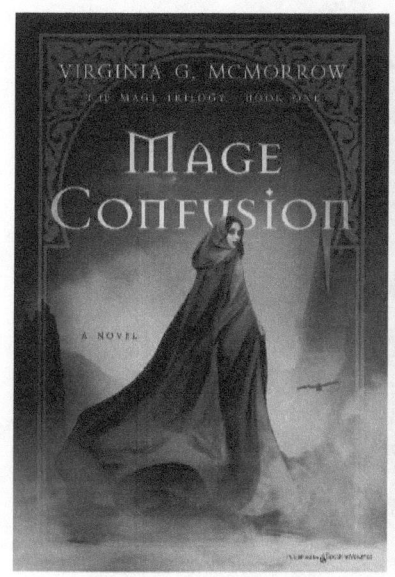 

**For more information
visit: www.SpeakingVolumes.us**

Now Available!

P.M. GRIFFIN

Star Commandos
Books 1 - 9

**For more information
visit: www.SpeakingVolumes.us**

Now Available!

JORDAN S. KELLER

Ashes Over Avalon Trilogy
Book One – Book Two – Book Three

**For more information
visit: www.SpeakingVolumes.us**

www.ingramcontent.com/pod-product-compliance
Lightning Source LLC
LaVergne TN
LVHW091629070526
838199LV00044B/993